A Star and a Tear

A Star and a Tear

A Mystery Novel
Exploring the Symbiotic Relationship
of Sexuality and Spirituality

Stephen McCutchan

PRIMIX
PUBLISHING
THE WRITE CHOICE

Primix Publishing
11620 Wilshire Blvd
Suite 900, West Wilshire Center, Los Angeles, CA, 90025
www.primixpublishing.com
Phone: 1-800-538-5788

Published by Primix Publishing   01/09/2024

ISBN: 979-8-89194-050-5(sc)
ISBN: 979-8-89194-051-2(e)

Library of Congress Control Number: 2024900920

CONTENTS

Chapter 1   A News Story 1
Chapter 2   Eric Ivory to the Rescue .12
Chapter 3   First Meeting with Police 20
Chapter 4   When You're Tired 31
Chapter 5   Reggie's Arrest and Frank's Response 39
Chapter 6   Digging for a Story 48
Chapter 7   Reconnecting with the Seminary 56
Chapter 8   Ivory Names Names 63
Chapter 9   Bearding the Lion 70
Chapter 10   John Knox Versus True Vine 76
Chapter 11   Judge Not That You Be Not Judged 86
Chapter 12   Speaking of Sin 93
Chapter 13   Temper Temper 101
Chapter 14   Amanda Doesn't Recognize Frank 107
Chapter 15   Explosion and Recreation 116
Chapter 16   The Apology 125
Chapter 17   Experiencing Church .132
Chapter 18   Jacob's Invitation 138
Chapter 19   Casting Suspicion 143
Chapter 20   Before the Lecture 152
Chapter 21   Jacob's Affirmation 159
Chapter 22   The Conundrum of Sex and Ministry 166
Chapter 23   Looking for a Pattern .173
Chapter 24   Clues Come Together .190
Chapter 25   Saints Preserve Us 200
Chapter 26   Preparation for the Park 206

Chapter 27   September 4 211
Chapter 28   Running the Trail .217
Chapter 29   An Altar to the Gods 229
Chapter 30   The Sins of the Father 236
Chapter 31   Epilogue. 240

CHAPTER 1

A News Story

*I*t's strange how a small, seemingly insignificant incident can rip open your personal universe and alter your life forever. Six years ago, Frank Sessions had forgotten to pick up some chocolate chip cookies as he drove home from John Knox Presbyterian Church where he was the pastor.

A cup of tea and a cookie were one of the special moments at the end of the day that his wife and he like to share before going to bed. "Not to worry," said Rosie. "You finish balancing the checkbook and put the water on to boil while I run down to the convenience store. I'll be back in a jiffy."

An hour later, there came a knock on the door. When Frank opened the door, a police officer was standing there. In a frozen moment of time, Frank heard that when his wife entered the convenience store, a robbery was taking place. A drug-crazed thief killed her as he had killed the store clerk.

Six years later, the sight of a chocolate chip cookie still made him sick. If he had just remembered to pick them up that evening, his whole life would have been different. He couldn't shake the guilt of that one moment of forgetfulness that had cost him his vibrant, sensitive, beautiful wife.

He managed to slog through the daily routine of ministry, but he had lost his passion for life. At his now young adult children's urgings, he had tried a couple of on-line dating experiences with disastrous results. Many of the community ministries that used to energize him now went on without him. His eating habits were horrible, and he had gained forty pounds, at least. He had also grown a full beard. He knew that his church had been very tolerant of his listless efforts as a pastor. The most he could do was meet the minimum responsibilities at his church and extend himself in pastoral ministry to his members. He still cared about people and their concerns and found satisfaction in helping them find resolution.

Maybe that was why he had agreed to meet with Brenda Sides, the reporter from the *Athens Record*. She had called on Monday afternoon and asked if there was any possibility that he could see her on Tuesday. She said that she wanted to clarify a biblical angle on a story that she was writing. What preacher can resist making room to talk to someone about the Bible, especially when there is a sense of urgency in her voice.

Marcie, his secretary, announced Brenda's arrival. When Marcie ushered her into his office, he was struck by the energy that she exuded. She was an athletic-looking woman with an untamed shock of fiery red hair. Her direct gaze, confident smile, and strong voice was modulated just enough to invite a positive response.

They exchanged pleasantries as Marcie offered them some coffee. He came around from behind his desk and invited her to join him in some comfortable chairs in one corner of the office. The bookshelves on all four walls were filled to capacity, and his large desk had books and papers everywhere. Brenda glanced around at the otherwise sparse decorations of his office. "I like that," she said, indicating a woodcarving of Abraham. "He started it all, didn't he?"

"In a manner of speaking," Frank said. "Three faiths trace their origin to his courageous decision to begin a journey based on trust more than knowing where it would end."

Brenda took a pen and notebook from her purse as she commented, "Religion is a powerful and mysterious thing. I guess that's why I'm here."

"So, tell me what's going on, Brenda."

"I'm working on a story that has some vague religious implications. It may go nowhere, but I think there is something deeper here. I confess, if I'm right, it requires a little more biblical knowledge than I have." Brenda shifted in her chair, rolled her eyes, and shrugged.

Frank knew that even many faithful members felt inadequate when it came to the Bible. He wanted to ease Brenda's discomfort. "Don't apologize for your lack of biblical knowledge, Brenda. I've studied it for thirty years and still find it an overwhelming mystery. Tell me more about your story."

"The story is about a rape this past Saturday. It may turn out to be just a straight out rape story," she grimaced, "as if any rape can be called commonplace. I think, however, there is something more here. I'm hoping by telling you about it, you can help me sort it out."

"Brenda, I'm glad to talk with you about it, but may I ask why you picked me." He tried to disguise his slight unease.

She looked away for just a second and then, as if catching herself, she turned back and said, "Reverend Sessions, I'm not a member of your church, or any church for that matter. At best, I'm one of your sporadic visitors. However, when I have been here, your sermons suggested that you were not afraid to talk about difficult topics."

Frank was impressed that while she continued to look directly at him, there was no hint of challenge, just honest exchange. If they were going to talk about rape, awkward for many, she seemed comfortable with herself.

"Help me understand what this rape has to do with religion?"

"If I'm correct," said Brenda, "the rapist has some weird religious fixation, almost like he thinks the Bible justifies what he's doing."

"The Bible and sex. Actually, several years ago, that was an area where I did a lot of work. Even did some lectures at the seminary. This sounds interesting. Tell me more about your story."

Brenda took out her recording device and set it on a table before them.

Frank felt himself stiffen. "Brenda, I'm pleased to talk with you about this, but if I'm going to be quoted, I may need to be a little more careful with what I say. Members of churches can get very uptight seeing their pastor quoted in the newspaper, especially on a subject as volatile as sexuality."

At first Brenda looked puzzled. "Oh," she said, shaking her bright red hair. "This is not to record you." She put her hand on the recorder button. "I have a recording I want you to hear. Sorry, I can understand how you could misunderstand.

Frank was embarrassed at his assumption. "My mistake. Please go on."

"First, let me give you a little background. One of my beats for the paper is the police station. Yesterday I was standing in the lobby of the police station when I saw this woman, later I learned her name was Carrie Breakstone, storm into the police station and declare that she wanted to report a rape. I knew that the police have a standard routine in such a circumstance: They listen to her story, lead her through their established procedures for any rape victim, and promise to investigate. It often leaves the victim feeling dismissed. I hung around in the lobby sensing there might be something unusual about her story."

Frank got up and reached for a pad of paper and a pen. "Now it's my turn. I assume that it is all right if I take notes?" he asked.

"As long as we agree that this is off the record and confidential." She paused a second. "Oh, wait, that's your line." Brenda laughed. "Sure, go ahead and take notes. It may help us sort this out."

What a winning presence she has, Frank thought. I wonder if anyone ever refuses to talk with her. Frank resumed his seat. "I'm ready, go ahead."

"I'm not picking on the police. They have to follow procedure, but sometimes, especially in the hands of an insensitive officer, it can seem too routine and leave the impression they aren't taking it seriously." She raised her hand palm up and gave a small shrug. "Call it a reporter's intuition, but I had the sense that this one was anything but routine.

"After the police had completed their process, I spotted her walking through the police lobby. She walked like a controlled storm ready to erupt. I tried to approach her in a way that wouldn't scare her. I said, 'Excuse me, I don't mean to intrude, but I'm doing a story on the responsiveness of the police to citizen's complaints. I notice that you are very upset, and I was wondering if the police were helpful or not?'"

"Nice opening," Frank commented.

"Wait till you hear what happened next. She spun around. I almost thought I was going to get a karate chop. Her words poured forth in a staccato like fashion. 'You …are…a…reporter?'"

"Yes I am," I said.

"With her spike-heeled boots, she was taller than I was. She bent over and thrust her chin to within inches of my face. It was all I could do not to back off, but I held my ground."

"Do you want a story about a crazy evangelist who spouts religious platitudes while he is stripping you of your clothes, and then shouts 'Hallelujah, Thank you Jesus,' while he is exploding into you?" Her voice rose as she spoke.

"Yikes, I can see why you thought the story had religious dimensions. Now I really am intrigued. Go on."

"We were standing in the middle of the lobby of the police headquarters and, like I said, she was talking rather loudly. People were walking all around us, some of them giving us strange looks. The desk sergeant was now staring at us from her desk about 30 feet away. I wondered if I'd stumbled on to a crazy woman, but there was something about her disciplined intensity, and my own reporter instincts, that caused me to take her seriously."

"Good move," Frank said. "Too many people miss what is important because they don't take some off-the-wall comments seriously and probe beneath them."

"I've dealt with rape victims before. I know they are both very vulnerable and can act a little crazy, so I decided to carefully direct her to a little more private place but one that wouldn't frighten her. I said, 'Ma'am, if you want to tell me your story, I'd be glad to buy you a cup of coffee and listen.'

"'Drop the ma'am stuff. My name is Carrie Breakstone, and you are about to hear a story that will make atheism seem a pleasant alternative in this screwed-up world.' As she spoke, she began to pump her fist in defiance. 'This bastard picked on the wrong woman if he thought embarrassment would keep me quiet.' Then Carrie paused and in a more reflective tone said, 'There was something in the way he behaved that, as I think about it, makes me wonder if there aren't others who've been afraid to come forward.'

"I led her to the cafeteria in the police building. That's probably not correct. As I think about it, she led me. Her high-heeled boots echoed on the tile of the reception area as she marched toward the cafeteria. She may have been a victim, but she seemed determined not to stay a victim.

"She chose a table fully visible to the public but slightly removed from others in the cafeteria. I got each of us a cup of coffee. 'Carrie,' I said, as I sat the coffee before her, 'If I'm going to tell your story accurately, I need to record it. Is that OK?'"

"So," said Frank, as he pointed to the recorder on the table, "this is what I'm about to hear?"

"That's right, this is her story, but there are some missing pieces that I'm hoping you can help me fill in."

Frank's head drew back and his eyes narrowed. "I'm not sure I understand, Brenda." He cleared his throat and tried to relax his hands that were gripping the chair. "How could someone who wasn't there possibly help fill in the blanks of your story?"

Brenda held out both hands in front of her in a gesture that indicated she was being misunderstood. "Wait, Reverend Sessions. I'm not being a sneaky reporter here. I know you weren't there. However, I think what Carrie remembered that the rapist said may have been from the Bible, and I'm hoping you can help me complete some of the quotes. Let me play the recording, and I think you'll understand."

Get a grip on yourself, Frank thought, this young lady is being straight with you. Stop being so paranoid.

"Sorry," said Frank. "Let me refill our coffee and then we can listen to the recording." As he moved towards the drip coffeepot, he consciously made himself relax.

After getting the coffee and regaining their seats, Brenda turned on the recorder.

The voice of a woman was speaking. "I had gone for a walk on a greenway near my apartment. I was admiring the beauty of a late afternoon with clear blue skies and trees in full bloom. I really do love spring.

"I'd stopped to watch some squirrels chase each other up a tree when I sensed someone behind me. Before I could react, this person had approached me from out of the bushes beside the trail and placed a cloth over my mouth and nose. I tried to struggle, but I could feel myself losing consciousness. The police tell me he probably used ether.

"When I awoke, I was traveling in a car. I was in the passenger seat. My seat belt was fastened, but that was all. I wasn't tied up or anything. All I remember is that I felt really strange. I was aware of what was happening, but I wasn't able to make any decisions. I guess he had given me an additional drug that made me lethargic. As I told the police, I could hear what he was saying, but it was as if I was under a spell and couldn't resist. They suggested it might be a new form of Rohypnol, a date-rape drug."

Frank could hear Brenda respond in a calm voice. "It's ok; just continue to describe what happened."

The woman's voice continued. "We must have driven for at least an hour or maybe it just seemed that way. Everything seemed to move so slowly. On one level, I kept trying to figure out what was happening to me, but I wasn't doing anything about it. I just sat there, as if we were out for a pleasant spring drive." You could hear the confusion in her voice.

"Anyway, he took me to some place out in the country. I have no idea where, but it was far removed. There was no chance that someone would see us. He stopped the car and led me into some woods where he had fashioned what he called his special altar on a fallen tree covered with branches and leaves. It was adorned with flowers." The voice paused then in almost a little girl's tone she said, "I still don't understand why I just let this happen to me. I'm a fighter. I'm not a wimp."

Frank interrupted. "It's almost like he had her under some kind of spell."

"Wait, it gets even stranger," Brenda said. The woman's voice, who Frank now knew as Carrie, continued to describe her experience. 'There was a portrait hanging over the tree next to his altar. It depicted a well-developed Jesus, bare to the chest, who was fondling the breasts of a woman near him.'

"Do you see that picture, my dear sweet Mary?" the rapist said.

"At least I wasn't so drugged that I didn't know my own name," Carrie said. "I told him he had the wrong person. That my name was Carrie.

"He didn't even hesitate but went on with his explanation. 'Don't you understand? God provides his special servants moments of pleasure as a reward for their devotion. God provided Eve for Adam, Bathsheba for David, and Mary Magdalene for Jesus. Now, dear one, he is providing you for me.'"

"Mary Magdalene is the source of sexual fantasy for lots of repressed religious nuts," Frank said. "Some scholars claim she was a prostitute that Jesus healed, and then she became part of Jesus' company of believers."

The recording continued with Carrie's story. "Even as he was saying this, he began to undress me. As he took off my blouse and began to unfasten my bra, he began to recite some weird poetry. He said something about how beautiful I was and that my breasts were like a fawn among the lilies."

Brenda paused the recording. "This is where I hope you can help me. During her description she remembers partial phrases and words that he said and since he seemed fixated on religious things, I wondered if it had something to do with the Bible."

Frank reached for a Bible and began thumbing through it as he indicated for Brenda to continue with the recording.

Carrie's voice continued, "What infuriates me is that I just stood there next to his so-called altar as he crooned poetry to me and began to lick and caress my breasts. I'm no prude but this was disgusting.

"Then he took off his own clothes in front of me as if I were a spectator at a strip show. He was fully erect, and he swayed as if in time to a tune as he approached me. I had on a pair of bright red shorts that he took little time in releasing and sliding down my legs." There was a moment of silence as if Carrie was trying to find words to continue.

Frank heard Brenda on the recording saying, "Carrie, I know this is very difficult. Take your time. I'm here to listen."

"You are really good at this," Frank said, as they continued to listen to the recording.

"Surely, if I can remember this so clearly," Carrie said, "I was awake enough to do something, but I just let it happen. It was as if I was having an out-of-body experience watching myself being fondled and degraded and did nothing." Her sense of shame and confusion was evident.

"It was the drug, Carrie," said Brenda, "It's not your fault."

Carrie continued her description. "He lifted my naked body onto his altar, still quoting his verses, something about a couch of cedar. Then he began to paw me and say something about my navel and wine, whatever the hell that had to do with it."

Frank held up his hand to stop the recording. "I think what he said was, 'Our couch is green; the beams of our house are cedar, you are a rose of Sharon, a lily of the valleys. Your rounded things are like jewels, the work of a master hand. Your navel is a rounded bowl that never lacks mixed wine. Your belly is a heap of wheat, encircled with lilies."

"That's in the Bible?" Brenda asked. "It sounds like something from the Kama Gita."

"It's from the Song of Solomon. It's one of the most erotic writings in the Bible." He indicated the recording. "Is there more?"

"Oh, yes," said Brenda. "She looked so traumatized that I asked her if she wanted to continue.

"She grabbed my arm with the desperate strength of a person who saw her last chance to avoid drowning. 'Keep that damned recorder on. Don't you dare run away now. I want to tell the whole vulgar story. He kept quoting his damned poetry even as he mounted me. Something about climbing a palm tree.'

Frank held up his hands to pause the recording. "Probably something like, 'You are stately like a palm tree, and your breasts are like its clusters. I will climb the palm tree and lay hold of its branches."

"She couldn't remember all of it, but that fits with what she did remember," said Brenda.

"So did he just let her go, or did she escape somehow?" asked Frank.

"That's the rest of the story," said Brenda. "Let me play it for you." She turned the recorder on, and Carry continued with her description of what happened.

9

"When he finished, he told me to get dressed, like a slave who had completed her task." Now there was fury in the tone of her voice. "He was through with me. Later, when he dropped me on a street corner, he said to tell others that I had been filled with holy love by an angel of God, and he gave me a cheap heart-like trinket with the words, 'Filled with God's glory' on it. 'Spread the good news, my beloved Mary,' he said and actually winked at me. Then he sped off in his car. And no, I can't tell you what type of car it was. It was just a dark two-door car." She was almost shouting again.

"What did you do then, Carrie?" Brenda asked.

"I wandered for at least another hour before the drug wore off enough for me to know where I was. I called a cab and went home.

"I live alone, so there was no one with whom I had to interact. I now know that it was a mistake, but I immediately took a shower, trying to scrub his filth from me. Then I found a bottle of scotch and got bombed."

Brenda's voice on the recording was hesitant and soft. "I understand."

Carrie continued, "When I finally sobered up, I took a cold hard look at what had happened. I was enraged." Her voice hardened. "I swore that no matter what the consequences, that bastard was not going to get away with this. I decided that I would start with the police station, and that's where you found me."

Brenda shut off the recorder. "While no rape should be dismissed as unimportant, you can see why I thought this one was unique. What do you make of his quoting all those Bible verses?"

Frank hesitated, trying to decide how much to say to Brenda. "I think, in his own mind, he is trying to justify his actions as part of God's special presence in his life," Frank said. "Now that you know where the quotes came from, what do you want to do with the story?"

Brenda picked up the recorder and placed it back in her bag. Then, she looked back at Frank.

"That's what Carrie asked me. She looked so drained and so helpless when she had finished. It was as if all her anger had built up to give her the strength to tell her story, and now that it was done, she was depleted.

I knew it would be wrong under the circumstances, but everything in me wanted to reach out and hold her."

"You were wise not to," Frank said. "Even another woman can be threatening at that point. What did you say?"

"I asked her if she was sure she wanted to be exposed by my printing the story. I wasn't even sure how much of it my paper would let me print," Brenda said.

"My hesitancy seemed to touch enough of her spent energy to give one more push. 'What I want, Ms. Sides, reporter for the *Athens Record*,' she had gone back to the formal address as if to remind me who I was. 'What I want is for you to tell my story with all of its details so that that bastard is exposed, and if he has done or is planning to do it again, the whole world will know.'"

"Where do people get that type of courage?" Frank asked, as he shook his head in wonder.

"I don't know," said Brenda, "but I think she's right that this may not be a one-time occurrence, and if she is brave enough to come forward, I want to help her all I can." She put her notebook back in her purse. "Now I've got to convince my paper to publish it in all its rawness."

"I know at least one member of their editorial board. If you have trouble convincing them, give me a call. Maybe I can help."

"You can't know how much help you've been already. Can I keep in touch with you as this proceeds. I think I'm going to need some spiritual counseling before this is all through."

"The answer is an emphatic yes," said Frank.

As he ushered Brenda to the church door, Frank felt a small spark reignite deep down in his soul. It wasn't much, but it was more than he had felt for a long time.

CHAPTER 2

Eric Ivory to the Rescue

Bob Godwin stood in front of his full-length mirror on his office closet. He checked his profile as he ran a brush through his blong hair. His six-foot, 175-pound body was trim and fit. Not bad for a 52-year-old man, he thought.

Bob had labored in the vineyard of conservative Christianity for more than 25 years. He disdained the complex ideas of theologians and the ambiguous thoughts of religious liberals. Bob preached that Jesus was a simple man. God understands that life is difficult, we all fail at times, but God gave us Jesus to pull us out of the muck and show us how to love and be loved. People flocked to his services and gave rapt attention to his messages filled with humor and simple directions for a better life. In the words of a more liberal colleague, "Bob played the guitar of faith that vibrated with chords that appeal."

Being pastor of the True Vine Church was demanding, but Bob took pride in how he had built this church from several hundred to its current 3,000 members. He was adept at managing a twenty-member staff, mediating when necessary, and maintaining a largely harmonious, smooth functioning program with the multiple offerings that appealed to his varied constituency. He had an innate sense of what would appeal to this media glitzed, often lonely, and easily distracted generation.

It was Friday afternoon. The design for the worship services had been completed and delivered to the music groups and sound engineers on Wednesday. They skillfully prepared the slides and appropriate musical accompaniment in a way that appealed to the digital generation. The sermon was ready, and Bob began to relax. Looking at his calendar, he was delighted to see that he had no appointments. Tomorrow he would practice his sermon and fine tune his delivery, but this afternoon was free.

He poured a fresh cup of coffee and sat in the specially designed contour chair that was placed near the window that looked out on the manicured lawn of the church campus. He picked up the *Athens Record* and turned to reread the newspaper's account of the serial rapist. It irritated him that the news media focused on the crazy lunatic's habit of quoting Scripture while he violated his victim. To label him the Sexual Evangelist bordered on the sacrilegious. While the rapist's atrocious actions horrified Bob, he also saw the story's potential negative impact on the church. Any scandal connected with religion served to confirm society's cynicism and made his work more difficult. As he planned to say in his sermon, even the devil can quote Scripture, but true Christians need to stand up for Jesus, who shows us a better way to live.

As he read the article, he jotted notes about ideas he might develop in future sermons. He knew the issue was not going away. He was tired and perhaps he even dozed a bit. He was surprised that when he looked at his watch, it was three o'clock. He flicked on his radio to listen to the Eric Ivory show.

For several years, Eric had hosted his own talk show over WHNT. By adding two vowels to the radio call letters, he titled his program *Why Not?* He saw himself as the defender of the true faith in a society that had reverted to animalistic paganism.

In a variety of ways, Ivory commented on the various issues of society always asking, *"Why Not* let the pure faith of Jesus guide your life?" Even though Bob saw Eric as a right-wing fanatic, he enjoyed Eric's jeremiads against the liberal churches in Athens. Bob found his show an entertaining break from the demands of the ministry. With Eric on the far right and the liberal churches on the left, he could appear as the moderate voice of reason.

Bob was a strong evangelical conservative and was amused by Eric's attempt to portray himself as standing above the fray and viewing society with the twenty-twenty vision of pure reason and truth. Like Eric's hero, Rush Limbaugh, he would pronounce his judgments on the failed leaders of his city, religious and political, and ominously declare that their day of reckoning was coming. He castigated the liberal churches of Athens and their preachers who watered down the faith in a vain attempt to be relevant. "These weak-kneed, people-pleasing preachers," Eric declared, "have sold out and compromised the faith for their thirty pieces of silver."

Today, Bob was interested in how Eric would respond to this new violence in the city. As Bob listened to the broadcast, it seemed that Eric saw the story of the religious rapist as a platform from which to launch a new campaign. While he had his loyal followers, Eric kept searching for a way to expand his influence.

"Friends, I've been telling you for several years now that those false preachers of liberal religion are leading us down the path to destruction," Ivory said. "Do we need any more evidence of the satanic pollution of our Lord's good news than this sick rapist who is terrorizing our fine city of Athens and spouting religious blasphemy even as he commits his vile acts?

Eric Ivory was on fire with the conviction of a true believer. Bob listened with a growing sense of unease. He knew enough religious history to be aware of the danger of fanaticism.

"I tell you I am fed up with the corruption of our blessed Lord's church. I am announcing today that I am calling all the faithful pastors, and I emphasize the word faithful, I'm calling all of the faithful pastors of the churches in our city to come together next Monday morning, June 3, to work with me to save our city from the Beelzebub rantings that have led to this sorry state."

Bob was sorting through his mail as he listened. His mind had begun to wander, but suddenly he heard his name mentioned.

"I haven't even had a chance to talk to my good friend, Bob Godwin, but I'm sure, at this time of dire emergency, he wouldn't object to our meeting at his True Vine Church."

The nerve of that pipsqueak, Bob thought. What right does he have to presume to call a meeting at my church?

"As The Reverend Godwin says from his fine pulpit Sunday after Sunday, we don't need the fancy theologians and the swishy politicians. We just need the simple words of Jesus to show us the way. And I say to you, my friends, Why Not – Why Not organize the power of this simple gospel to heal our fine city."

Even as Bob's anger grew, there was a part of him that was impressed by the skill with which Eric sought to manipulate both him and the situation. "Spread the word, friends. Let your pastors know that they should be at the meeting next Monday at nine a.m. and become real shepherds of their flocks. We need to protect our city from the wolves in sheep's clothing that have sold out the faith for a mess of pottage."

Bob knew he was being set up, but there was little freedom to maneuver. Eric knew how to push all the buttons. How could Bob explain that in this time of crisis, he wasn't going to cooperate because he hadn't been asked first? He was sure that the other conservative pastors also would feel coerced but they would come to the meeting. They might be upset, but they wouldn't want to be left out if the campaign caught fire.

There goes whatever chance I had to catch my breath on Monday. Who can oppose the new incarnation of John Wayne riding to the rescue of the fair damsels in our city? I can only hope, Bob thought, that some of my pastor colleagues can help moderate Eric's growing extremism.

* * * * *

During the Saturday and Sunday services, Bob spoke to about 2,500 worshippers. He made clear that he had invited Eric Ivory, host of the *Why Not* radio show, to meet with the clergy of the city to discern God's will. "I believe that it is critical for us to respond to the blasphemous outrage that has been perpetrated on our beautiful city. I ask you to keep the pastors of this city in prayer while we gather to listen to God's bidding."

Later, as he thought about it, his irritation at Eric subsided. It was presumptuous, of course, and he would certainly let Eric know that he had stepped over the line. Still, it was good to visibly demonstrate Bob's True Vine Church in a leadership position in the city. People who listened to Ivory might be a little confused as to who had initiated the meeting, but it would be clear that Bob was stepping up when the city was in need.

* * * * *

As Ivory had hoped, with the city on edge, over the weekend the other news media had broadcast his invitation to the city's pastors. The serial rapist was headline news, and his Scripture quoting made the churches' response news as well. Both the broadcast and print media sent reporters to cover his forum. Rhetoric overrode reason as the gathered pastors, under the glare of the media in attendance, vied with each other to demonstrate that they wanted to cleanse the city of heresy and save the women of the city from violence in the process. Most of those in attendance were from the conservative churches, but there were also some pastors from more moderate churches. They listened but did not get into the debate.

The pastors joined Bob in being concerned that the rapist's extensive use of Scripture and religious symbolism had a negative effect on their own ministries. "It's that type of blasphemy that can destroy our churches," one pastor said. "Somehow we need to help people see the difference between faithful churches and those pseudo-churches that have perverted the true Gospel of Jesus Christ, our Lord, and Savior."

Another pastor quoted a letter to the editor printed in Sunday's paper. "In his tirade," the pastor said with disdain in his voice, "the writer repeats adnauseam the old charge of how the church has oppressed women from the beginning, and now churches are paying the price." There were audible groans from others. "It gets worse," the pastor said. "Listen to this, 'Look out when you are near a preacher, You never know when he might seek heavenly bliss in a more physical manner.' That is slander," said the speaker.

The audience of preachers agreed. This was a clear challenge to the integrity of their profession.

"How do we fight that type of falsehood?" the next speaker asked. "The Gospels make clear that even Satan can quote Scripture, but we need to restore our people's trust in the true church."

Eric Ivory, at 5'5" and 220 pounds, was not as commanding a figure in public as his deep voice conveyed on the radio. As he had hoped, however, the pastors were desperate to hear any voice that might guide them in responding to this attack on their character. So, after several hours of plaintive exchanges, Eric Ivory recovered the mike. "My brothers and sisters in Christ, I believe the time has come for the faithful to separate themselves from the pagans, even those wolves in religious sheep's clothing. I have been promised substantial financial backing for a concerted effort by the true believing churches to make use of the media and the best speakers available to begin a crusade that will expose the heretics and invite the faithful to join together in Christ."

There was applause, and some cheers of relief, but Bob could see there was also some hesitancy, especially among the more experienced pastors. They clapped because they weren't ready to challenge Ivory in front of the media. At the same time, they had been through many religious campaigns before, and like a suitor once burned, twice shy, they wanted to know more before they signed on. Enthusiasm was not enough for them.

Eric, caught up in his own rhetoric, hadn't noticed. He took the applause as affirmation and was prepared to plunge ahead. "We need to draw up a plan of battle to cleanse the Body of Christ of this malignant cancer that threatens us."

Again there were some cheers.

"Towards that end," Eric continued, "I would propose that we first form a steering committee to draw up a plan and that we come together again in two weeks to lift up the banner of Christ over this great city of Athens. As our Lord and Savior declared, his faithful people are the light to the rest of the world. This immediate threat is only the tip of the iceberg, as you and I know, but maybe we can allow the fear in this city to wake its citizens to the greater danger around us. Let this be the beginning of a great revival of the faithful and a full exposure of those who have betrayed the faith of our Lord."

Bob watched as those gathered began to give assent to Eric's proposal. Some of the younger pastors gave enthusiastic support. Others of the more seasoned pastors were considering how much control they were willing to turn over to such a campaign.

"Been there, done that revival thing," said one of Bob's more seasoned colleagues. "Everybody's excited now, but I've watched these waves hit the beach before. They always recede. When they do, my church will still be standing. What about you, Bob?"

"I'm with you, Carl," said Bob, "but we got to play along for now. This Sexual Evangelist has really got people spooked."

Eric was watching the crowd's response, and as it began to subside, he acted to retain control of what was happening. "I would like Bob Godwin, Carl Hutchins, Billy Jameson, and two others that you can choose to work with me on a strategic plan. We'll caucus before we leave today and set some dates to begin meeting."

He's done it again, thought Bob. Does it ever occur to him to consult with people before he appoints them to his caucuses? There's a time coming when our Mr. Ivory is going to get his pearly whites shoved back in his silver throat or some where else that is even less visible. For now, however, I need to reestablish that this meeting is taking place in my church.

"I know its old fashioned," Bob began, "and many of you are lifting the roof with your exciting contemporary music, but I'd suggest that Bishop Ferguson lead us in a rendition of 'Shall We Gather at the River' to conclude our meeting."

It did not occur to Bob that he had just volunteered Bishop Ferguson without asking. True to his nature, the Bishop swallowed the insult and demonstrated more grace than was deserved.

Bishop Ferguson, pastor of a large independent holiness church and one of the few African Americans present, began to move forward. Even as he walked, his rich baritone voice began the gospel tune, and young and old joined in with enthusiasm.

The media rushed forward seeking comments from both Ivory and Bob. One had the temerity to shout out the question, "Do you think the rapist is a clergyman?"

A sudden silence fell over those who had heard the question. It had been the elephant in the room from the beginning, and now it had been voiced.

Bob had an idea. He stepped to the microphone and asked for silence. "Some of you may have heard a question from one of our guests from the media. He asked whether we thought that the rapist was a clergyman."

There was a chorus of boos from some of those near the back.

"Wait a moment," said Bob. "Clearly this reporter thinks that we have better knowledge than the entire police department of the city of Athens."

There was some laughter and some cat calls.

"I would like all those clergy present who have raped someone in the last year or know a clergy who has to please raise your hands."

There was an uncomfortable moment of silence. Then Bob continued. "There you have it, Mr. Reporter, among the faithful pastors gathered here, there are no candidates. While we await the work of the police, you may report that our churches are in the hands of faithful, hard-working pastors."

There was a strong response of applause.

CHAPTER 3

First Meeting with Police

Brenda Sides and Carrie Breakstone were right in their gamble. Brenda had pushed hard to get the story told in its uncensored form. The paper agreed but, at the police's request, they withheld some details like the rapist's misuse of names. The paper did emphasize the rapist's use of quotes from the Song of Solomon. They even dubbed him the Sexual Evangelist.

Because of the Scripture quoting aspect of the crime, the *Athens Record* story was quickly picked up by both the print and the television media around the nation. The bloggers on the Internet had a hey day offering different theories as to the significance of this blend of sex and religion. The city of Athens quickly gained a notoriety that they didn't appreciate.

The mayor tried to reassure the public as to the safety of the city while demanding quick action on the part of his police department. The combination of fear by many and embarrassment by the city leaders quickly ramped up the pressure on the police to catch the rapist. Even greater fear and unwanted publicity erupted when Carrie's suspicions proved accurate.

In a follow-up story, it was revealed that three prior victims found the courage to come into the police station and report similar experiences. They said they had been reluctant because they felt like they had cooperated in some way and were ashamed. Carrie's refusal to be silent gave them the courage to come forward. By the week end, the police knew they had a serial rapist.

Under growing pressure to show progress in the investigation, the police combed the city looking for likely suspects. As part of the investigation, they examined their records for registered sex offenders in the area, and their attention was drawn to Reggie Pardella. Reggie's arrest back in 1998 was a major scandal within the education system of Athens. Reggie was a physical education teacher in the South Park Middle School as well as an assistant soccer coach. He also ran a popular sport's camp during the summer for middle-school children. When it was revealed that Reggie had molested several middle school children over several years, there was a strong outcry, and more than one administrator in the school system was forced to resign.

Fifteen years later, Reggie Pardella was released from prison in response to a plan of careful supervision sponsored by the John Knox Presbyterian Church in negotiation with the parole board. The prisons were overcrowded, and there was interest in a program that might demonstrate the possibility of new beginnings for some of the nonviolent prisoners and thus provided space for the violent ones.

The parole board, after careful consideration, in consultation with the courts and his psychiatrist, agreed to Reggie's provisional release. Everyone agreed that he had to follow the legal procedure of being registered as a sex offender, but it was hoped that working with the church, he could demonstrate good conduct and be reintegrated into society. As part of the plan, they agreed to release him quietly so as not to arouse negative public pressures. His release came three months before the rapes began. The timing seemed ominous.

Now both the courts and the mayor were fearful that the blow back from his release could prove devastating. The police chief, under tremendous pressure from the mayor, chose one of his best detectives, Lieutenant Carl Bryson, to follow up on Reggie as a possible suspect. Bryson, with his blond hair and blue eyes, was almost Hollywood handsome with a big smile and a quick wit. On first impression, Bryson often appeared to be brash and a little arrogant. Those who worked with him, however, knew that he was both canny and thorough. It was accepted among the officers that you could trust Bryson to always have your back.

As part of building background for his investigation, Bryson decided to begin with the local prison. When he told the prison operator what he was interested in, she connected him with the Superintendent of the prison, James Kramer.

"This is Superintendent Kramer, Warden of Marshall Prison, how can I help you?"

"This is Lieutenant Carl Bryson of the Athens police force. I'm investigating our recent rash of rapes in the city and the name of Reggie Pardella came up. I understand he was a resident of your prison."

"Should have kept him here, if you ask me," Kramer responded. "I don't know about you, Bryson, but as far as I'm concerned, we should cleanse the earth of these perverts."

Bryson knew he was talking to someone who wanted to vent, and he decided to give him plenty of space in which to do it. "Well, Superintendent Kramer, I can give you the usual bullshit that this person is not a suspect or even a person of interest at this point, but I wonder if you can give me any background that might be of use to me."

"He didn't particularly cause any problems," Kramer responded, "but I've been at this game a long time. I keep up with what the experts are saying. I believe most people can change but not these perverts, so I'm not fooled."

"Fooled?" Bryson said and let it hang.

"Religion, he got religion," Kramer said. "He's not the first to suddenly see the light if they think it will improve their chance to get parole."

His words caught Bryson's attention. "Tell me more." Even though Bryson assumed that Kramer probably had read the stories about the rapist in the *Athens Record*, he didn't want to lead Kramer's response but rather see how it would unfold.

"Some bleeding-heart pastor was leading a Bible study here at the prison and good old Reggie saw his opportunity and latched on to him. Don't get me wrong, Bryson, I'm all for churches leading Bible studies here at the prison. It can even straighten some of these guys out but not the perverts. No one has come up with a cure for them. There really isn't anything you can do for them, if you ask me, except lock them up and throw away the key."

"So you don't think he was sincere?" asked Bryson.

"In his own demented mind, maybe," said Kramer, "but I wouldn't want my daughters near him, if you know what I mean."

This guy is a real Neanderthal, thought Bryson. I wouldn't want my daughters near Kramer either. He could be right about Reggie though. He decided to probe a little further.

"But he convinced the parole board," Bryson said.

"He and his pastor buddy," said Kramer. "They worked out some fancy plan that the parole board bought. It's not the parole board's fault. They're under pressure to make more room here at the prison without spending the money to build more space. But releasing these perverts is asking for trouble."

"Can you tell me more about the plan and who the pastor was?"

"The pastor is Reverend Sessions from John Knox church; Presbyterian, I think. One of those liberal churches who can't accept that anyone is all bad," said Kramer.

"I know the type," Bryson said. "What was their plan?"

"Don't know a lot about it," Kramer said. "It was called 'New Beginnings' and had something to do with finding a group of men who would meet regularly with Pardella and agree to be by his side whenever he went to church or other public places for a period of time. I guess they forgot to tail him when he went to the park."

"So you think he might be our guy?" Bryson asked.

"Don't really know about that, detective. Guess that's your field. But whether he's guilty this time or not, he's still part of the cancer that is destroying our community."

"Thank you, Superintendent Kramer, you have been very helpful."

Good luck, detective. You catch him and I'll be glad to put him in solitary for you."

Now, thought Bryson, I need to do a little research on our good Reverend Sessions. I wonder why he is so interested in helping sexual predators in our society.

Frank knew that Brenda's story would kindle a firestorm of emotions in the city. He hadn't anticipated the national interest that it triggered. The more the national media and Internet commentators focused on the story, and, therefore the city of Athens, the more the pressure built on the city leaders and the police department. The media and the Bloggasphere seem endlessly captivated by the synergism of religion and sex, he thought. If you throw in a little violence, as long as people can view it from a distance, the public is enthralled.

The story made people in Athens very nervous, but it also made the police aware of the serial nature of the rapist and about that Frank felt good. He was also pleased that Brenda had been sensitive to his desire to leave his name out of the story. Once he might have enjoyed being in the fray of such events, but not anymore.

Frank was not prepared for a phone call from the police on Monday afternoon asking if they could come by on Tuesday morning. Normally he handled pressure well, but their call had put him on edge. Since he trusted that Brenda had not been the source of their interest, he worried about what could have brought his name to their attention. Logic would suggest, and he hoped it was true, that their interest centered around the prison ministry program that his church sponsored. A couple of the parolees that they sponsored were registered sex offenders, and he assumed that was the source of the police's interest. He was confident that none of them fit the profile of the rapist, but the call still made him nervous.

Frank arrived at his office at 6 a.m. on Tuesday. Before the police arrived, he wanted to get the bulletin ready and some preparation for his budget meeting that night. A slight cold had developed over night. He hoped some extra vitamin C and lots of water could help him ward it off, but it did nothing to help his mood.

As he was completing the budget preparations, he began to muse about how best to respond to the police visit. He didn't want to let his irritation show. After all, they were just trying to do their job. Then Marcie's voice came over the intercom.

"Frank, your 10 a.m. appointment is here."

Frank recognized the tautness of his secretary's voice. It reinforced his own nervousness. He wanted his emotions under control. The last several years, since Rosie died, the emotional control in which he once took pride had slipped. As one of his early mentors said, "A good pastor can 'suffer fools gladly' if the end result is to advance the larger purpose." The larger purpose in this case was to satisfy the police's inquiry and move on in life.

"I'll be right out, Marcie."

His office was small and crammed with books on all sides. His large desk was the central piece of furniture that dominated the room. There was space that allowed for a sitting area off to one side. He straightened some chairs in the sitting area. He had considered making them sit across from him in front of his desk. No, I'm still a pastor, he thought. I should demonstrate hospitality. He opened his office door.

As he entered the outer office, he saw there were two police officers standing stiffly by his secretary's desk. One, an imposing officer with sergeant stripes, was about six-foot-four and easily topped 220 pounds. Beside him was a physically less imposing lieutenant with blond hair and a natural smile who appeared clearly comfortable with himself. He advanced and stuck out his hand.

"Reverend, I'm Lieutenant Carl Bryson. Thank you for meeting with us. This is Sergeant O'Riley." He laughed and said, "I tell him he's the only African American in the city with an Irish name."

Sergeant O'Riley, who had obviously heard the joke many times, managed a small smile as he held out his hand. "It's a pleasure to meet you, sir."

"Won't you gentlemen come in?" Frank said. He ushered them into his office. He indicated the small circle of chairs and asked if they would like some coffee.

"No, Reverend," Bryson spoke for both of them. "That won't be necessary. We just have a few questions, and we'll be on our way." He glanced around the office and commented, "You sure have lots of books. You must do a bunch of reading."

Frank was annoyed but also amused at the attempt to put him on the defensive. "I do have lots of books, Lieutenant. I like to read them to relieve stress when I'm not doing real work." He hoped that Bryson hadn't noticed that one whole section of the bookcase on the wall behind his desk was filled with books on various aspects of sexuality and religion.

"I like to exercise, myself," said Bryson.

Frank maintained a steady gaze directly at Bryson and was pleased that it seemed to make him uncomfortable. "Have you made progress in the serial rape case, Lieutenant? It will certainly relieve anxiety in the city when that happens."

"We may do that soon, Reverend." He took out a small notebook and pen and prepared to write. "As part of our investigation, we've come to ask you about someone that I believe you know. His name is Reggie Pardella."

Frank tried to hide his anger. He knew that as the pressure grew for the police to solve the serial rape case it was very likely that Reggie's name would come up. As both a registered sex offender and part of a scandal that had rocked the city fifteen years ago, Reggie was a likely target for this investigation. Frank had been proud, if a little nervous, about Reggie's participation in the New Beginnings release ministry sponsored by his church. A psychiatrist member and some dedicated men in his church agreed to form a support group to help Reggie adjust to his release in society and provide supervision. Reggie had been very honest about his sickness and seemed to be making good progress. Yet it was understandable that a registered sex offender might become a suspect for police who were desperate for a lead.

Since Frank had not been asked a question, he did not respond but continued to look at Bryson.

Bryson waited for a moment and when the silence continued, he finally asked, "You do know Mr. Pardella, don't you, Reverend?"

"Yes, I know Mr. Pardella," Frank said and then waited in silence.

Bryson wrote a note in his pad and then looked up. "I gather from your visits to him in prison and your proposed plan with the parole board that you know that Mr. Pardella is a registered sex offender?"

"I am aware of that," Frank said. He had learned the silence game a long time ago and drew some pleasure in seeing that it irritated Bryson. Normally this would be the police's tactic, but Frank had reversed it on Bryson. He wasn't sure but he sensed that O'Riley was a little amused that his Lieutenant was not intimidating Frank.

"Are you in the habit creating plans for perverts in your congregation?" Bryson said.

Frank noticed that Bryson watched him closely to see how he would react. So, thought Frank, we are moving from silence to aggression in this chess game. OK, I can play that as well.

"You may not be familiar with the nature of a Christian congregation, Lieutenant. We are a hospital for sinners of all types. As Paul put it, 'God chose what is foolish in the world to shame the wise; what is low and despised in the world so that no one may boast of his goodness before God.' We would be most pleased to welcome you and Sergeant O'Riley to worship with us any Sunday morning. Our services begin at 11 a.m."

Bryson stiffened a little. "I have my own church, Reverend. Our congregation is made up of people who try to lead a moral life. We believe in condemning sin as sin."

Frank decided to reverse the gamesmanship that had raised the tension level in the room. "Lieutenant, let me make it simple for you. Reggie Pardella, while not a member, does come to worship with us at this congregation and is part of our New Beginnings ministry. He knows and we know that he is a sick individual. After all, his sickness destroyed what had seemed to be a promising career at South Park Middle School. With his agreement, we take some special precautions when Reggie is here, but he is welcome as one sinner among many sinners."

"Do you know where Mr. Pardella is now?" Sergeant O'Riley asked.

That question caught Frank off guard. "I assume that he is at his apartment building, but I'm not sure," said Frank. "Is he a suspect in your investigation?"

"He is a person of interest," Bryson said.

"Well, I don't know his whereabouts, but I will make inquiries and see if I can help you," Frank said. "However, from what is being reported in the papers, I seriously doubt that Reggie is your man."

"And why do you say that?" Bryson asked.

"First, your rapist seems to evidence a high intellect, and Reggie, though once a physical education teacher, doesn't show that capacity. Second, though the reports of the women have been conflicting, it is consistently reported that the rapist is a physically strong individual and that doesn't match Reggie as well. Though he was a soccer coach and rather agile with his feet, he has a childhood injury that damaged one of his arms. Reggie is not going to be able to lift women up on those makeshift altars."

"And how do you know so much about the rapist, Reverend?" Bryson asked.

"In addition to books, I also read the papers, Lieutenant. While fanatics do memorize portions of Scripture, as the rapist has done, some of his rantings evidence a higher intellect than just memorization."

"Very interesting," Bryson said as he made another note on his pad.

Sergeant O'Riley, who had been quietly sitting off to the side, spoke up. "Reverend, you seem uncomfortable with our questions. Do you think that perhaps you have an authority problem?"

Frank studied him for a few seconds.

Bryson, still writing in his notebook, looked up. "You didn't assume that my almost racist joke at the beginning of our conversation indicated that I lacked trust in O'Riley's uncanny ability to read people, did you, Reverend?"

Frank was quick to recognize that he had been outmaneuvered. "Let's say that I now recognize that you both are better at chess than I gave you credit for, Lieutenant."

O'Riley continued to watch as Bryson resumed control of the interview. "I'm interested in your analysis of the rapist, Reverend. As I recall," he glanced at his notes, "you suggest that it would be an intelligent person, very strong, and with a knowledge of Scripture."

"And Reggie doesn't fit that description," said Frank.

"No, that's true, but you would, wouldn't you, Reverend?"

Frank felt the blood rush to his head. For a second he even felt dizzy. Determined not to lose control of himself and realizing that his reaction to this veiled accusation could be critical, he paused, looked at Bryson, tilted his head, raised a quizzical eyebrow and said, "Are you accusing me of something, Lieutenant, or just trying to be irritating?"

Bryson allowed a small smile to curve his lips upward. "You're not a bad chess player yourself, Reverend."

Now it was Frank's turn to smile. "I apologize, Lieutenant. I've had a rough couple of days. I'll try to be more cooperative. What else can I help you with?"

They all stood up. "Nothing at the moment, unless you do hear from Pardella. Do you mind if Sergeant O'Riley and I look around your church for a few minutes?"

"Not at all. Would prefer to do it by yourselves, or would you like me to give you a tour?"

"A tour would be nice. You probably have a set of keys that would be helpful."

"In case you want to look into some closets or other secret hideaways," Frank said, but this time his tone was playful. "I will be most happy to show you anywhere you would like, Lieutenant. Again, I apologize for our rough beginning."

Frank ushered them out of his office. "Marcie," he said to his secretary, "I'm going to give these officers a tour of our church. I'll be back in a few moments."

Frank was a little ashamed of his own behavior. He had decided that the best defense was a good offence, but realized now that he had enjoyed the joust too much. It made him stand out rather than fade into the background as he desired.

He was still rattled by Bryson's statement and wondered if there was more behind it. Had he made note of Frank's collection of books on sexuality? How much had Bryson looked into Frank's past? Were the questions about Reggie Pardella just a cover for what Bryson really wanted to know? My behavior this morning, Frank thought, hasn't done me any favors.

They proceeded to take a tour of the church.

As the officers were concluding their visit, Frank said, "I wish you the best of luck in tracking down this rapist. He has given religion a bad name."

"Well, we are working hard on this case. The commander has even brought in a detective who specializes in this area to help us. She may want to talk with you once she gets moving on her investigation.

"I will be glad to help in any way that I can," said Frank.

As Frank watched the officers drive away, he chastised himself. Control yourself, Frank, this will all be over soon, and you can return to your little dungeon.

CHAPTER 4

When You're Tired

Bob Godwin was tired. It was 3:30 on Tuesday afternoon, and he had stopped at a Wendy's for a Coke. Many people would be thinking that they had three more days until the weekend, but for Bob, a pastor of a mega church, it meant three more days until *Show Time*.

He was hoping for a sugar jolt to get him through his next appointment. The people bustling around him seemed so full of zip and vigor. They had just come off a three-day weekend while he had preached five times, once on Saturday and four times on Sunday. He knew he had preached a good sermon, but what mattered now was what he would come up with for next weekend.

The only thing that mattered was whether you kept pleasing them. It was the monster that haunted all pastors and weighed on them continually. Last Sunday was quickly forgotten. By Sunday evening, the prospect of beginning all over again left him mildly depressed.

The Bible-quoting rapist had freaked out the whole city and put all churches on edge. Some of Bob's members thought they were being funny when they cracked jokes on Sunday about watching out for the preachers in the city. Bob wanted to cram their pitiful attempt at humor down their throat, but he smiled instead.

Many pastors take Monday off to recover but not Bob. He tried to slow down that day, but yesterday did not offer that opportunity. That blowhard Limbaugh wannabe, Eric_Ivory, messed up that possibility when he called his forum at the True Vine Church. As Bob expected, there was more rhetoric than action, and the meeting had gone on and on. If preaching drained him, listening to a bunch of pastors whose speeches sounded like warmed over sermons, left him in despair. Then to top it off, Ivory announced that Bob was a member of the steering committee to plan the next steps. The forum plus the steering committee occupied most of his Monday.

The majority at yesterday's forum were conservative pastors, but what could you expect from the liberals. Most of them had already lost their faith and were just tilting at the latest windmill hoping that someone would recognize they were relevant.

As he thought back on the meeting, he was intrigued by what took place. The rapist, dubbed by the media as the Sexual Evangelist, gave Ivory a platform to advance his agenda by mounting a crusade. Ivory was on a roll, and no one, including Bob, had had the courage to try to slow him down.

Bob returned home Monday evening bone tired. After supper, he had made twelve phone calls to visitors who were first time attendees at the weekend services. When he finished, he invited Barbie, his wife, to watch a movie, but she claimed she was too tired and went to bed early. Even good movies aren't much fun to watch by yourself.

After a few hours of sleep, and a breakfast with Barbie where neither said much, he went to the office and did some initial research on his sermon. Then he met with a couple to plan their marriage service, had a luncheon meeting with some members of the outreach committee, and met with the steering committee Ivory had established to implement his plan. Now, he hoped the Coke would give him the energy for his last visit of the day.

Felicity Marshall, a widow who had lost her husband three months ago, asked him on Sunday if he could come by for a visit. He assumed she was having trouble coping with her husband's death and uncertain about her future. She probably also felt lonely and in need of some decent conversation. He had thought a lot about how to cope with loneliness. Maybe he could offer her some helpful suggestions.

Few people understood how lonely it was to be a pastor of a large church. They assumed that your life was fulfilling because you were surrounded by people seven days a week doing the Lord's work. They didn't realize that each of those people asked something from you and it was rare that anyone ever stopped to consider what you needed; rarer still that someone would treat you like a normal adult rather than pigeon-hole you into the role of pastor.

In many ways, Barbie was the perfect wife for a successful pastor. He recalled with pleasure how beautiful she was at their wedding now over twenty-five years ago. His six foot, 175 pound, well-conditioned body would be considered handsome, but she was a knockout. She still was beautiful, popular with the congregation, and focused on what would advance his career. His only regret was that they were both so busy filling their roles that they often neglected giving attention to each other.

As he passed through the gate of the Marshall residence and drove down the long tree lined driveway, Bob chided himself for whining and refocused his attention on the pastoral needs of this recent widow in his congregation. He knew that he often felt better after he helped someone through counseling, so maybe this visit would also get him out of his pity party. The landscaped yard was a thing of beauty. Strategically located, tiered gardens gave off an array of color. The house was a mansion with a beautiful stone facade. Sculptures guided one's gaze towards the large entrance veranda. Bob spotted a six-car garage off to the side. A Lamborghini sat in front of the garage.

The Marshalls were not shy about displaying their wealth. At least, thought Bob, it seemed to be in good taste. It's nice that the wealthy can bring some beauty into the world.

The Marshalls had joined the congregation three years ago, but Bob really didn't know much about them. Floyd Marshall was a very successful banker. People were shocked to hear that he had died of a heart attack while away on a business trip. Bob heard rumors that Floyd was not always faithful during his business trips, but his tragic death silenced such gossip.

Parking his Chevy Impala in the circular driveway in front, Bob recovered a bounce to his steps as he approached the massive oak door at the entrance. He admired the oversized, artfully crafted brass knocker on the door but chose to press the doorbell. It was five till four. Better early than late, he thought. He heard the musical chimes begin to play, and the door swung open.

Felicity Marshall greeted him with a big smile. She was a slim, attractive woman in her early forties. Her blond hair was tied back in a ponytail and she wore dark blue slacks and a scarlet red silk blouse. A delicate silver chain and pendant was at her neck.

"Rev. Godwin, it is so nice of you to come."

"I'm glad to visit, Mrs. Marshall. I'm sorry that we didn't have a chance to get better acquainted before your husband's sudden death."

"I certainly understand you can't know all the thousands of members of your wonderful church. As a beginning to our becoming acquainted, why don't you call me Felicity."

"Certainly, Felicity, and please call me Bob."

"That's awfully nice of you, Bob." She blushed and looked down at her feet. "I wasn't sure that it was right to call a reverend by his first name."

Searching for words that would ease her discomfort, Bob smiled and said, "We are human like everyone else, Felicity. In fact, sometimes it's nice to have people drop the reverend and just respond as two friends would."

"Then let me invite my good friend, Bob, into my home." She bowed and waved her hand as a gesture of invitation.

As she bowed, Bob noticed cleavage under her form-fitting blouse but quickly shifted his eyes toward the interior of the house as he stepped through the door. The foyer had a Brazilian cherry hardwood floor and a high ceiling that opened onto a second floor balcony. There was an attractive painting of a sailing ship buffeted by the wind on one wall. A large palm plant was off to the right side. A cut-glass chandelier reflected soft light overhead.

Felicity directed Bob toward a small sitting room. A large picture window overlooked a manicured flowerbed at the rear of the house. Bob didn't know flowers well, but he recognized roses, gladiolas, and several others that provided a panoply of colors. Felicity took a seat on a small couch, and Bob sat in an overstuffed chair facing her. A coffee table separated them.

"Would it be naughty of me to suggest that my good friend Bob share an afternoon glass of wine with me at the end of what I imagine has been a very full day?" She tilted her head down slightly, paused, and looked up through her eyelashes. There was a puckish grin on her ruby red lips.

Bob knew that Barbie wouldn't be home for supper till after 7. "It has been a long day, Felicity, and I would love to share a small glass of wine with you."

"Oh, goody," she said and bounced up to get a bottle of wine from a wine cooler on the credenza. "How about a French Chateau de Nages? Floyd loved to bring back bottles of quality wines from his travels. This one says it is a Rhone blend that delivers a concentrated nose of blackberries, dried herbs, and licorice." She tittered lightly. "It sounds like a perfect afternoon wine, don't you think?"

"I think it sounds delicious," Bob said.

She placed the bottle in a clever little device that effortlessly removed the cork. She poured two glasses with ample portions of wine.

Handing one glass to Bob, Felicity sat on the couch and raised her glass. "Here is to friendship. God knows I need a friend." Then she looked surprised at what she had said. She flushed slightly. "Oh, I'm sorry. I shouldn't say such things around a reverend."

"You've been under a lot of stress with Floyd's death. I don't want you to feel you have to measure your words, especially," he smiled, "around a friend."

"Thank you, Bob." She took a sip of wine, savored it for a couple of seconds, and swallowed. "My life has certainly been turned upside down. I guess it taught me that what you think is a secure future can change in an instant."

Bob spoke softly but with conviction, trying to convey support and comfort. "I know that you have suffered a great loss, Felicity, and the future looks rather uncertain, but you must trust that God will be with you in this difficult time. I hope the church can provide you with good support as well."

"The church has already been wonderful." She paused, as if searching for the right words. She drained her wine glass and refilled it. She offered Bob more wine, but he declined. "What I say to you, both as a friend and as a pastor, is confidential right?" Her left hand reached for a small pillow that she pulled onto her lap.

"Of course, Felicity. It would be very natural for you to have many confused emotions at this time. Sometimes trying to tell someone what you are feeling can help you understand what is happening in your soul. You can trust that whatever you say will be held in confidence."

She sat her glass down, gripped the small pillow more tightly, looked out the window for a few seconds, and then spoke softly. "It's true, you know."

I'm not sure I understand," Bob said as he leaned in to hear her words.

"I know what people are saying." Felicity looked back at Bob. "I have no doubt that Floyd was with another woman that night when he died. It's happened before."

"I'm sorry," Bob said. "That must make this very difficult."

"It makes it both difficult and confusing. My feelings are all over the place."

"Paul advises us to be angry but not let the sun go down on our anger," Bob said. "I think he was telling us that feelings of anger are natural, but we mustn't let them fester inside ourselves. Talking them out can sometimes help."

"You want to know how angry I am, Bob? I'm almost glad he's dead. He's been dead to me for several years. I put up a good front, the picture perfect couple, but it was lonely as hell." She tossed the pillow back to the corner of the couch, grabbed a Kleenex with one hand, and undid her ponytail with the other.

Bob reached out and covered her hand with his.

At first she didn't respond and then she turned her hand around and clasped his hand. "Barbie's a very lucky woman," she said. "I haven't had a man touch me with tenderness for years."

"Floyd was a very foolish man not to recognize the treasure he had," Bob said.

"All those years being the good girl. Sometimes I would lie awake at night and wish some stranger would come through my bedroom window and ravish me just so I knew what it felt like." Again, she looked up through her long eye lashes at Bob. "Aren't I just the most horrible person you've ever met?"

"I don't think you are horrible. I think you are a very lonely person. We all need to be touched and valued."

"You do understand, don't you? Oh, thank you." With her free hand she used a magazine to fan her slightly flushed face. "Would you think it was terrible of me to ask if you could sit beside me and hold me just for a minute?" Then she blushed deep scarlet and almost stammered "I'm sorry, I should never have asked that of you. Please forgive me."

Bob hesitated for a second, released her hand, and stood. "There is nothing to forgive, Felicity. I understand your need for comfort. We all need that from time to time." Then he moved around the coffee table and sat beside her with one arm around her shoulder. She melted into him and began to cry softly.

"Thank you, Bob. You know you are the one who made God real in my life. I don't know how I would have made it through these last several years without the faith you helped me discover. In a way, this is like God holding me in his arms."

Bob felt her softness and was warmed himself as she cried softly on his shoulder.

Then she began to giggle. Her one hand began to feel his chest. "I know I'm being wicked, but it feels nice to touch a man. It's a lot better than having a stranger ravish me. You're sort of my knight in shining armor."

Bob knew he should resist, but he didn't want to. All his own loneliness made his body ache for the soft touch of this woman. "I'm not sure my armor is very protective at the moment."

She sat back slightly. "My goodness, it's so hot in here."

Bob tried to respond with some supporting words. His eyes widened, and he felt his lips part as he saw her reach up and unbutton a couple of buttons on her blouse. She snuggled back in and spoke in a childlike voice. "I know that Felicity is being bad, bad, bad, but you really feel good, good, good. You are sooo strong."

He tried to shift slightly as he became aware of the bulge appearing in his own pants.

"Oooh, naughty, naughty Felicity. Me, oh my, open my eye and see what I spy. I think you have a wrinkle in your pants, Bobby. Let me see if I can smooth it out."

An hour later both Bob and Felicity became almost shy as they turned their backs and replaced their clothes.

"Uh, Felicity, that was truly wonderful, but I hope you understand that as your pastor this can't continue."

"OK, my good friend Bob has changed back into my faithful pastor. Actually, I do understand. I've never done anything like that with anyone except my husband when we were in the early years of our marriage. However, I want you to know that it really felt good, and I will keep this afternoon in my fantasies forever. If occasionally you feel lonely, as I know you will from time to time, just remember the time that Bob escaped being a pastor for one afternoon and took a lonely widow to the moon and back."

They hugged briefly, and Bob left the house. As he got into his car, he glanced back. He couldn't believe what he was seeing. She had opened her blouse and was flashing her breasts at him. Then with a big smile, she blew him a kiss as he drove off. Somehow the tiredness of early afternoon had entirely left him.

At one level, he knew he had sinned. It had happened before. Several years ago a voluptuous counselee had invited his supporting touch but later brought accusations to his church board. He confessed to the board that she had caught him at a weak moment, and a couple of wealthy benefactors offered her a settlement for the good of the church. His tearful confession had convinced his board, and he vowed to be stronger the next time he was tempted. He knew it was wrong, but part of him wondered if occasionally God made special allowances for those who worked so hard for him. At least he hoped so.

CHAPTER 5

Reggie's Arrest and Frank's Response

Frank was the first to arrive at his small, cluttered office at the John Knox church. Being alone in his house, he saw no reason not to arrive early and he enjoyed the smell of fresh coffee as he plugged in the coffeemaker so that it would be ready when others arrived.

He set aside Thursday morning to outline sermon topics and other program ideas for the remaining Sundays before Pentecost. With all the excitement, even national attention to events in Athens, he wanted to help his members gain some perspective. Yet, even as he worked, niggling doubts kept invading his thoughts. *Who am I to offer anyone perspective when I can't even see beyond my own dark shadow? What do I have to say to these people? They are already coping with life's challenges better than I am.*

He once had been a good preacher, full of passion and conviction. Since Rosie's death, he had wandered in a dark haze. At best, he was keeping up appearances and going through the motions. He admired his loyal church members for continuing to come to worship and endure his anemic attempt to preach. *If you can build up points in heaven, he thought, these people who have endured their pastor's unresolved grief with great patience deserve to have their share.*

Brenda's interview and the excitement following her story, reminded him of what it used to be like. He didn't have fiery red hair like she has, but once he shared her passion for the truth and maybe even a little bit of her courage. *If nothing else comes out of this mess in Athens, he* hoped that the national attention to her story would give a boost to her career. With her type of spirit and the skills she demonstrated in the interview, he thought, she should have a bright future in journalism.

He turned back to the project before him. He wanted to reward his faithful members with at least a pale reflection of what a real sermon was like. Do I even remember how to do that, he thought?

Many churches feel a letdown after the excitement of Easter. Part of the challenge for the pastor is energizing the congregation as they approach the Pentecost season. Unfortunately for the pastor, the Pentecost season is also the spring season when people's attention is drawn to other things than the church. As Frank jotted down notes, he thought about how contemporary Christians demonstrate problems that were similar to the original disciples. After the cross, the disciples seemed to lose their commitment and just wanted to hide away. Hey, maybe that would be a good theme for a series of sermons. Maybe we all are in need of being visited by some Pentecostal fire.

For the next couple of hours, he worked on his notes trying to expand on the idea. His intercom buzzed. He knew that Marcie was trying to protect his morning, so he figured this must be important. "Yes, Marcie, what is it?"

"It's Andy, one of your legal-eagle buddies, and from the sound of his voice, I think it's important." Andy was one of the lawyers who had bought into the idea behind the prison ministry. He wasn't a criminal lawyer, but he had a good legal mind and a conscience that allowed him to see those in prison as real human beings who had messed up. The prison ministry at John Knox organized volunteers to visit those in prison and offer them some hope. They also offered support to the families who were waiting for the prisoner's release. A third part of the program was to be mentors and resources for the prisoners upon release. The goal was to help them reintegrate into society as productive citizens.

Frank pushed the button to connect his line. "Andy, what's going on?"

"Find a TV and turn it on. They've arrested Reggie."

"Damn, I was afraid of this. Thanks, Andy, I'll get back to you."

Frank found the remote in his desk drawer and flicked on a TV in the corner of his office. He moved a vase of artificial flowers sitting in front of the screen. The mayor of the city was speaking. City officials and the police chief surrounded him. "I know that the city has been under terrible stress since learning about the rapist who has been assaulting the women of Athens. I am pleased to report today that through the excellent work of our law enforcement team, an arrest has been made. While everyone is innocent until proven guilty, there is reason to believe that our city is safer because of our alert, hard-working police force." The comments continued but were mostly self-congratulatory attempts to demonstrate what an excellent job the mayor was doing and how wise he was in appointing the current police chief. Frank knew that the mayor was also trying to build a hedge around himself. He had gone along with the courts and parole board in allowing Reggie to be released quietly as part of the church's experiment in redemption. If Reggie proved to be the rapist, the political price for that decision could be high.

Frank stared out his window and thought about Reggie. As sick as Reggie was, Frank had seen in him a glimmer of humanity. He once had been a good public school teacher and despite a withered arm due to a childhood accident, he became a decent middle school soccer coach. His agile feet, he once told Frank, had made up for his mangled arm.

Thinking of Reggie reminded Frank of the lepers in the Bible. As a sex offender, Reggie was marked as untouchable. He didn't ring a bell to warn people not to come near, but he registered on a public website. There is little tolerance for someone who takes advantage of children. Each time Reggie sees that look of revulsion in people's eyes, something must die in him, Frank thought. Reggie seemed to be making some progress. Now he was arrested. He must really be scared.

Frank dialed Andy's direct line. "Thanks for the alert, Andy. I tried to convince the police when they were here that Reggie was an unlikely suspect. I guess the mayor was under a lot of pressure to make a quick arrest to calm the city."

"'Fraid so," Andy said. "What do you want to do now?"

Frank pulled out a fresh pad of paper to begin to itemize the next steps to be taken.

"You and Larry are the two lawyers in our support group. Do you think the two of you can decide who will take the lead in representing him and can you do it pro bono at least for now?"

"I don't do much criminal work, but I'm sure Larry and I can come up with something to get us started."

"Good. In the meantime, I'll go down to the jail and see if they will let me see him. He's probably coming off the wall. Then maybe we can convene his support group and organize some regular visitation while we get this worked out."

"Frank," Andy continued. "I'm all for us following through on this, but you need to be open to the possibility that it may be true. People with this type of sickness don't suddenly get cured because some people support them."

"I know, Andy, but this just doesn't smell right. As I told the police, Reggie isn't strong enough to lift those women, and he isn't smart enough to quote all that Scripture."

"You're probably right, and this may well be the result of the political pressure the mayor and the police are feeling. Whoever this lunatic is, he has really spread terror, and people don't act rational when they are panicked. However, we both need to keep open to the possibility that we may be wrong. Sometimes people are stronger than they look."

"I hear you, Andy. In the meantime, let's make sure that Reggie gets a fair hearing."

As Frank hung up, he began to think about how all this had started. Long before he became pastor at John Knox, while he was an associate at First Church in Willington, SC, Shirley Paddington, a member of the church had asked him to come by for a Friday afternoon visit.

When he arrived at 3 p.m., he thought he smelled alcohol and noticed that Shirley was dressed in a rather revealing and tight-fitting dress, but he didn't pay attention to the warning bells that should have gone off. She invited him in and, at first, the conversation was a pleasant exchange about her experience at the church. She excused herself to retrieve some snacks from the kitchen. When she returned, he noticed that she had removed a clasp from her blouse making it more revealing when she bent over to place the tray of snacks on the coffee table in front of him.

It became obvious that in addition to the snacks, the kitchen allowed Shirley to fortify herself with a strong drink. "I think I'll just kick off my shoes and get a little more comfortable," she said. After removing her shoes, she turned on her most brilliant smile and said, "Why don't you loosen your tie and relax a little bit. Here, let me help you."

Subtlety was not part of Shirley's arsenal. While he thought he was being cautious by sitting in one of the large armchairs across from the couch, Shirley decided that sitting in his lap as she loosened his tie might facilitate the conversation. Frank immediately stood up, with the result of dumping Shirley on the floor.

He apologized and reached out to help her up while keeping his distance at the same time. She tried to make a weak joke about Jesus' command to love your neighbor as she tried to pull him back towards the couch. Still trying to be diplomatic, Frank helped her sit back on the couch and spoke firmly but gently to her. "Shirley, you are a lovely woman, but I am both your pastor and a happily married man. This cannot happen. Please try to understand."

Shirley did not understand. Her face became very red, whether at first from embarrassment or not, it soon morphed into a look of anger. She began to shout at him. "What's the matter? Afraid you're not man enough?" She ripped open her blouse and began to flaunt her breasts before him. "Bet you haven't seen any as nice as these for a while."

"I'm leaving now, Shirley. I recognize this is the effect of the alcohol and not a part of who you really are."

A stuffed animal came hurtling past his head as he reached for the door. He quickly exited the house, jumped into his Volkswagen, and drove out of her driveway. Once he was several blocks away, he pulled over on a side street and stopped. He felt himself trembling. What had just happened, he wondered? Had he done something to suggest that he was open to such a proposition? He began to take several deep breaths, slowly exhaling and willing himself to calm down. When he felt more in control of himself, he headed home to talk to Rosie, the one person who always helped him stay centered in life.

Rosie took one look at him as he came through the door and saw that something was wrong. "You're pale as a ghost. What happened?"

Many times, as a matter of professional ethics, he avoided telling Rosie the details of his conversations with others. This time, however, he recognized that he needed to tell Rosie everything.

As he thought back on that incident now, he recognized that he made a very wise decision. Not many hours later, the police arrived at his doorstep. When Shirley's husband, Arthur, returned later that afternoon, Shirley was sobbing in their living room, blouse torn and evidence of wine and snacks scattered on the floor. She was very distraught but her story as to who was the victim in what had taken place was very clear. Now it was the young associate pastor who had accosted her, and she was in shock.

Arthur, whose legal firm recently had handled a sexual abuse case involving a nearby Catholic Diocese, did not hesitate about what to do. He immediately called the police and filed rape charges against Frank Sessions, Associate Pastor of First Church, Willington. He threw enough legal language around in making the charge that the police were persuaded they had a credible case to secure a warrant for Frank's arrest.

The senior pastor of First Presbyterian Church in Willington, with whom Frank worked as an associate, was on vacation and communication about the event was confused. Since it was late Friday afternoon when Frank was actually arrested and the wheels of justice turned even slower on the weekend, it was Monday morning before bail could be arranged and Frank released. The church had been shocked at the accusation but trusted Frank more than the Paddington' accusations.

Then it was over almost before it began. Shirley moved from drunkenness to sobriety; from anger to embarrassment; and finally confessed to Arthur a version of what had happened that cleared Frank even though it did not fully disclose Shirley's actions. Arthur immediately withdrew the charges and apologized profusely to Frank. Rosie was willing to have Arthur and particularly Shirley roasted over a barbeque pit, but Frank convinced her that there was nothing to be gained from pursuing it further. The Paddingtons did not return to the church.

Now, as Frank thought of that rather traumatic chapter in his life, he realized how significantly it had shaped his ministry. His couple of days in jail convinced him that Jesus' statement about visiting those in prison was more than a metaphor. Whether guilty or not, those in prison were God's children and needed to be treated as such. He developed a prison ministry in every church he served. However, more than that, he discovered the profound impact that such a ministry had in developing the faith of the members who made the visits.

Then there was the sexual component to the incident. The following spring the church granted him a three-month sabbatical, and he spent it at Auburn Seminary in New York reflecting on the strange symbiotic relationship between sexuality and spirituality. It eventually led to his thesis for his Doctor of Ministry degree on the search for transcendence in both sex and religion. Several years ago, he was invited to the local seminary as a guest lecturer, and his topic was "Climax and Conversion: The Song of Solomon and the Religious Search for Ecstasy." At the time, he felt he was being bold and a little rebellious. The students loved it, and the faculty seemed pleasantly amused.

Now that lecture was coming back to haunt him. While he hadn't revealed this to anyone, it was clear from what Brenda Sides had told him that the rapist had read either his thesis or at least the copy of the lecture he had given at the seminary. The quotes he helped Brenda find on the day she told him of the Breakstone rape were the same verses he had used in his seminary lecture.

He had been hiding in a cave of self-pity and unresolved grief for the last several years. He didn't have Rosie to help give him perspective. He glanced at her picture that hung prominently on his office wall. He could almost hear her say, "OK, big boy. You held it together for the children until they were grown, and you've demonstrated your grief long enough. Get over it already and get on with your life. The church and the world need what you have to offer."

He grimaced and then stuck his tongue out at Rosie's picture and gave her the raspberry. That used to be a familiar gesture that he would make when Rosie had told him a truth he didn't want to hear but he knew was right. "Ok, dear heart," he said to the picture, "I'm going to try, but it would be all right if you occasionally visited me in my dreams."

He stood up, took off his tie, hung his coat in the closet, and opened the door to the outer office. Marcie looked up from her computer. She would not ask but was clearly curious about Andy's call.

"They've arrested Reggie," Frank said. "The mayor is making a big deal over it as if he has personally saved Athens from disaster."

"I'm sorry," she said. "I know you and the others have worked so hard to help him."

"I don't think this is over, Marcie. I'm sure that the real rapist is still out there, and I'm betting that he is too sick to stop now and let Reggie take the rap. However, until I'm proven right or wrong, Reggie is still in jail, and, guilty or not, he deserves to be treated as a human being. I'm going over to visit him. Send an email to the support group and see if we can gather tomorrow evening about seven here at the church."

Driving to the jail always made him nervous. He was a frequent visitor because of the jail ministry, and most of the personnel knew him and treated him with respect. Still, it always evoked some knots in his stomach, left over, he believed, from his own brief experience in the Willington jail. It was only for a couple of days, but he experienced the impact of being caged and treated like a number. If only briefly, he was prisoner number 52648.

As he walked through the door into the jail lobby, he saw the desk sergeant seated behind a glass enclosed reception area. As he made his way towards the reception desk, he passed a number of people who seemed to be waiting patiently to visit their family member. What a dreary life, he thought.

"Hello, Rev. Thought you might be coming over for a visit."

"Hey, Sarg. Yeah, I heard they've arrested Reggie and thought I'd stop by to see how he's doing."

"I tell you, Rev., I respect you and think it's good that you and your people visit these prisoners. Actually, it makes it easier on us. But honestly these sex perverts need to just be thrown in a hole and forgotten. Even the fancy psychiatrists tell you there's no cure for them. You'd be better off spending your time with some of the others."

"You may be right, Sarg, but he is still a child of God, and Jesus touched the lepers even though people believed there was no hope for them either. At least what Reggie's got isn't contagious like they thought those lepers were."

"Hey, that's deep, Rev. I'm going to lay that on my pastor. He'll think I'm getting religion."

"Be kind to your pastor, Sarg. Clergy have a rough job. How about checking me through so I can have a few minutes with Reggie?"

Having placed his wallet, keys, pens, and change in a safe-deposit box, Frank heard the door buzz releasing the lock and allowing him to enter the hall that would lead to the visitors' room in the jail. An officer directed him to the room and instructed him about how to use the telephone that would allow him to talk to Reggie, who would soon be on the other side of the Plexiglas partition. A door opened and a guard brought Reggie in. He was dressed in the familiar orange jump suit used by many jails. His face was pale, and he shuffled in, hampered by the chains on his wrists. When he saw Frank, his face brightened a little, but he still looked confused.

They both picked up their phones, but Reggie quickly laid his down and began to cry. Frank waited for him to regain some control.

"I didn't do it, pastor. You've got to believe me. What I did may have been even worse, being children and all, but I never attacked no women. At least they ought to punish me for something I've really done."

"I believe you, Reggie. Andy and Larry are already looking into it for you. Just hang in there."

"Tell them to hurry, pastor. It isn't safe in here. Prisoners have their own form of punishment for people like me. I'm scared. Even the guards don't like me."

Frank knew that was true and didn't know how to respond. "They'll work as fast as they can."

"I got me a Bible, pastor. I'll just keep reading it and praying a lot."

"I'll pray for you too, Reggie. Do you want me to have a prayer with you right now?"

"'Preciate it, pastor. God is about the only hope I have now."

Frank had prayer with Reggie but he felt very uneasy about the situation as he left the prison.

CHAPTER 6

Digging for a Story

Brenda Sides had been a reporter since she left college. It was what she always wanted to do. Her father had been a journalist with a newspaper in the Midwest, and he had infused in her the joy of discovering a good story. "It's like being a detective," he said, "only you don't have to carry a weapon, and you can expose evil without having to wear a uniform that makes people nervous." The other thing that she remembered him telling her was that the art of the interview required patience and silence interspersed with a few open-ended questions.

She majored in journalism at UNC and found some excellent mentors along the way. When she got her degree, she went to a small town newspaper where a friend of her father worked and asked to intern at modest pay so that she could hone her skills. She knew that newspapers were being challenged by the Internet, but she figured that if she had good skills, there would always be a need for a good investigative reporter.

After spending a year as an intern, she managed to get hired by the *Athens Record* to cover crime and politics in the city. The pay wasn't great, but she didn't need much to live on. This was an opportunity to build her platform as a seasoned reporter. As her father had pounded into her, a good reporter works hard, isn't afraid to do her homework, and has the courage to trust her instincts.

It was instinct that caused her to hang around the Athens police headquarters that Monday afternoon in May. That was one time when instinct triumphed over desire. She had been invited to join a Monday Let's-Start-the-Week-Together happy hour with friends. She really wanted to go. Friendships as a young, single person with erratic work hours were hard to form. She was about to call it a day when the woman she would come to know as Carrie Breakstone stormed into the police station. She'd seen victims come to the police station before, usually beaten down and scared, but Carrie came storming in like a locomotive firmly on the track and headed for a destination.

She remembered how she was dressed. Tall black boots with high heels to give an already tall woman the ability to look down on others. A woolen skirt that tastefully reached the knees while still emphasizing the black boots that suggested there was plenty of leg yet to be revealed. A bright orange blouse, tight but not too tight, and a brown vest that gave some extra warmth on a chilly spring day. Her dark hair would have been the envy of any woman. It bounced on her shoulders as she marched to the station desk. Her face was flushed with anger, but it didn't hide the beauty of her skin. No make-up but none was necessary.

Brenda, with her fiery-red hair and athletic build, together with an innate self-confidence, appreciated beauty when she saw it in man or woman. It was more than just a statuesque woman that drew Brenda's attention. She saw the set in her stride and the determination on her face that suggested she was someone to be reckoned with. She stepped closer to the intake station to see if she could overhear the complaint, but she didn't need to. Carrie was not careful in how she announced that she had come to report a rape, her own rape, and wanted to talk to someone now.

Brenda had watched others come in with similar concerns. She knew the standard procedure for processing Carrie's complaint was going to take a while. A woman being raped in this city might bear mention in the paper, but it was hardly a big story. She wanted to leave for her party, but something held her back. Maybe it was because Carrie was such a commanding presence, or maybe it was just that mysterious instinct to which Brenda had learned to pay attention. While she waited, Brenda planned her approach so that she wouldn't scare Carrie off before she got the story.

The result is now history. Thanks to her instincts, Carrie's courage, and the sympathetic assistance of a pastor that she had only known by listening to him from the pew, she broke a story that had vaulted her into the limelight. Even the Associated Press and United Press International, as well as national television networks, picked up her story. Suddenly her name was known by many news journalists around the country. She even had some feelers from larger newspaper chains. On dark nights when she crawled into bed by herself, she fantasized on where this could lead.

That was late at night. During the day she was running hard to try to keep up with new developments of her unfolding story. The story broke in late May. Within days there was a follow-up story when several new victims of what had been dubbed the Secular Evangelist came forward with their stories. It was probably the religious angle that caught the nation's attention. Not only did the rapist insist on quoting Scripture while he was raping his drugged victims, but a radio talk show host, Eric Ivory, had decided to make this story a foundation for his crusade against liberal churches in the community. The national networks were also working the angle of how churches in recent years had been faced with many cases of inappropriate sexual encounters between clergy and their membership. Late night comedians delighted in telling jokes about clergy escapades. One comedian she heard was riffing about clergy and suggested that one should no longer call a minister father unless one had absolute proof. Athletes, he suggested, might need to have drug tests but clergy should have blood tests to establish paternity.

Brenda, in seeking how to develop some follow-up stories while the investigation awaited further development, began to wonder about the impact on those who were in the process of preparing for the ministry. She knew that it didn't take many stories about reporters fabricating stories to make all reporters nervous about their reputation for integrity. She wondered how potential clergy felt about this religiously oriented serial rapist. Since she lived in a city with a prominent Protestant seminary, she decided that she would visit the campus and do some interviews.

She went on Thursday, June 6, right as the story of the arrest of Reggie Pardella was breaking. He was a registered sex offender. Brenda wondered if that wasn't a little too convenient. Still, she knew that the police were doing the best that they could under enormous pressure. She hoped that they were right this time. As each new victim had come forward, she could feel fear sweep over the city. Even she, who was not one given to fear, became much more cautious about where she ran for her daily exercise.

She drove down the spacious driveway that offered entrance to the seminary campus and stopped at the administration building to announce her presence on campus. The person who was in charge of development and public relations for the seminary was cautious at first. She referred her request to the president of the seminary who, when it became clear that Brenda would not approach the story from an anti-religious bias, saw some benefit to the story.

He offered to invite some students to come in for interviews. She agreed that that would allow for some deeper inquiries, but she also asked if she could just wander around the campus and spontaneously speak to some students while he arranged for the more in-depth interviews. He agreed.

She left the administration building and walked onto the quad around which most of the buildings were built. It was a lovely June day, and there were a number of students playing Frisbee, sunning themselves, and simply enjoying the beauty of outdoors. The quad was bright with a bed of orange and yellow marigolds and white begonias. Near the chapel were some bluebeard shrubs with their blue flowers and what she thought was a potentilla bush with red blooms. The flowers made up for the trampled grass where students frolicked as well as a couple of well worn paths marking shortcuts across the quad.

She interviewed three women students and two men. She was just finishing talking to an engineer who was starting a second career in seminary when he looked up and said, "Hey, why don't you interview Jacob. If there is anyone who would have a considered opinion on this, he would." She turned and saw a tall young man emerge from the school library and begin to walk down the sidewalk towards the chapel. People spoke to him, and he seemed friendly enough, but he also appeared to be somewhat of a loner.

She walked over to greet Jacob. "I'm told that you are Jacob. My name is Brenda Sides, a reporter for the *Athens Record*. Could I speak to you for a few moments?"

He looked a trifle uncomfortable, but he stopped when she spoke to him. Rarely had Brenda ever looked at a man and had her first thoughts be, wow, but she felt her face grow warm as he removed his sunglasses and looked at her.

"You have the reddest hair I've ever seen on a person. Is it real?"

"Real, of course it's real. What type of question is that?"

"Not a very good one, I guess," he said with a sardonic smile. "Maybe it would be better if you asked the questions, you're the reporter."

"Yes, I am the reporter," she said with more ice than she wanted in her voice. "I'm interviewing students about how they think the recent story about the religious serial rapist, together with the sexual scandals involving clergy that have proliferated in recent years, will affect their ability to build trust with members of their congregations?"

"One more hurdle to cross, I guess. Good reason not to get involved with women," he said.

She did her best to hold her tongue. She knew that a reporter's best friend is to keep silent and see what a person will say to fill the void.

"Look," Jacob said, "I've not given much thought to women or sex lately, so I don't have much of an opinion. Is there anything else that you would like to know?"

Brenda was irritated by his seeming disinterest. "Are you telling me that you are gay?" She'd never been that abrupt with anyone she was interviewing. What's going on with me, she wondered.

"No, I'm pretty sure I'm not." He didn't seem offended by the question. "Just never met a woman that interested me that much, I guess." He glanced down at her hand. "Guess you haven't met a special guy either. Doesn't make you gay, does it?"

Brenda was speechless.

"Sorry if I upset you. Guess I'd better be moving on."

Jacob walked on down the sidewalk.

Brenda stood their breathing hard but speechless. Her mind wouldn't focus.

A woman who had observed the interchange walked up to Brenda. "Don't let him get to you. Actually, he must like you. He usually doesn't spend that much time before he finds an excuse to escape."

Brenda began to sputter. "He's arrogant, rude, and, and ..."

"And hot, hot, hot." the other woman said. "Every single woman on this campus recognizes that, but, for whatever reason, he doesn't let a woman get within ten feet of him. You actually did pretty good. That may be a record for his longest interchange with the female species."

"So why does he act that way?"

"Most people just assume that it has something to do with what happened to his mother."

Brenda was calming down, and the reporter's curiosity kicked in. "What happened to his mother?"

"Oh, you mean you don't know who he is?"

"Other than some rude dude who is studying for the ministry? No, who is he?"

"That's Jacob Sessions. He's the son of a local pastor. Weird, isn't it? His father is rather famous around here for his lecture on sex and faith, and his son is scared to death of the opposite sex."

"Weird is right. I've actually talked to his father about that very subject. You said people thought he was reacting to what happened to his mother. What happened to her?"

"I wasn't in the city at the time, but I understand that she had gone out to a convenience store to pick up some cookies or something. When she got there, some nut case was robbing the place. I think he killed her with a knife." She shivered. "It was pretty gruesome."

"That's awful. But what does that have to do with Jacob's relationship with women?"

"Apparently her death really tore up Jacob's father. It's just speculation, but some think that when Jacob saw what it did to his father, he vowed he'd never let himself get that close to a woman so that he wouldn't have to suffer like that himself. Of course, maybe he's gay, or there's some other reason."

"Whatever his reasons, he really set me off. Thanks to you, I'm calmer now."

Brenda excused herself and went to the administration building to conduct the in-depth interviews that the President had set up. When she finished the interviews, she had plenty of material for an excellent article, but she was drained. She decided to stop off at the campus center and get a strong cup of coffee.

She ordered a large coffee of dark roast. As she paid for it and turned to leave, she saw Jacob sitting in a far corner buried in a book. She stared at him for several seconds as she sipped her coffee. Then she made up her mind, drew in a large breath, and walked towards his table.

She did not wait for an invitation but pulled out a chair, set her coffee down, and reached over and closed his book.

He looked up, reached over, and took her coffee and had a sip. Then he said, "In addition to the reddest hair I've ever seen, you also have green eyes that match. Are they real also?"

"I really make you nervous, don't I?" said Brenda.

"I guess I wasn't very polite. Sorry about that. To be honest, you do disturb me, but I'm not sure why."

"Do you know how hard it is for a single girl to put green dye in her eyes so that it coordinates with her hair?"

Jacob leaned back and guffawed. "Yeah that was really a dumb remark." He looked down at the table and then back up at Brenda. "If you still want to ask your questions, I think I owe you a more considered response."

Brenda had lost all sense of being a reporter. She knew she was stepping across all professional lines of objectivity. She had never been shy around men, but she couldn't believe what she heard coming out of her mouth. "I think you owe me more than that. I think you owe me a dinner, and tonight would be an excellent time for you to pay up."

She had both her hands loosely around her cup of coffee. She watched as he reached over, laid one hand on her wrist, with the other gently removed the cup from her hand, and took another sip.

She repressed a shiver and said, "Hey, that's my coffee."

"Yes it is, so in addition to a dinner, I owe you an extra cup of coffee. I guess we will have to have two meetings; not more than one of which can be as a reporter and an interviewee."

"Maybe neither of them. But you are right. We do have to establish some ground rules, so we both know when I'm being a reporter and when not."

"I'd suggest the first night be just new friends," Jacob said, "and we can work out the ground rules from there."

"By the way, so that you know, I've been to your father's church and heard him preach. He was the one who helped me work out those quotes by the rapist for that first story."

"He's a good man. If he'd lose forty pounds and shave off that beard, he isn't bad looking either."

As they started to get up from the table, they became aware that there were many people watching them and whispering among themselves.

"From what someone told me," said Brenda, "I may have just set a new Ripley's record for time you've spent with a woman without bolting out the door."

"For people who spend a lot of hours studying the Scriptures that condemn gossiping, they spend a lot of time violating that admonition," said Jacob.

They moved through the tables with Jacob acknowledging many of his friends and accepting some ribbing in the process.

CHAPTER 7

Reconnecting with the Seminary

Frank was working on designing a new member class when Marcie buzzed him on the intercom. "Yes, Marcie, whose on the line?"

"It's the dean of your son's seminary. Hope he's not in trouble." Her soft laugh reminded Frank of what a valuable gift he had in Marcie being his secretary. She was a tough lady with a deep faith, laced with a healthy dose of cynicism that helped her keep perspective. Frank knew he could say anything to her, and it was held in deepest of confidence.

"Not Jacob," Frank said. "He's got his head screwed on far better than his dad does."

Frank looked at the picture of Jacob and Rachel on his desk. They were now young adults, and raising them after Rosie's death had probably saved his sanity. The couple of occasions when he considered joining her in death had vanished when he thought of Jacob and Rachel.

If there were moments when the pain had been so great that faith seemed unreal, his son's and daughter's trusting presence made living real. When he wanted to resign as pastor or curse the heavens, there was always a call from the school counselor, a sports injury to be treated, or even a spontaneous hug that made him realize the reason to keep on living.

When Jacob chose to do graduate studies in theology and ethics, Frank was thrilled. Jacob had a good head on his shoulders, and Frank had little concern when he heard that the seminary dean was calling.

Frank shoved some books aside on his desk and grabbed a fresh pad of paper as he reached to push the button on his phone. "Dean Fairington! I hope all goes well at the seminary."

"Hi, Frank. I realized as I was making the call that I hadn't talked with you in a couple of years. How are you doing?"

"Truthfully, the church has been very tolerant, and I'm hanging in there. What can I do for you?"

"I'm sorry for your pain, Frank, and if what I've called to ask of you is too difficult at this time, I will certainly understand."

"Doesn't hurt to ask, Ken. Maybe something new would be good for me."

"Remember the seminar you gave a few years ago on the Song of Solomon – *Climax and Conversion* I believe was your title. In fact it is one of the more popular reprints in our library."

"I'm afraid that the Song of Solomon has been a little too much the topic of conversation lately."

"That's really why I called," Ken said. "A rapist on the loose is scary enough for anyone but his habit of throwing religion into the mix has really thrown this campus into turmoil. It doesn't do much for your self-confidence when the profession you are planning for is the butt of jokes for late night comedians. Your previous lecture on religion and sexuality makes you a good person to help the students process what is happening."

"A month ago, I wouldn't have been interested, Ken, but some things have happened recently that have reawakened my interest. Not only have the police mishandled this, but that idiot on the radio has really stirred the pot. What type of lead time can you give me to prepare?"

"It's important that we not put this off too long. The students are anxious. Could you possibly do it within the next couple of weeks?"

Frank pulled out his calendar. "Sure, let's set it up for a week from this Thursday, that's June 20th I think, in the evening. How does that sound?"

"That's great, Frank." There was an audible sigh of relief in the dean's voice. "I really appreciate it. By the way, we've really enjoyed having Jacob on campus. I'll miss him when he graduates."

"Thanks, Ken. He's a great young man. I'm afraid I haven't been too available to him in the last couple of years, but I intend to remedy that."

As Frank hung up, he felt the vibrations of energy too long repressed – a memory of a time almost forgotten when he had enjoyed engaging in the battle around important issues. Maybe there is some fight left in this old dog yet, he thought.

As he turned again to the new member class design he had been working on, the ideas seemed to fall into place with greater ease than before. He even found some space for some humor, which hadn't been part of his repertoire for a long time.

He hit the save button on the computer and shoved back from his desk. He glanced at the clock. It was eleven-forty. With a smile on his face, he walked into the outer office where Marcie focused on putting together the church newsletter. "Marcie," Frank said, "It is about noon, and I would like to buy you lunch and finish it off with a hot fudge sundae."

For a moment, Marcie just stared at her computer. Then she slowly turned her head and looked at him. "All right, I'm trying to remain calm and consider what is taking place. I have several options to choose from. One, I've fallen asleep at my computer and am dreaming. Two, I've entered a time-continuum and am living in an alternate universe. Three, God has finally gotten her divine act together and is answering this congregations repeated prayers for a miracle. I've pinched myself and don't think I'm asleep. I've never been interested in that science fiction crap. So that leaves me with choice three, which may mean I'll have to modify my skepticism about prayer."

"Don't get your hopes too high. This may only last for the day, but I'd like to show my thanks for your faithfulness during this time when I've acted like a turtle who can't get out of his shell. Let's go enjoy a nice lunch."

Marcie shook her head and smiled. "Not that I'm complaining, but what in the world did that dean say to you?"

"He wants me to talk to the students about this religious crazy who has been terrorizing the city."

"How do I explain to my husband that, in a city terrorized by a Bible-quoting rapist, I've accepted a date for lunch with a pastor who wants to talk about sex?"

"I've never known you as a lady at loss for words, so I'm sure you will find a way. Come on, I hear that hot fudge sundae calling my name."

* * * * *

When they returned from lunch, Frank began thinking about the seminary lecture. He wanted to provide perspective, but he also wanted to offer some practical advice and to encourage the students to believe they still had a measure of control over their lives and ministry.

He thought about who might be a useful sounding board to brainstorm possible ideas. The first person he thought of was Oscar Ramerez. He was embarrassed to say that he had not talked to him in a couple of years, but he could think of few others whose intellect, practicality, and humor he trusted more.

Even as he looked up his number, it excited him to think about renewing their friendship. When he heard the familiar Hispanic accent, he said, "Oscar, this is Frank Sessions. How are you doing?"

"Frank Sessions? I once knew a Frank Sessions, a righteous dude as I recall, but I haven't heard from him in years. You don't suppose the two of you are related somehow?"

Frank chuckled, leaned back in his chair, and put his feet up on an open desk drawer. "Actually I think we are mirror twins, and the dark one has been dominating for a while, but I'm hoping his double is beginning to assert himself."

"My God, that might even make a liberal like me believe in miracles. I've really missed working with you, Frank. Whatever the cause, I'm delighted to hear from you? What's on your mind?"

Dean Farington called me and asked if I would speak to the students and faculty about this crazy religious rapist and his impact on our profession. I thought, if you had some time in the next couple of days, I could bounce some ideas off you."

"Fantastic. We need your leadership in this. That blithering idiot, Eric Ivory, and his lackeys are fueling the fire of an already dangerous situation. We need to offer something more substantial in return."

"Thanks, Oscar, when can we meet?"

"Two thoughts on that. First, if you are free, I could meet you this afternoon at the Starbucks over on 5th Street about four. Second, Ivory has called for a second forum on this subject next Monday at True Vine Church. You know, the church where God wins with the Reverend Godwin. How about you and I attending and stirring things up a bit?"

"The first thought sounds great, and we can discuss the second one over coffee. Since Bob Godwin is the convener of the forum, I don't know whether I can take that or not. I'll see you at four."

Now, Frank thought, What is it that I want to share with those students so that I might be helpful.

* * * * * * *

At four o'clock, Frank entered Starbucks. Since he was still full from lunch and feeling a trifle guilty about the hot fudge sundae, he thought he would forgo a frappuccino and stick to some decaf coffee. As he was ordering, Oscar came through the door and waved as he set his laptop and briefcase down at a table.

"Oh, you're no fun at all," Oscar said, as he saw the plain coffee in Frank's hand. "In celebration of a friend come back to life, I'm going to have a caramel latte with a dash of peppermint thrown in. That's the closest I can come to a resurrection drink."

For the next fifteen minutes, they tried to catch each other up on events in their lives and reestablish frayed bonds of friendship. Then Oscar said, "OK, enough catching up. This is serious business going on in our city, and it has strained relationships among the churches that were not very strong to begin with."

"To use an overused cliché, sex, violence, and religion have converged to form the perfect storm," said Frank. "From what the dean said to me, not only the young students but also the more seasoned second career members of the student body are really disturbed by what is happening and don't have a clear sense of how to respond."

"The sexual scandals that have exposed the churches over the last decade have shattered the trust between clergy and the larger society. We used to be rated as one of the most respected professions in our society. Not anymore," said Oscar. "The good book invites us to be fools for Christ, but no one is laughing."

"It also feeds into Ivory's campaign to cleanse the churches of liberalism," said Frank. "I was furious when he tried to use this scandal to malign the progressive churches in the city. Now it's even worse since the police have arrested Reggie Pardella."

"You don't think he's guilty, do you?" said Oscar.

"Not for a minute," said Frank. "While the police and the mayor are sitting around congratulating themselves, the real rapist is still out there."

"Even liberals are afraid of sexual perverts," said Oscar. "It will be easy if the police can pin the rap on him. All we need is a good scapegoat and then none of us have to examine our own lives."

"I think the rapist is too sick to stop. When he strikes again, the fear in the city will escalate. If the rapist turns out to be a deranged pastor, it won't be just liberal pastors that society mistrusts."

"I can understand why some of the students wonder what type of profession they are getting into," said Oscar.

"That's precisely the point I want the seminarians to understand. There is no pure place where any of us can stand and toss rocks. Sex is one of the most powerful forces in the universe, and it can be used either for good or for bad. To deny its power in your life is to make you vulnerable."

Oscar played with his cup for a few seconds while he gathered his thoughts. "I've had three prominent members of my congregation wreck their families and careers by becoming involved sexually in the past six years. What is it that makes us willing to risk everything for that illusive intimate encounter?"

"While I think our faith can help resist such temptations," said Frank, "I also believe that spirituality taps into an energy that when misused can make us even more susceptible, especially to the temptations of sex."

"That may help explain," said Oscar, "why our conservative friends get more upset over sexual issues than other sinful possibilities. Surveys suggest that they have as much, if not more, trouble in responding to the issue of sex among their constituents as we do."

"Sinclair Lewis had a point when he made the protagonist of his novel, Elmer Gantry, a conservative member of the Christian community," said Frank.

"I know that in my head," said Oscar, "but it still shames me that so many clergy get themselves in trouble. No wonder the seminarians are scared as they listen to all this hysteria."

While they were speaking, three attractive women in stiletto heels and suits that flattered their slim forms came into the store. As the women chatted among themselves and walked to the counter to place their orders, Frank and Oscar both looked at them and then back at each other.

"That's part of the world in which the new pastors will be ministering," said Oscar. "The other part is the other 80 percent of the world that wants to look like them."

"And the males" said Frank, "that want to shore up their fragile egos by winning a woman's attention."

"I wonder what Eric Ivory would say about such ladies in public," said Oscar. He paused a second, "and in private."

"I've been thinking about your second suggestion, that we attend Ivory's forum. If you'll go with me and carry some extra barf bags in case I get overcome, I think it may be a good idea for us to go."

Oscar smiled and then reached out and touched Frank's arm. "It's nice to have the old Frank back. It's been lonely out here on the hustings."

"Thanks, Oscar. It feels good to be reengaged again. It has been a long dark alley. Rosie was the lodestar for my life, and without her, I sort of lost direction. I'll never be the same again, but maybe I can still make a contribution."

"I'll be in touch about the details of the forum."

They shook hands and hugged each other.

There is a hand of providence in this, Frank thought, as he moved towards his car to return home.

CHAPTER 8

Ivory Names Names

Why Frank tuned in to the Eric Ivory show on Friday, the 14th, he couldn't say. He had listened a few times in the past but generally felt it only upset him, and he didn't need any more upset in his life. As he sat in his office thinking about the second pastor's forum, it occurred to him that it might be a good idea to know more about what Ivory was thinking. It wouldn't be the first time, Frank thought, that someone had taken advantage of a tragic event to advance a personal agenda.

The program began with a strong version of "America the Beautiful." Of course, Frank thought, begin with patriotic music and suggest that your opinion is the only truly patriotic viewpoint. It irritated him even before he heard Eric speak.

"This is Eric Ivory speaking to you. Unlike the theological pinheads in some of our liberal seminaries, this Eric Ivory does not come "Out of the Ivory Palaces." I am down here in the streets where life is lived and people need a true faith to help them get through the day."

Frank felt like gagging.

"You've heard, my friends, about the excellent work of our fine police force in arresting a scumbag named Reggie Pardella." A sound of a crowd roaring their approval came over the radio. "If you are new to our fine city of Athens, this poor excuse for a human being masqueraded as a teacher and a coach in our school system until about fifteen years ago. Then we discovered that his real agenda was preying on our vulnerable children. Yes, friends, it looks like our streets are safer." The sound of the roaring crowd was played again in the background.

Fake sound effects, Frank muttered, what a testimony to truth in advertising.

"Now I'm sure the A C L U," he exaggerated each letter for effect, "will cry lots of wet tears that he's just a poor *furner* that we are picking on, but I say *Why Not* have a safe city for Americans. After all, we built this great Christian country. Don't our children deserve to be protected against the garbage of our society? Don't we deserve a safe place in which to live?"

Furner, Frank fumed, you idiot, we are all immigrants except the Native Americans, and we killed off most of them.

Not much concern about being innocent until proven guilty, Frank thought. Where's the love of our justice system let alone any Christian thoughts of grace and forgiveness?

"After we take a station break, I will fill you in on another chapter in this whole sordid saga of the liberal church's betrayal of the clear message of our Lord and Savior Jesus Christ. It's what our dearly departed friend, Paul Harvey, would call the rest of the story."

The station broke for identification and a series of advertisements. Well, thought Frank, you've learned your craft. Always leave them with a teaser that will cause them to stay tuned and listen to the advertisements. Frank pulled out a pad of paper and a couple of good pens just in case he wanted to take notes on what Eric would say. He assumed that it would be some type of buildup towards the second forum Eric had called for next Monday, June 17.

Like the first meeting, this forum, too, was at Bob Godwin's True Vine Church. Frank was sure that given the emotional tension in Athens and Eric's trumpeting his cause on his program, the attendance at this meeting would be even better than the first one. None of the conservative pastors would want to be left out, and many of the moderate pastors might feel the pressure to be present as well. While many of the more liberal pastors would be contemptuous of what Eric was doing, even they would feel the heat from his rhetoric.

As he waited for the program to resume, he thought about Oscar's invitation to attend the forum. Frank wasn't sure he wanted to walk into that lion's den, but he appreciated Oscar's suggestion that we should know our enemy. Oscar was a canny pastor, and it might be fun to beard the Ivory lion right in his own den.

"This is Eric Ivory, back with you to share the rest of the story of what is happening in our fine city of Athens. I tell you this story with a deep sadness in my heart. When churches name Jesus Christ as their Lord and use religious language to disguise what they really are after, my friends, it dishonors our beloved Lord and contaminates the pure gospel that all of our faithful churches are trying to share with this woeful world. That is why we must expose their perfidious behavior in defense of our true gospel. I take no joy in what I am about to tell you, but it is necessary to speak the truth in love."

Man, what a buildup, Frank thought. I hope some of my more thoughtful colleagues are listening. It sounds like we are going to all be taken over the coals. What could he possibly say after that entree?

"I refer you back to the perpetrator of this vile act on our city, one Reggie Pardella. I don't know what country he is from or even if he is a legal resident in this city. However, if he is an illegal resident, I don't know why our taxes should pay for his room and board. That whole immigration mess is a topic for another day. He is here, he committed a despicable crime, he was convicted of molesting our sweet children, he went to prison. Now why was he released into our fair city to wreck his mayhem on our people? That is the rest of the story."

Clever, Frank thought. Without any evidence, he has named Reggie an illegal alien but in a way that allows him to deny he said it.

"I do know," Eric continued, "and this information is available to anyone who wants to inquire on line, that our Mr. Pardella is a registered sex offender. In fact, it is because our police have this information available to them that they were able to identify Reggie so quickly. Take that A C L U–The All Criminal Liberation Union. Some of us want to have safe streets and aren't afraid to have the police keep good records."

O, brother, thought Frank, that was a cheap shot, but I bet it will get some play in the media.

"Does such knowledge prevent our liberal churches from joining the ACLU, babying the criminals of our society, and risking our safety?" continued Eric. "It does not. This is the incredulous story of how Reggie was free to roam our streets and place our citizens at risk?"

Uh-oh, thought Frank, I think I see where this is leading.

"The rest of the story, my friends," Eric paused to build up the tension among his listeners, "is that Mr. Pardella was safely behind bars where he should be until the John Knox Presbyterian Church and their ultra-liberal pastor, the Reverend Frank Sessions, came up with a plan to set him free."

Frank stared at the radio. While he knew that the church's prison program was generally supported by the congregation, he also knew that it had its detractors, and this would strengthen the opposition within his congregation. Not only that, but such irresponsible allegations would make many of the members of John Knox uncomfortable. While they support the prison ministry, and many similar ministries of the church, quietly, they are not prepared to be associated with public controversy. They are good people and want to be on a Christian journey, but they are not prepared to join a journey to the cross at this stage in their lives. For many their faith is part of a quiet journey, an internal relationship with Jesus Christ, and not part of a public confrontation with others.

"Yes, my friends," said Eric, "sad to say this church, instead of focusing on saving the souls of the millions of spiritually hungry people in our society, chose to develop a plan to set this sick individual free to roam the streets and wreck his mayhem on our fair city. They convinced the parole board that they would pal around with Mr. Pardella and keep the city safe while they reformed this deviant. Maybe you haven't read the literature, Reverend Sessions, but I have, and let me tell you that even the most liberal psychiatrist will tell you that there is no cure for this type of sickness. Like the good book says, if you try to cast out one demon from such a person, six other demons will come and take up residence making him even more dangerous than before. It looks like that scriptural wisdom has been fulfilled as this demented sicko from whatever country he comes from began with helpless little children and now has moved on to the women of our city."

Frank had heard about out-of-the-body experiences, but he had never experienced one. Now it was as if he was floating above his body and viewing himself frozen to his chair. He saw his fingers beat on the arms of the chair, but his arms were immobilized as if strapped to the chair. His face became rosy red, and he could hear himself snorting as if his sternum was clogged. He wanted to scream, but no sound came out of his mouth. Somewhere, outside his body, the thought occurred to him that he might be having a stroke.

How could he possibly begin to respond? Reggie, where this all began, is being condemned as being beyond redemption. Frank's church is being charged with perpetrating a monstrous crime on the city. His own integrity as a Christian pastor is under attack.

Eric Ivory wasn't through. His voice grew smooth and took on a tone that suggested he was taking his listeners into confidence. "But there is more to this story, my friends. I'm not one to pass on rumors, but I have it on good authority that our good Reverend Sessions may be more of a wolf in sheep's clothing than many realize. The Bible tells us that we should confront our brother within the community of faith and speak boldly that the truth will make us free."

Eric paused as if he were now turning to speak directly to Frank. "Is it true, Brother Sessions, that early in your ministry, you took advantage of one of your innocent parishioners and even spent some time in prison before some powerful voices in your congregation were able to pull strings and get the whole thing covered up?"

There was another period of silence as if waiting for Frank to respond. Then Eric continued, "I don't know whether Brother Sessions is listening, but if so, I want to be fair, so he is free to come on this program and respond if he desires. Though most people who engage in such nefarious activities prefer to operate in the dark, so, my friends, I wouldn't hold your breath."

Frank continued his out-of-body experience, hovering over his body, wondering if it might explode.

"I'm not accusing anyone, but I do think the citizens of Athens need to know if Reggie Pardella acted alone, or whether there is more to his partnership with the John Knox Church and the Reverend Sessions than meets the eye. Perhaps the police have a little more investigating to do."

Frank's whole body began to shake as he stared at the radio while Eric unctuously concluded with a prayer for the purity of the church and signed off.

In the back of his awareness, Frank knew that the phone was ringing in the outer office. He saw the door open. Marcie was standing there, but he couldn't comprehend what she was saying.

Finally some of her words broke through to his awareness.

"Pick up the phone, Frank."

"Marcie, I can't speak to anyone at this moment. Go back to your office, and tell them I'll call them later."

Marcie put out her hands and held the frame of the door as if for support. "Frank, I've always done what you asked of me but not this time. I'm not leaving this room until you pick up the phone. Either that or I'm calling 911."

"Who is it?" He croaked.

"It's Oscar Ramerez. He was very clear that I should not talk to you over the intercom, but I was to come into your office and stand there until you picked up the phone."

The mention of Oscar's name broke through his paralysis and released him. Still feeling weak, Frank lifted the phone. All he could say was "Oscar."

"I'm assuming that you were listening to Ivory's broadcast," Oscar said.

Frank did not respond.

"I will take your silence for a yes," Oscar said. In a calm but firm voice, Oscar continued. "Frank, don't move out of your chair, breathe deeply, and hold on to your desk. I will be there as soon as the speed limit will allow. Now, return me to Marcie."

Frank felt numb. He turned to Marcie and held out the phone. "He wants to talk with you."

Frank could hear Oscar give instructions to Marcie. "Marcie, this is important. I will explain more later, but Eric Ivory has just attacked Frank personally on his radio broadcast. It was really nasty. Even if he asks you to leave, stay in his office so that he knows that you are with him until I can get there."

Frank had often spoken of the importance of the ministry of simply being present to someone. He now felt first Marcie's presence. She had no healing words to say. She looked very frightened, but, like a rock, she was not to be moved. Frank knew that he was being held together by someone who cared, and he was grateful.

CHAPTER 9

Bearding the Lion

Frank sat like a statue staring at his desk. He wasn't paralyzed. He just could not summon the will to move. He knew Marcie was there, but his vocal chords wouldn't operate. He wasn't thinking. There were no specific thoughts in his brain. It was as if he was existing in a vacuum.

Then he saw Oscar come through his office door. Oscar pulled a couple of chairs in front of Frank's desk and indicated for Marcie to take one of them. Marcie started to say something, but Oscar indicated that she should remain silent. Oscar placed his hands on the desk near where Frank's hands were but without touching him. He looked directly at Frank. "There is no need for you to say anything at this moment, Frank, but when you are ready, we are here. Breathe deeply and get in touch with your own body for a few moments."

The silence was a gracious gift. Frank recalled when he was told that his wife had been killed, an innocent bystander in a failed convenience store robbery. That was worse, but some of the feelings were the same. He wanted to rush out and do something, but anything, but time was frozen. His mind was disconnected from his body. He sat there and tried, as Oscar suggested, to get in touch with his own body.

Maybe fifteen minutes passed before he looked up and noticed that the lights on his phone were all lit up indicating several people were trying to call the church. Neither Marcie nor Oscar made any move to answer the phone. It was as if the phone was in another world, and they were in Frank's world and determined to stay there as long as necessary.

70

He looked at them and drew power from their unspoken compassion. "Thank you," he said. "I remember in those first minutes when they told me that Rosie was killed, it was so unbelievable that I couldn't comprehend what people were saying. I needed time to process what I'd heard, but everyone was talking, and I couldn't breathe."

"It's OK," said Oscar. "You don't need to talk until you are ready."

"Did you hear the broadcast, Marcie?" Frank asked.

"No, I don't even know what we are talking about. I just got a call from Reverend Ramerez, and he told me to come right in here and not to leave. You looked so strange, immobile, almost catatonic. I didn't know whether you were having a stroke or what."

"In short," Oscar said, "Eric Ivory, on his *Why Not* broadcast, named Frank as Reggie's cohort in crime and offered as evidence a suggestion that Frank had a guilty past."

"I know the incident that he was alluding to," said Frank. "While I was exonerated, even the suggestion of sexual impropriety feeds the gossip mills. What I want to know is where he dug that up?"

"Gossip is like mercury," said Oscar. "It's bright and attractive to the eye, but every time you try to gather it up, it slips away and finds a new location in which to shine."

"Can't you sue him for defamation of character or something like that?" asked Marcie.

"That's a tricky area," said Oscar, "especially with public figures. He is probably counting on the fact that Frank won't want his past brought up."

"Right now it's not my past, but his future survival that's at risk. Even though it goes against everything I believe, I want to ring his neck."

Oscar looked at various parts of Frank's face, shoulders, chest, arms, and hands, as if giving him an examination. When he finished, he said, "I've got a more immediate concern." "Today is Friday. Do we need to find a substitute to conduct worship for you on Sunday?"

Frank rolled his neck and shoulders and then grinned. "No, both friend and foe will expect me to respond on Sunday. I'm sure we'll have a packed house. Maybe we should take up two offerings: one from those who support me and one for those who believe the gossip. Maybe that way we could retire the debt."

Marcie shook her head. "How can you joke at a time like this?"

"It's a survival technique," said Oscar. "Think back on those old episodes of Mash on TV. Sometimes things are so bad that if you don't laugh, you'll go insane. In that vein, I would suggest a third offering."

"A third offering?" Frank said.

"One for the media. You don't think they're going to stay away from something as juicy as this, do you?"

"What a nightmare," Frank said. "Marcie, I'm sorry, but I will need you to field the phone calls. I will leave it to your judgment, but unless it's an emergency, I'm not available. Do place a call to Wiley for me." He turned to Oscar. "He's our faithful clerk of session. We may need to decide if we want a brief session meeting before worship to answer any questions and think through our next steps."

"OK, at least you are thinking organizationally again. I think that means you have survived the first shock wave," said Oscar. "I'm really sorry that this is happening to you, Frank. What else can I do?"

"If you are still willing, I'd be pleased to have you with me at the meeting on Monday," said Frank.

"You still want to go to the pastors' forum?" asked Oscar. "Now I'm the one who is not so sure that is a good idea."

"No, think about it," said Frank. "Where better to respond to his accusations than in the company of pastors? Of course, probably we should pass the word to some of our more liberal colleagues, so we will have some support. Unlike his radio program, Eric won't be in total control. And, I'll bet there will be plenty of media present."

Marcie got up from her chair. "This is above my pay grade. I think I'll get back to my desk."

Both Oscar and Frank rose as Marcie began to move towards the door. Then she paused and came back to where Frank and Oscar were standing. "I know this is not normally appropriate," she said, "but you really scared me, and I am glad you are all right." Then she threw her arms around Frank and gave him a hug. Then she turned and hurried towards the door.

"Hey, don't I get a hug too?" Oscar said.

Marcie turned, blinking back tears, "Just so it's clear that I normally don't go about hugging preachers." She gave Oscar a quick hug and returned to the office.

"Que barbardidad," said Oscar. "This guy really goes for the cajones, doesn't he?"

"It doesn't sound like 'no hitting below the belt' is in Ivory's book of rules," said Frank. "This may work to our advantage. I wonder if those who might support him will think that he has crossed the line. It's amazing how our egos can trip us up sometimes."

"Who's in charge of this Monday meeting?" asked Oscar.

Frank smiled. "Oscar, you are brilliant. Eric thinks he's in charge but he announced that Bob Godwin, the pastor of the True Vine Church, was hosting the meeting." Frank began pacing the carpet while he rubbed his hands together. "I've never considered Godwin to be a very deep thinker, but he has a sensitive radar that picks up any signal that he might be thought a patsy."

"Yeah, with the media present," said Oscar, "he won't want it to look like he's not in control, and he will be sensitive to any appearance that he might be unfair."

Just then Marcie stuck her head back through the doorway. "Frank, do you remember that young reporter that broke the story on the patterns of the initial rapes? The one who interviewed you."

"Sure, her name was Bonnie, no, Brenda Sides. A young woman with fiery red hair."

"Well, she's on the phone and wants to know if you would like to have an opportunity to respond to Mr. Ivory's accusations."

"Sometimes it pays to be nice to reporters," Frank said. "Yes, Marcie, tell her if she will call back in five minutes, I will take her call."

Marcie returned to the office. Frank turned and gave Oscar a high five. "What do you think, Oscar? How about if instead of hiding from this fight, I take the offense?"

"My only counsel is to make sure that you don't overreach, Frank. Don't try to best Ivory in a single quote. Take it one step at a time."

"Did you ever read much Shakespeare, Oscar?"

"I have enough trouble understanding contemporary English. Besides, we have enough great Hispanic writers that I don't need to add that English dude to my repertoire."

"Occasionally he came off with a good quote, and I think I have just the right one as my response to Mr. Ivory."

The intercom buzzed, and Marcie announced that Brenda Sides was on the line. Frank held up his hand and said, "Watch this." He put his phone on speaker, so Oscar could hear both sides of the conversation.

"Brenda, this is Frank. I guess neither of us knew where this story was taking us when we first sat down to talk, did we?"

"Reverend Sessions, before I assume the role of a reporter, let me just say that I think what Ivory did on his radio broadcast was despicable. Now, as a reporter, I want to provide you an opportunity to respond for tomorrow's paper, if you wish."

"Thank you, Brenda. I will make a brief response now and then have more to say later. I have been intrigued with Mr. Ivory's increased obsession with anything to do with sex in recent months. There are many more valuable issues to be debated among the churches than just sex, but Mr. Ivory doesn't seem to be able to get beyond that one topic. In the words of William Shakespeare, 'Me thinks he dost protest too much.'" Frank paused and let some silence fill the air.

There was a slight giggle on the other end of the phone line, then regaining her composure, Brenda said, "Is there anything else you would like to say for the record?"

"One thing more, Brenda. While I haven't had an opportunity to talk with Bob Godwin, who is hosting the clergy forum on Monday, I am sure that as a fellow Christian brother, he will want to provide me ample opportunity to respond to Mr. Ivory. We may have our differences, Brother Godwin and I, still I think we both recognize that speaking the truth in love requires us to be open to listening to each other."

"Are you suggesting that Mr. Ivory may not fall into the category of Christian brother?"

"There is great variety among those who call themselves Christian across the globe. I'm not familiar with all of them. I think you would have to pose that question to Mr. Ivory."

"Wow, anything else you would like to say, Reverend Sessions?"

"No, that's probably enough for now, Brenda. Thank you for calling."

"One more thing, no two more things before I end this conversation," Brenda said.

"What's that?"

"I value the relationship we were establishing when this whole thing began, and I hope that I can still talk to you both as a reporter and as an emerging disciple. I think I'm discovering there is more to this Christian thing than I had assumed."

Frank laughed and said, "Brenda, my offer for continued conversations continues in effect regardless of where this goes. Good luck with your story. What's the other thing?"

"Just so you know, I had the chance to meet your son the other day when I was doing some interviewing on campus. Seems like a nice guy. Look forward to talking with you again soon." Without waiting for a response, she hung up.

Frank replaced the phone and turned towards a grinning Oscar Ramerez.

"Mama Mia," said Oscar, "I do believe the waste products of animals have entered the rotating blades that stir the air of life. The old Frank has returned, and I have new hope for the world."

"Oscar, I will never forget that you came to the office today in my time of need. I'll let you know how Sunday goes and let's plan to meet at Panera's on Monday at eight before we go to the clergy meeting at nine."

Oscar rose from his chair, did a little dance on the carpet, and headed for the door. "Hasta Lunes, entonces."

CHAPTER 10

John Knox Versus True Vine

History might one day speak of Sunday, June 16, in Athens as the Sunday of dueling churches, but on this Sunday, most people in the city were focused on their own concerns and not aware of the drama building between John Knox Presbyterian Church and the True Vine Church. Those who were interested in churches at all had grown accustomed to church leaders engaging in a war of words. It often embarrassed members and fed the cynicism of those who did not attend any church. Some sought a spirituality apart from the organizational church, while others tried to make it through the week without referencing faith or religion at all.

What did concern the people of Athens was the serial rapist who they were told was now in jail. Religion had become part of people's thoughts because the rapist insisted on quoting the Bible during his rapes. Even if they didn't understand how it all fit together, the mixture of sex, religion, and violence was the perfect recipe for capturing people's attention.

The Reverend Bob Godwin knew that sprinkling references to either sex or violence into his sermons often grabbed people's attention. Because of what Eric Ivory had said on his Friday broadcast and because the second pastors' forum that Ivory called for was scheduled for the True Vine Church, Bob was not surprised to see a large attendance at his worship services this weekend. Even if the rapist was in jail, they wanted to understand how to make sense out of this strange connection between rape and religion.

Bob was still chafing at the way Ivory had manipulated him into supporting Ivory's campaign, but he was smart enough to take advantage of a new leadership role. Ivory was a purist, bordering on fanaticism. Bob knew that such an approach might initially galvanize a following but would soon grow thin when the initial ardor began to cool. He'd heard Ivory's broadcast where he virtually accused the Presbyterian pastor, Frank Sessions, of at least being complicit in the violence plaguing the city. He didn't know Frank personally but quietly had some sympathy for the complexity of ministry and the frailty of Christian leaders. He agreed with Ivory that liberalism was diluting the power of the faith, but his recent experience with the widow Marshall made him wary of being too self-righteous.

He decided urging compassion for even sinful pastors while being a resolute defender of the pure gospel would play well with his listeners while building a little bit of distance between him and Ivory's sensationalism. It allowed him to appear to be a true leader above the fray who worked to bring the warring parties together without compromising the true gospel. Ivory would be irritated but couldn't say much because he had already publicly affirmed Bob as a leader in his movement.

Bob, upon reading Frank's quote in the paper, recognized that Frank Sessions was no fool. The article by Brenda Sides this morning had shown Frank to be a clever strategist as well. His not too subtle hints that maybe Ivory's accusations reflected on Ivory's own character was very clever. In addition, he knew that Frank was trying to manipulate

Bob by publicly professing Bob's sense of fairness. Bob thought that might work to his advantage as well. There would be a lot of media attention at the meeting Monday. Bob would appear to be a fair and strong leader at a time when the city needed to experience competent people who were in charge.

The sanctuary in True Vine Church held about 1200 people. Bob did not see many empty seats as he glanced out before the first service began. The theaterlike seats and the slightly inclined aisles provided Bob with a clear view of each person. Unlike church pews, theater seats allowed people just enough distance from their neighbors to protect personal space. It's weird, Bob thought, how all our modern communication media have made us both hungry for and afraid of touching each other. Even when we do touch each other, with our socially correct hugs, it has a sort of faux sense of intimacy that says you can touch my body but my soul is private.

The band was building a sense of enthusiasm among those who had gathered. Bob tapped out the rhythm on his leg as he watched people's bodies move with the strong beat of the music. It was almost as if they were being infused with energy. He enjoyed the contemporary worship trend that built on the power of simple melodies and powerful rhythms to bind people together in community. Its association with the rhythms of secular music was also attractive to the younger set.

Occasionally he envied the more liturgical churches, however, with their invitation to probe the depth of people's humanity and its connection with the Divine mystery. Such churches had lost ground because they failed to recognize the power of emotion in worship, but Bob knew that too much focus on emotions can be like always eating rich desserts and forgetting the importance of the main meal.

He observed his associate pastor building on the music to guide the people into an awareness of events in the life of the church. "We have an exciting series of summer events to bring our family together in faith at our Wednesday night suppers and prayerful study groups. We also have some exciting mission trips planned for both adults and youth. It is our opportunity to both bless and be blessed."

The associate continued his invitation to the programs of the church as Bob turned his thoughts inward in preparation for his sermon. He raised up on his toes a couple of times and shook his hands to relax them. Like a singer preparing to sing, a good preacher had to focus his energies and shield himself from any distractions.

Courageous leadership in times of fear was his theme. As he walked in front of the people, there was a hush. He could sense their intensity. Even those who had not heard the Ivory broadcast knew the basics of what Ivory said. The city was taut with anxiety. They hoped that the rapist had been caught, but they wouldn't rest easy until it was clear that the guilty person or persons, as Ivory had alluded to, had paid a price for the fear that had enveloped the city.

There was still a question that hung there like a ripe peach waiting to be picked. Why did the rapist quote Scripture during his violent act? How can the wonderful words of life be used in such a vile way? Even if this rapist was caught, his blasphemy needs to be answered and people's faith in the gospel restored. People hungered for their pastors to answer that question in the weeks ahead.

* * * * *

Across town at the John Knox Presbyterian Church, Frank met with the elders that formed the governing board or session of his church. Frank though normally pleased and strengthened by their discussions, was a little nervous about how this conversation would evolve. While the majority of them were moderately liberal, there were two or three who could be counted on to represent a conservative perspective. Elmer Ewalt, one of the conservatives, was the first to speak up when the meeting convened.

"Frank, as you know, I have not always agreed with some of your more liberal positions and wasn't comfortable with some aspects of the church's prison ministry."

Here it comes, Frank thought. I think I'm about to get the I told you so speech.

"However," Elmer continued, "no two-bit, right-wing radio dingbat is going to publicly embarrass our church and our pastor without hearing from us. I'm conservative and am proud of it, but that idiot is an embarrassment to all conservatives."

Frank shifted in his chair slightly. He felt that warm glow that comes with knowing that a battle you dreaded was not going to occur. "Thank you, Elmer. I appreciate your support."

Earnest Balsworth spoke next. "I agree with Elmer, Frank. You've had some rough years since Rosie's tragic death, but you've hung in there. Your integrity is beyond question. Even if," he smiled and looked at Elmer, "sometimes you aren't as liberal in your thinking as I would like."

Sally Dillenger continued the conversation. "We got bushwhacked with Reggie's arrest. I knew from my husband's participation in our prison ministry that we were risking touching lepers in that work, but it burns me that everyone is so ready to assume he's guilty. I'm a lawyer and that is not the way it's supposed to work."

Others nodded in agreement. They looked at Frank to see what he would say.

"I've talked with Reggie," Frank said, "and I'm convinced that we will eventually find that he is innocent."

"That means," added another elder, "that the rapist is still out there. Do you suppose he is smart enough to lay low now and let Reggie take the rap?"

"Boy that creates a Hobson's choice doesn't it?" said Sally. "You want Reggie to be released, but you surely don't want another woman to be raped to accomplish that."

The other elders murmured assent as they recognized the complexity of what was before them.

"I think we have a couple more immediate concerns for this morning," said Earnest. "Frank tells me that it is likely that some members of our wonderful fourth estate will want to be here because of the dustup that Ivory character created. How do we prevent our worship service from becoming a media circus?"

While they were the church governing board, they looked to Frank for leadership. Again, they turned to see what he had to say.

"I'd like to suggest a way to proceed," said Frank. "What we would all like to do is have this to be a nonstory as far as the media is concerned. As our policy has always been, anyone can attend worship, but we will not allow cameras or film to be taken."

There was unanimous agreement. Frank noticed their body language. The tension in the room seemed to dissipate. They had a plan.

"I have one further thing to say before we adjourn," said Martha Flaxson. "Frank, you know that we all support you. There is nothing more unifying than being attacked from outside."

"Thank you," said Frank, "I've always felt supported by this church."

"That's the other thing," continued Martha. "We all know that you have been through a difficult time since Rosie's death, and we appreciate that you have not given up. It's given us a model for courage. But what I want to say is that though I wish it hadn't been caused by these events in the city, you've shown more life and strength in the last month than we've seen for some time. I guess what I am saying is, and I think I speak for all of us, it's nice to have you back, Frank."

Frank was at a complete loss for words. He tried to say something but just stammered.

Sally said, "I would suggest that we conclude our meeting with prayer and allow Frank some time to get ready for worship."

Following the prayer, each elder reached out and touched Frank with a gesture of support. In some cases it was a handshake, in others a pat on the back, and for some a solid hug. This was a congregation worth standing up for, Frank thought. The ersatz religion that Ivory was trumpeting was not going to stand without challenge. He felt energized and ready for the worship service. In the words of his elder, Frank thought, it was nice to be back.

* * * * *

If one could have had a split screen showing the worship services of John Knox Presbyterian on the left and True Vine Church on the right, one would have seen a striking contrast. The music at John Knox was robust but traditional. The words were a narrative probe of faith's complexity. At True Vine the band played, and the song leaders led with enthusiasm. The words provoked feelings of praise and celebration.

At John Knox people followed the music in their hymnals; at True Vine they craned their necks to follow words flashing on screens without the help of musical notations. Frank's congregation confessed their sins, prayed for their neighbors, and listened to two passages of Scripture. At True Vine Bob read a brief passage of Scripture on which he based his message. One congregation placed their money in offering plates while the other placed gifts in baskets that passed among them.

Both congregations anticipated that the sermon would enrich their lives.

* * * * *

Frank spoke of the frightful time they had been through and suggested that, like the Israelites in the desert, they still had a long way to go and needed to be alert to God's guidance. "The accused, Reggie Pardella, has worshiped among us," he said. "While I personally believe he is innocent of this vile crime, innocent or not, we need to pray for him and not be too quick in our judgments. I, myself, am accused of contributing to this fearful event in our city. My accusers say I am too open to those judged unworthy in our society. In my defense, I say that it is not easy to love the neighbor who is seen as unworthy. I take comfort in the thought, however, that Jesus himself was accused of associating with the wrong types of people in his society."

* * * * *

Bob reminded them that they had been through a frightful time, and through God's grace and the effective work of the police department, they had reason to believe that their nightmare of fear would soon be over. "The rapist may be in jail, but the blasphemy of the Scripture he quoted while performing his hideous acts needs to be answered by the true disciples of Christ. The Bible itself tells us that the devil may quote Scripture, but the true Word of God finds its home among the faithful that praise God with their whole heart and soul."

* * * * *

Frank's eyes moved across the congregation. "I'm glad to see so many of you here to worship God today." There was a slight chuckle that rippled through the congregation. "Perhaps we should hire Eric Ivory as our recruitment agent." This time open laughter moved across the congregation. "I hope the reporters among us won't be disappointed that when it comes to commenting on Mr. Ivory's slanderous comments or probing the Scriptures for God's guidance for this congregation, I choose the latter." There was a smattering of applause. "Later in the service, when we pass the peace, I hope that if you happen to greet reporters, you will make sure they know they are invited back to worship God on both good days and bad." Frank was amused to see some reporters in the congregation slowly lower their notepads out of sight.

* * * * *

Bob turned to the subject of the forum of pastors to be convened on Monday and reminded his members of the importance of strong pastoral leadership as they responded to the corruption of society all around them. Alluding to Ivory's accusation of the watered-down faith of the liberal churches, Bob spoke of how even in our churches we are not free from sin. "Each of us needs to be pure in heart and faithful in the practices of our faith trusting that God will give us the power to walk unharmed among the briar patches of the world." He paused for a second. "However, we must be cautious of the danger of judgementalism. Like you," he reminded them, "we pastors are human and make our mistakes." He pointed to examples of David's missteps and how God had used him for good.

* * * * *

"With all the ranting about liberal and conservative churches," Frank continued, "and who needs to purify whom, let me remind you of some fundamental truths of our faith." Frank moved out from the pulpit and stood before the congregation, looking at them intently. "First, in the competition about who is the most pure in the faith, let us confess that we lose. As Jesus said, 'Those who are well have no need of a physician, but those who are sick. Go and learn what this means, "I desire mercy, not sacrifice." For I have come to call not the righteous but sinners.' Mr. Ivory can speak for himself, but I, along with all of you I suspect, am an imperfect sinner in need of Jesus as our physician."

* * * * *

"The strength of a good leader," Bob reminded them, "is seen is our ability to see the light in time and bring our flock with us. I have certainly sinned," he said. "Just ask my wife," he smiled at Barbie sitting off to one side of the sanctuary. The congregation gave an appreciative chuckle. "But by God's grace, I will help convene a very human band of pastors tomorrow, and we will trust God to lead us out of our moral quagmire and organize our churches to help Athens move to a better and more faithful tomorrow."

* * * * *

Frank reached over and picked up the Bible that lay on the pulpit. "Most of you know that this congregation is involved in a prison ministry that includes, along with others, those who have been charged with sexual crimes. The Bible is relevant to our lives today because the same types of sins continue to infect our souls. In Jesus' day, one of the untouchables was the leper. It was assumed that he was virtually incurable and the burden was on him to announce his presence wherever he went. Who is our leper today? Is it not those sexual deviants who psychiatrists say are incurable? Like the leper, our laws demand that they warn us of their presence in the community by registering in a place available to the public."

* * * * *

"We live in a society," Bob proclaimed, "where we are afraid to call a sin a sin and confront the sinner with his deeds." Bob turned and placed his hand on a rough-hewn cross near the center of the stage. "The gift of God's beloved son was rejected by sinful men. The True Vine church understands that God loves the sinner but God does not love the sin. We reject this sinner's blasphemy and support our courts in condemning and punishing people for their crimes."

* * * * *

Frank paced back and forth as if in deep thought. "We at John Knox make no pretense that we have a cure for leprosy, but in a limited way, we have tried to treat a couple of admittedly sick people as children of God, in hopes that God would do what we cannot. At this moment I, urge you to pray for Reggie Pardella and let the courts decide on his guilt or innocence."

* * * * *

In both congregations, the people listened intently. Both pastors noted that even the reporters seemed to listen rather than take notes.

* * * * *

"I feel God's spirit moving in this city," concluded Bob. "God is present in the midst of this tragedy urging the churches to come together and proclaim the Gospel truth. Are you with us?" There was a chorus of yeses from the congregation and several shouted amens. "Then pray for the pastors of this city in the coming days that we might be faithful to God's word."

* * * * *

"What you and I have to determine," said Frank, "is whether we live this faith even when it is uncomfortable? Shall we associate with those Christ loved even when society says they are unlovable? Or, like the Pharisee in the temple, are we content to say, 'God, I thank you that I am not like other people: thieves, rogues, adulterers, or even like this tax collector.'"

Frank raised his voice as he moved toward the front of the chancel. "There are enough self-righteous prigs tearing our society apart. The rapist will be caught and this chapter in our city's life will be concluded. But there will be other challenges after that, and we need a faith that transforms us rather than seeks the cheap thrills of maligning others."

The overwhelming message Frank received at the door from long-term members was a simple phrase, "Welcome back, Frank."

He wasn't sure what tomorrow held, but he was glad to be part of a congregation of sinners that had held him together as he moved through his journey of grief. Now he was determined to hold them together as they faced this threat to their city.

CHAPTER 11

Judge Not That You Be Not Judged

Oscar picked Frank up at eight on Monday, June 17. "Look at that Carolina blue sky," said Oscar. "I know that we have to plan our strategy for today's forum, but did you read in the paper how the Demon Deacons stole a top recruit from Duke's wish list. It's a sign, I tell you, that God is on the side of the little people."

"I'm not sure I've ever heard someone equate the signs of the heavens with the recruitment score card of the ACC conference," said Frank.

"Hey, Amigo, in North Carolina you don't read the tea leaves, you read the sports page. As the good book says, tailgaters sit down to eat and drink, but coaches rise up to play. The problem is, like the game of faith, some are dazzled by the flashy player who gets caught up in his own fame. Smart coaches look beyond the press reports. They are looking for the good athletes who exercise self-control in all things. God recruited you for a reason. Let's run the good race."

When Frank finally stopped laughing, he said, "When Karl Barth said we should read the Bible in one hand while holding the newspaper in the other, I don't think he had the sports page in mind."

"OK, maybe I paraphrased a little bit," said Oscar. "But both the bit about self-control and running the good race are not only from Scripture but also are good words for us today."

"OK, great guru, point well taken. Hey, there's a Starbucks, and, for your good advice, I'm buying."

"Like the good book says," Oscar continued, 'Cast your bread upon the waters and it will return to you' in the form of a latte grande."

"Enough with the Bible quotes, already. I need help thinking about how I'm going to handle this meeting." Even as they continued their banter, Frank knew and appreciated that Oscar was trying to ease his feelings of tension.

Like many Starbucks, there were several people focused on their laptops while they sipped their coffee. The aroma of the coffee and the bright smile and greeting of the barista reminded Frank of the ordinary routine of life that was oblivious to the challenges that were stressing him. "Two latte grandes, extra hot," he said. They moved to the section of the counter where they could pick up their drinks.

Then they went outside and found two chairs touched by the early morning sun. Sitting with drinks in hand, Oscar looked at him and said, "So, whatcha going to do, jefe?"

"I was furious when I heard Ivory's attempt to slander me. It was a cheap way to build support for his campaign to malign the liberal churches. As I said, my first impulse was to haul him into the street and wring his neck. Having had a chance to cool down, however, I think I will try to hold my tongue and see if he doesn't overreach himself."

"Te acuerdo. Need I remind you that if the media spot you today, they are going to want a response," said Oscar.

"I know I have to be ready for that, but I'm even more interested in making sure that Bob Godwin knows I'm there."

"Watch out," Oscar said, "Godwin is a master at playing to the crowd. If Ivory's campaign catches fire, he won't want to be left behind."

"True," Frank said, "but I'm counting on the fact that he doesn't want to be seen as Ivory's patsy. Remember, and I have no doubt that Bob will be aware, this is a clergy meeting. Many will like what Ivory is doing but, with the media present, they will not like to be seen as lemmings. If they know I'm there, my guess is that someone will want me to speak."

"OK," said Oscar, "as the good book says, you need at least three smooth stones and a sling shot if you're going to defeat Goliath. The question that continues to baffle even the best philosophers is, if an ivory palace falls in the vineyard, and no one is around, will it make any noise? In the words of that great radio theologian, *Why Not* be present and see if Ivory is as slippery as some mineral experts say."

Frank chuckled and shook his head as he looked at Oscar. "What scares me is that some of your mangled quotes are beginning to make sense."

Oscar drained his coffee cup and said, "Let us go to the church of the true vine and ask in the words of the good book, 'Is there any balm in Gilead or shall we look for the fruit of the vine in some other place?'"

"Do you ever record any of this stuff?" said Frank. "Maybe you could put it on YouTube or something?"

"In another career at another time, my friend, but today let's go forth and proclaim the Gospel and see if anyone has ears to hear."

"As the good book says," said Frank, grinning and slapping Oscar on the back.

"Vámanos," said Oscar and headed for his Ford Escort.

"Where's the van with the big sign *Iglesia de Jesús Cristo, donde todos son aceptados?*"

"If I drove into the True Vine parking lot with that van, the police would stop me and ask for immigration documents, and all the gringo pastors would want me to translate for them. Today, we arrive incognito."

* * * * *

As Frank and Oscar drove into the spacious parking lot of the True Vine Church, it was already filled with lots of cars and groups standing around in clusters talking.

"As the good book says, the vultures will gather if they sense blood in the water," said Oscar.

"I think it's sharks that gather because of blood in the water," said Frank.

"Look's like vultures in those media vans to me," said Oscar. "Maybe they don't read the same translation as you do."

Frank and Oscar deliberately parked away from the media vans. They agreed that they didn't want to get tangled up with interviews by the media, but they did want colleagues to know of their presence at the church.

"OK, Oscar, let's go press some flesh. Any clergy that we meet, make sure they know my name. When Ivory starts his rants, I want people to know that I'm hearing it."

Frank was pleased to see that many of his more moderate colleagues chose to be present. He greeted them along with some conservative friends who recognized him.

"Hey," said Oscar, "there's Bob Godwin in that cluster. Do you want to greet him?"

"Oh yeah," said Frank, "especially him."

A couple of the clergy in the group surrounding Godwin recognized Frank and Oscar as they approached. They moved apart to let Frank approach Godwin.

"Reverend Godwin," Frank said, "I'm not sure we have ever officially met. I'm Frank Sessions of the John Knox Presbyterian Church. Allow me to introduce you to my friend and colleague, El Reverendo Oscar Ramerez, of La Iglesia de Jesús Cristo."

Bob took a step back and his eyes widened, but he quickly recovered and stretched out his hand in greeting. "Reverend Sessions. It's good of you to be present at this meeting. I think Reverend Ramerez and I met at last year's Evangelical Conference in Charlotte. It's good to see you again, Reverend Ramerez."

Oscar looked around. "There seems to be several police cars present. Are you expecting trouble?"

Bob followed his gaze. Some of the police were directing traffic, but there were also additional officers near the church entrance, all in full uniform and very visible.

"I'm afraid this rapist issue has got everyone on edge," said Bob. "With the media present, I think they just want to make sure everything stays calm. They also help with traffic. We often have some officers present when we hold large events."

"Since I'm sure that we will soon find out that Reggie Pardella is not our serial rapist," Frank said, looking directly at Bob, "and since it is likely that the rapist is someone with a strong religious bent, it is certainly possible that he may be among us. Maybe it is a good idea to have police present in case he identifies himself."

One of the other clergy in the group turned and stared at Frank. His voice was taut as he spoke. "Are you seriously accusing one of us of being the rapist? I find that offensive."

"I'm sure you do," said Frank. "Just as I found it offensive that Ivory all but accused me of being complicit in this crime. I hope you will join me in letting Ivory know just how offensive he's been when we go into the meeting. Now, if you'll excuse us, Oscar and I want to go in and find a seat."

Frank and Oscar left them standing there and headed for the building where others were gathering. Brenda Sides saw them coming, but when Frank held up his hand in caution, she did not alert the other members of the media to his presence.

"Man, that's jungle fighting," said Oscar. "Did you happen to train with Che Guevara in your younger days?"

"I intended to slip in quietly and just listen. Not a very good start, was it?"

"It'll be interesting," said Oscar, "to see if Bob alerts Ivory to your presence."

They walked up the steps towards the large glass entrance doors. Each of the doors and large windows had religious symbols or partial quotes from Scripture etched on them.

"What, no flashing neon signs saying Jesus saves?" said Oscar in a soft voice.

"Behave yourself," said Frank, though he was grinning as he reached for the door. Before he reached the handle, the door opened with a smiling greeter with a True Vine nametag.

"Welcome to the True Vine Church where we put Jesus first. Please make yourself at home and feel free to ask me if I can answer any questions for you."

As Frank and Oscar entered the spacious lobby, they noticed a large welcome counter off to their left. On the counter were numerous brochures about different events and behind it was a smiling hostess greeting visitors.

Over their heads, both to the left and the right, were large screens seeming to hang in midair. The screens alternated between announcements of forthcoming events at the church and pictures of various church events filled with smiling faces of people enjoying themselves.

Oscar paused to look at some of the church scenes as they rolled by. While most of the pictures were populated by Caucasian individuals, there were a smattering of both Hispanics and African Americans. "They all look young, prosperous, and happy," said Oscar.

Several plates of morning pastries surrounded a coffee bar serving Starbucks coffee. It had attracted quite a few pastors who were chatting among themselves. In a couple of corners, local TV stations had set up places in which to conduct interviews. A few clergy were speaking to the attractively dressed media reporters.

Frank and Oscar moved quietly through those loitering in the spacious foyer and entered the large auditorium.

"Mama mia," said Oscar. "Both of our churches could fit in here with lots of room left over."

Spread before them were innumerable well-cushioned theater seats set on a sloping floor that provided each occupant a clear view of the stage.

"I hear that they can seat about 2,000 if they use the balcony."

"We'd better hurry and sit down, or we might not get a seat," said Oscar.

"Where do you want to sit?" asked Frank.

"As the good book advises, let's sit at the back, off in the far corner where we can't be easily seen, and wait to be invited forward," said Oscar.

They moved towards some empty seats in a corner near the rear of the auditorium. "You Bible Thumpers are devious."

Soon the auditorium began to fill. The media had already staked out some spots for their cameras and set up some boom mikes to be able to pick up people's comments from various spots in the room. In what is often called a chancel area in more traditional churches was a large stage that allowed space for a contemporary band and a clear, Plexiglas podium for the speaker. Large screens were strategically placed so that everyone in the large room could comfortably read the messages that were being broadcast.

Some comfortable chairs for guest speakers were set off to the side of the stage to allow for easy access to the podium. A couple of strong men, apparently bodyguards, came in with Eric Ivory as he parted the curtains at the side of the stage and assumed a seat. Bob, who had entered the building by another door, was greeting some of the clergy seated near the front. As Frank and Oscar seated themselves, they saw Bob ascend the steps to the stage and walk to where Eric sat. Bob said a few words to him, and Ivory quickly looked up and began to scan the audience.

"Me thinks thou hast been outed," said Oscar.

"Outed but not spotted," said Frank. "You picked good seats. This pillar provides excellent cover from that part of the stage."

CHAPTER 12

Speaking of Sin

Bob Godwin wanted to dance a little jig as he approached the mike to begin the meeting. He watched Eric Ivory blanch white as he informed him that Frank Sessions was in the room. It confirmed Bob's opinion that Eric was braver when he was in charge and was the one who controlled the mike. The advantage of radio broadcasting is you can imagine your opponents quavering at your brilliant comments and never have to face their response.

In Eric's broadcast, he challenged Frank to come today, but it appears, Bob thought, that he never believed Frank would actually come. Welcome to the big leagues, my friend.

Out of the corner of his eye, Bob saw Eric furiously making notes. He wondered how he would alter what he was going to say knowing that Frank was in the room.

How brave would Eric be if Sessions storms the stage and demands to be heard? His impression of Sessions from the incident in the parking lot was a man who was not easily bested in an argument. The fact that he came to the meeting in the first place was evidence of his courage.

This could get interesting, Bob thought. Whatever happens, the Reverend Godwin will be the peacemaker among the warring children and be seen by the media as the reasonable one. Just in case, however, he was glad that his associate had thought about calling the police for crowd control.

As more people began to flow into the room, several uniformed police positioned themselves strategically and visibly along the aisles. While he didn't think any of these clergy would risk looking foolish in front of the media, a strong leader needs to be prepared for the aberrant nut.

Bob stepped to the mike and greeted his guests. "Let me greet you this morning in the name of our Lord Jesus Christ. While what we are talking about is a serious matter, I have to say that it makes me proud to see the clergy of our city coming together. What a statement to this city that her spiritual leaders are willing to recognize that when the going gets rough, we pastors get going."

There was a smattering of applause and a few shouts and whistles.

He chuckled a little. He knew that some of these pastors disliked each other intensely and had no interest in cooperating on anything. However, today events had brought them together, and Bob was giving the world the impression that he was in charge of making that happen.

"As the Word of God tells us," Bob continued, "there is 'one God and Father of all, who is above all and through all and in all.' As a reminder that we are all God's children and that even though we are here to discuss difficult matters, we do it in the context of our praise of the almighty God. I have invited my praise band to lead us in some songs as we gather in His holy name."

The band began to play and a set of four praise singers came forward. Bob stepped back. "We are overwhelmed with joy and honored by the privilege to lead this amazing body of God's holy servants in praising the almighty," said one of the male singers of the group. "We invite you to join with us singing the chorus on this first day of the rest of our life and lift the roof with our praises to our amazing God who has called us together."

He stepped back as an attractive young woman began in a low contralto. At first one could barely hear her words, and people leaned forward even as they read the words off the screens. She had their full attention as she slowly raised her volume, and they felt the power of her words as the screen indicated that they were approaching the chorus.

When the rest of the band joined her in leading them in the chorus, even those clergy unaccustomed to such contemporary music were fully involved. It was a young man with a tenor voice that led the second verse. He, too, began in a very soft voice, and then, as if being lifted by an invisible hand, his voice became stronger and stronger with words of praise to the God who lifts us on high. With the second chorus, the whole body of pastors were feeling united in praise. As Frank looked around, he noticed that even the reporters seemed caught up in the moment.

When the last note played, it was as if everyone was sad that it was over. For a moment, they forgot that there might be a divisive conversation ahead. Bob paused a few seconds to allow the pastors to savor the moment and then moved to the podium. "While I'm sure that you will all agree that we have just experienced a powerful musical prayer, I want to also humbly invite you to join me in a verbal prayer." Without hesitation, all bowed their heads.

"Jesus, we just feel your presence this morning. How amazing you are. You have gathered so many of your servants together this morning from all across this great city of Athens. We just want to thank you. We know that evil is strong and the wily Devil will even quote your sacred Scripture to try and lead us astray. But we just want to say this morning that your faithful pastors gathered here will not be fooled and that right will prevail.

"We make this prayer in the strong name of Jesus, our king and our savior.

"And let all God's servants say, 'Amen'"

The whole auditorium resounded with the strong sound of amen.

At the end of the prayer, Bob looked up and with a big smile on his face said, "Amen. Thank you Jesus. What a wonderful gift this band has dedicated to the praise of God. I'm grateful every week for their offering."

People began to shift in their seats. The musical experience had lifted them, but they mentally shifted to face the issue that brought them together. Bob cleared his throat and said, "My brothers and sisters in Christ, as you all know, the members of our congregations, along with the rest of the people of the city, have been through a terribly frightening experience. Not only that, but also this vile creature who has assaulted the women of our city has defiled the Holy Word of God by quoting Scripture as he performed his despicable acts. In doing so, he brought shame and disrespect on all of the servants of God who labor so hard to bring salvation to this city." Bob paused and scanned the audience, noting their nodding assent.

"The cynics in our city and even a few cultural members of some of the churches have begun to make disparaging remarks about trusting the clergy in our city. My brothers and sisters in Christ, we cannot allow Satan to insidiously plant seeds of distrust and suspicion among us. Even if this contemptible person is now behind bars, the power of the Gospel has been dishonored. Satan has left confusion and doubt in his path."

Frank gripped the arms of his seat. He noticed that the lights in the auditorium had dimmed slightly and that a spot now focused on Bob at the podium. He was incensed at Bob's aspersions about cultural Christians. His whole body was tense.

Oscar reached out and placed his hand on Frank's arm. "Easy does it, Amigo. We haven't even got to the headliner yet."

At the feel of Oscar's hand, he slowly turned, nodded, took a deep breath, and let it out slowly.

"One of our colleagues in the faith has offered us a strong challenge as churches to take advantage of this unforgivable act and allow God to use it for good among us. You all know Eric Ivory, the host of the *Why Not* radio program, and have undoubtedly heard his bold challenge to Christianity in the last couple of weeks. We met as a steering committee and wrestled with the challenge that he presented, and I invited him here to speak about his plan and allow us to reason together.

"I present to you, Eric Ivory, host of the *Why Not* radio broadcast."

A spotlight came on and found a short, portly figure rise and wave in recognition.

"Eric, please come forward and address this body of pastors who strive to bring the true Gospel to this city."

Eric could not have failed to notice that there was polite but hesitant applause as he approached the podium.

Frank leaned over towards Oscar. "A little heavy, don't you think? He should get away from his mike and those Krispy Kreme donuts and get more exercise."

Oscar raised an eyebrow and tried to project a look of disapproval. "Be careful with your bigoted attacks against fat people. You aren't exactly a bean pole yourself."

"I greet you in the name of Jesus Christ, our savior," began Eric. "I'm not a pastor. I'm just a humble servant of the Lord, but I believe that God has given me a word for you."

"I'm just a poor, unworthy soul," Frank whispered, "but God has given me a message for you. If you don't like it, tell God."

"As Ecclesiastes said, 'The heart of the wise inclines to the right, but the heart of the fool to the left,'" Oscar said.

"Whose side are you on?" asked Frank.

"I am but a servant of the Lord who brings the word to those who have ears to hear."

They turned their attention to Eric who was saying, "Who among you would deny that despite our best efforts, there is confusion among our people? Who would deny that some have tried so hard to accommodate the Gospel to the values of our society that it appears that society, full of envy, lust, and greed, is dictating the values of our families rather than the gospel truth? When we are offering the most powerful word on earth, a chance to defeat evil and promote good, a chance for healing and salvation, a chance to welcome our glorious savior home, why is it that many of our sanctuaries are only half-full on Sundays?"

"Actually, that's a good question," said Frank. "Why is it I don't expect a good answer will be forthcoming?"

Eric pressed his lips close to the mike so that even though he spoke in low tones, his words echoed throughout the auditorium. "Why is it when the Bible is abundantly clear about the difference between sinful behavior and faithful behavior, the seminaries educate our future pastors with thoughts that fill their heads with doubt and dissension?"

Ivory continued with sets of rhetorical questions designed to gather a consensus for action. "My good friend, Bob Godwin, spoke eloquently about our gathering together in unity under the Gospel of Jesus Christ today. I am grateful to him for calling this forum. But, we need to do more than just talk and sing, my friends. Our city is still trying to catch their breath from this horrible experience we've been through. They need leadership. They need pastors who are true to the faith and willing to courageously expose the heresies that have permitted this type of blasphemy to occur."

There were several "Amens" scattered across the room.

The media quickly swung their cameras around to pick up some faces in the audience.

"It galls me to the bottom of my soul that anyone in this city can get the impression that our churches approve of sin, and especially the sin of sexual depravity." As he said this, a look of disgust spread across his face. "We don't need a debate about such issues in our churches. That leaves our people confused. We need a clear and united statement that those who choose to live outside the bounds of human decency have already committed themselves to the fiery furnaces of Hell." He was in a groove now, and his words were bouncing off the walls of the room. "We don't need any wishy-washy, let's love everyone and forget that evil is real, activity from our churches. Evil killed our Lord, and we should be willing to stand in defense of our Lord."

More "Amens" rang out as the crowd was caught up in the rhetoric.

Frank began to notice those who weren't yelling their support but rather were sitting tight lipped with their arms crossed, as if they were holding something in.

Ivory's words cascaded over each other like a waterfall, but as he got more specific, more clergy began to show signs of uneasiness. Some, even very conservative pastors, knew the danger of fanaticism among the faithful. Some had been victims of members who questioned their purity in the past. Ivory didn't seem to notice it, but some of the clergy began to whisper to each other and cast furtive glances behind them.

Oscar was sitting more toward the aisle, and when he saw Bob look in his direction, he raised his hand and wiggled his fingers in a mock wave.

Eric had been clever enough to make his accusations in a form that would allow him to deny he was specifically accusing Frank, as he had on his earlier radio program. Oscar figured that Bob must be wondering if Frank would make a move now or would wait until people started asking questions.

Eric went on for another fifteen minutes outlining his vision for a campaign to cleanse the churches of heresies and present to the city a united and powerful witness. Bob had seen Eric grow visibly nervous when he told him that Frank was in the room, but now Eric seemed so caught up in his presentation that he had forgotten Frank's presence.

Eric then turned to the media. "I have not objected to the media being present at this meeting. After all, I'm part of the media, and many of you are my friends. However, let me tell you directly that the media shares in the responsibility for what has happened in our fine city. It is obvious that a rapist like Reggie Pardella feeds off publicity. If we hadn't given the story so much publicity and instead allowed the police do their work, some of this nightmare might not have happened."

Frank saw several of the reporters turn and stare at Eric. One could sense that he was not their favorite colleague.

"However, we all make mistakes. The challenge is always what we do once we have discovered our mistakes. I invite the media to give as much attention to the revival of churches in our city as they have given to this despicable animal."

Bob moved to stand beside Eric and reached out for the mike that Eric was holding. "The steering committee felt it was important for you to hear from Eric directly. All of us want to see the witness of our churches be strong in the city. Eric has offered his vision and some first steps for this to happen. It is perhaps time for some questions to clarify what we are proposing before we break into some working sessions to make this a reality."

Brenda Sides popped up immediately and waved her hand to be recognized.

"I had hoped that we might allow the clergy to ask some questions first, Brenda," said Eric, "but since you are so anxious, what is your question?"

By the stiff smile on his face and his grip on the podium, it was obvious that Eric knew he had made a mistake by recognizing Brenda.

As she started to speak, he moved back to the microphone and interrupted her. "Do try to be brief, Brenda, out of respect for the many clergy for whom this meeting was called. There will be plenty of time for the media when we have concluded."

Brenda's smile did not suggest appreciation of the paternalistic remark, but she did not hesitate to continue with her question. "You made some rather harsh statements about the pastor of John Knox Presbyterian Church on your radio broadcast this past Friday. Is he and what he believes part of what you think needs cleansed from the churches?"

There was a rustle in the audience. Many knew that Frank was present. Bob recognized that the meeting had come to a decisive moment. He pulled Eric to the side away from the mike and said in a soft voice. "Frank Sessions is seated in the left corner of the rear of the auditorium."

CHAPTER 13

Temper Temper

Sometimes everything slows down, and you watch events unfold on two levels. On one level, Frank watched Bob Godwin pull Eric away from the mike to consult on how to handle this new challenge. They were like marionettes jerkily moving back and forth across the stage as their strings were pulled. Eric's portly body seemed to vibrate. He was bouncing up and down on his toes, and his hands would move up and down as he argued his point of view.

At the same time, from his view in the rear corner, Frank could see multiple little conversations taking place among the people in the theater seats ahead of him. The audience, made up of pastors plus a scattering of media, sensed a turning point in the conversation. These pastors were veterans of many battles in the past. Whether conservative or liberal, they knew the problem of enthusiasms getting out of control and turning to bite them. Frank wondered if Eric had overplayed his role as the crusader for a campaign to cleanse the churches.

On another level, Frank was trying to visualize his own response. Should he stand and demand to be heard or should he wait to see if Bob would call him forward. Better to be called forward, he thought, but what if they tried to ignore him and move on. He looked around. The restless audience and the fact that many knew he was present didn't make it likely that they could ignore him. He decided he would only speak if they invited him to come up front where he had some measure of control over the microphone.

How should he behave when he got up front? Should he be outraged and excoriate Eric? There were some good biblical quotes about gossip and bearing false witness that he could use. Or, should he be magnanimous and suggest that surely Eric didn't mean what he had said? He could even hint that perhaps Eric wasn't as experienced as these pastors were in recognizing the consequences of a loose tongue, and perhaps we should all cut him a little slack. Oh, I like that, thought Frank: cunning, devious, and cruel.

Of course, I could always live out what I have preached, turn the other cheek, and invite us all to reflect on the witness we are making by our behavior. That would be the mature thing to do. He wasn't sure that he really wanted to be mature right now.

While these thoughts were playing across the screen of his mind, he felt Oscar's hand rest lightly on his arm. "I believe it is about to be showtime, Amigo." Oscar pointed towards the front where Bob was approaching the mike.

"Brothers and sisters in Christ, while it is true that our main agenda is to plan together on how to make the witness of our churches effective, Brenda has raised a serious question about what it means to cleanse the church of heresies. There have been times in our religious history when there have been witchhunts that have seriously damaged the witness of the church." Bob paused to let that message sink in. "The antidote for that is given to us in Scripture where we are told to speak the truth in love.

"I understand that Frank Sessions of the John Knox church is present today. Perhaps we can invite him to identify himself and respond briefly before we move on." Bob glanced around the auditorium. "There he is over in the rear corner. Greetings, Brother Sessions. Can one of the ushers provide him a mike so that he can speak?" A spotlight shifted to pick him up.

An usher rushed forward but Frank ignored his attempt to hand him a mike and began to walk towards the stage in front. There was murmuring in the audience as Frank moved forward. Several hands reached out to him in support as he passed by their seat. The audience's attention was no longer on the sage but on Frank as he walked forward at a deliberate pace.

"Brother Sessions, you don't need to come all the way up here. We can provide you a mike so that you can be heard," Bob said. It was clear that he didn't like the fact that he was losing control of Frank's participation. Frank ignored the attempt to hand him a mike and continued his slow, journey down the aisle towards the stage.

The cameras switched to pick him up. I wish I had shaved my beard this morning. I must look like a fat revolutionary. Lord, he whispered, help me not act like a fool or at least like a damn fool.

He could see the look of agitation on Eric's face. Bob also had a frown but was making his way towards the steps to greet Frank.

As he mounted the steps, he received Bob's outstretched hand and offered a polite smile. He turned towards Eric who was standing by the mike. Frank knew that his back was to the audience, and no one saw him wink at Eric as he approached the mike.

Eric cleared his throat. "Of course, you are welcome to bring greetings to this gathering of pastors, Reverend Sessions. If I have offended you by some remark I have made, I offer you my apology. I do hope you will be brief so that we can devote our time to the main topic of this meeting."

Frank moved between Eric and the mike, effectively moving him back from the podium. "Let's see, Eric, if I am correct, this past Friday you implied that I might have at least contributed to if I was not complicit in the rapes that have terrorized this city. If I remember correctly, you also left the impression that I had a dark past perhaps filled with some sexual sins of my own."

There was a small gasp in the audience. Eric was clearly stunned by Frank's directness. He moved towards the mike to respond, but Frank held up his hand and gave no room for Eric to move towards the mike. Sometimes having too much weight can have its advantages, Frank thought.

"You asked that I be brief so that we can devote ourselves to the main topic of the day. I'm assuming that you are referring to this power-washing campaign of yours to correct the errors that we as pastors may have made in our ministry in this city." Though the questions were directed at Eric, Frank ignored his presence as if he were merely part of a radio audience.

"In listening to you describe your crusade to rid our city of heresies, am I right in understanding that you believe the liberal churches, including the faithful people of John Knox Presbyterian, spread heresies that have diluted the purity of the faith and may have helped create an atmosphere in which vile sexual acts are seen as acceptable?"

Again, Eric tried to move towards the mike, but Frank was not willing to make room for him yet. Even without the mike, many could hear Eric complain as he turned to Bob. "Bob will you please tell your guest that I should at least be given a chance to respond to his off-the-wall comments."

"You want to respond, Eric?" Frank said. "You mean as you gave me a chance to respond to your scurrilous remarks this past Friday on your *Why Not* broadcast? Well I would say to you, why not let me complete what I came to say? You had a chance earlier to go on and on, correcting these pastors for their past failures. Why not, I ask?"

There was a ripple of cynical laughter that rolled like a wave across the audience. A few even clapped, although it was clear that some pastors were disturbed by the way that the momentum of the meeting had changed.

"I don't know where you go to church, Eric, and I don't know what painful sexual experiences are in your history that have triggered the intensity of your response in this case . . ."

"How dare you?" Eric lunged for the mike, but Frank had planted his feet firmly. He slightly dipped his shoulder and then raised it just as Eric made contact. Like a well placed block by a lineman, Frank's movement sent Eric bouncing back while Frank continued to hold his ground.

"I dare, Eric, because like these pastors, we are certain of two things as we work with our congregations. First, none of us are pure, and we are cautious about those who are so eager to cast the first stone. Didn't you ever wonder what secrets those would-be-stone-throwers were hiding when Jesus asked the one without sin to cast the first stone?

"Second, I dare, Eric, because the Gospel proclaims that we all are dependent on God's grace, not our purity. The Pharisees sought purity, Eric, and it was God who took the sinful response of the cross and transformed it into a sign for our salvation. All our churches need transformation, Eric, but it comes not by dividing us against one another but by a renewed focus on the cleansing spirit of God."

By this time, Bob was physically holding Eric to try to calm him down. Eric's face was splotched, and for those who could read lips, it was clear that Eric was not speaking blessings to Frank. Bob glanced towards a policeman who was standing off near the front of the church trying to decide if things were getting out of control.

In that moment, when Bob was distracted trying to decide if he needed to call the policeman forward, Eric broke from Bob's grip and charged towards Frank. Even as large as Frank was, Eric's momentum and outstretched arms shoved Frank away from the mike.

"Get thee behind me Satan," Eric screamed at Frank. "God has given me a message for the churches of Athens, and I will not have you block our hearing of it."

Frank stumbled but put his hand out and caught himself on a chair on the stage. Eric's behavior was becoming almost manic and not winning him any admirers. Frank decided to come off as the more mature one and let Eric defeat himself. Then he heard the chirp of his cell phone and knew a message had come in.

Sometimes pastors have automatic responses like a mother who cannot refrain from responding to a baby's cry. While he knew that now was not the time to read emails, the pastor in him wanted to be alert to possible crisis in his congregation. Attention was focused on Eric who was ranting into the mike. Frank tried to slip the phone out of his vest pocket and hide it in his hand as he glanced at his phone. His face went white as he read the message.

This time it was Frank who charged towards the mike, knocking Eric out of the way. He barely noticed that Eric went sprawling on the stage. "I have just received a message that should make us all ashamed. Another victim, a young lady named Erica, has been raped. That means the rapist is still roaming our streets. Not only that, but

Reggie Pardella, who is innocent of the crime of rape, has been killed by another prisoner."

He rounded on Eric, who was just getting himself off the floor. "You now have blood on your hands, you self-righteous prick."

Eric was so angry at being humiliated by being shoved out of the way that he probably didn't even hear what Frank had said. Rather, he flung himself at Frank again, screaming and trying to pummel him with his now clenched fists. Soon they were rolling on the floor kicking and screaming. Bob quickly motioned for the police to come on stage and break up the fight.

The police, having been alerted by the initial physical exchange, were quick to charge the stage. Being trained to control a potential crowd problem through the quick exercise of overwhelming force, they quickly pulled Frank and Eric apart. They placed both in handcuffs and hustled them off the stage and into separate patrol cars.

Bob approached the mike and tried to calm the audience. "Obviously we will not be able to continue our meeting this morning. I am very sorry this embarrassing event has erupted, and I am sure both Frank and Eric feel the same. Let me dismiss you with prayer and encourage you to enjoy some lovely refreshments that the ladies of our church have prepared while we try to sort this out and decide on our next steps.

CHAPTER 14

Amanda Doesn't Recognize Frank

Frank was ashamed of himself. Both he and Eric had totally lost control of themselves. Like two overweight walruses, they rolled on the stage, flailing at each other, and hurling venom without restraint. Of course, the cameras kept rolling, and the reporters delighted in the live action. What a spectacle this will be on the evening news, Frank thought, and groaned.

He thought he was being bold in confronting Eric Ivory in front of his clergy colleagues, but they ended up in a brawl like a couple of immature teenagers. Even as the police pulled them apart, Eric continued to shout and even spit saliva at him. The police decided it was wisest to sort it out at the police station, so, now in handcuffs , each was riding in a separate police car towards the police station.

As Frank rode in the backseat of the cruiser, he felt humiliated. With all the media present at the meeting, the thought of his congregation hearing about his behavior on the evening news made him cringe. The people of John Knox Church deserve better than this from their pastor, he thought. What type of hypocrite preaches love of enemy on Sunday and then on Monday engages in a public uproar?

In a way, he was grateful for the swift action of the police that prevented others from getting involved as well. What had he been thinking? How could he have let himself get so far out of control? When he reached the police station, he decided, he would immediately apologize to Eric and to the police for acting in such a childish manner.

Then his next act would be to offer the church his resignation. As difficult as it had been for the people of John Knox to put up with his long journey of grief and depression, they surely preferred that to being embarrassed publicly by his antics today.

The police car pulled to a stop at a street light. The police officer turned around and looked at him. "Are you all right, sir?"

"If having publicly disgraced myself like a complete idiot can be said to be all right, I guess you could say that I'm calmed down."

The police officer pulled over to the curb. Exiting the car, he opened the rear door. "We are told to act fast in such situations, but there is no reason for you to continue to have those handcuffs on. Here, let me get you out of them." He quickly unlocked the cuffs. "There, I'll bet that is more comfortable."

"Thank you, officer. You are being more kind than I deserve."

"Frankly, sir, I was present, and you did not throw the first punch. We'll get it all straightened out at the station."

"Not a great example of turning the other cheek, though, was it?" said Frank.

"I'm a Lutheran, pastor. I think that is why we have a confession of sins in our service. None of us, 'cept Jesus, live it all the time. Even he got ticked off occasionally as I understand it."

Frank was astonished by the officer's simple but powerful words. Sometimes, he thought, you don't have to have a long sermon to convey the truth – just the right person in the right circumstances.

"Do you suppose, after this is all over, I could ride with you during one of your tours of duty? I think I could learn some things from you."

"I'd be honored, pastor, but first let's get this incident straightened out. When we arrive at the station, I will take you in, and they will question you about the incident. My guess is that that will be about all there is to it. Either of you could get fined for disturbing the peace or one of you could file charges against the other, but that's up to you."

"I don't know about Mr. Ivory, but I'd like to get this behind me as soon as possible, and I'm not interested in filing charges against anyone."

"I figured as much, but you can't tell about Mr. Ivory. People like that sometimes feed off publicity, even negative publicity. Well, here we are."

Both police cars pulled to the side of the station, and both men were ushered into the building. Each was taken to a separate interview room.

* * * * *

Frank was taken into interview room number eight and told to wait there. This is just like on TV, he thought, except the room is a little smaller. There was a cheap white table made of inexpensive plastic and four orange stackable chairs at the table. The room smelled stuffy as if it needed a good airing, but there were no windows to open. The scratches and even some cigarette burns on the table suggested heavy use and deep feelings of anxiety. The room was grey and devoid of any decoration. He noticed a small camera and recording device in one corner. He remembered a few years ago when it was decided that all police interviews should be recorded as both a protection of the person arrested and the police.

A woman officer opened the door and entered with a clip board in her hand. "I need to get some basic information, sir. This is just for our records."

"I understand. What do you need to know?"

"Just basic information. You are the Reverend Frank Sessions of the John Knox Presbyterian Church. Is that right?"

Frank nodded.

"And this is in regards to an incident that took place this morning at the True Vine Church, correct?"

Again Frank nodded assent.

She proceeded to get some more routine information and then asked, "Can I get you some coffee or a soda?"

"No, I'M fine. What happens next?"

"An officer will be with you shortly to ask you some questions. You need to understand that you have a right to have a lawyer present, if you desire."

"I doubt that that will be necessary but thanks for informing me."

She moved one of the chairs over to the corner of the room. "We have a consultant from Virginia who will sit in on this interview unless you object," she said.

"No, that's fine," he responded. Frank was feeling so embarrassed that he didn't believe he had a right to object to anything.

"OK, make yourself as comfortable as possible." She looked around the room with a look of disgust on her face. "That's not too easy in a room like this. It won't be long. I believe it will be Lieutenant Bryson that will be here shortly."

The officer exited the room and left Frank to think about all that had happened.

The door opened. Lieutenant Bryson, who had conducted the earlier interview at the church, came in. He had a slight smirk on his face. "Well, Reverend, it looks like we meet again; this time on my turf."

Frank started to turn and felt the blood drain from his face. Standing slightly behind Bryson and to his right was a woman in uniform that he hadn't seen for years. Despite over twenty years intervening, the light olive skin and the slight Asian slant to her eyes left no doubt in Frank's mind who this was. The woman wasn't looking at him directly because her attention was drawn to the information on her clip board. Without even looking up, she sat on one of the plastic chairs the first officer had placed in the corner.

"I hope you don't mind, Reverend, but I have asked Criminal Psychologist Singletary from Richmond, Virginia to sit in on our interview. Since your assertion that Pardilla was innocent seems to have proved right, we have invited Psycholigist Singletary, who specializes in these types of crimes, to serve as our consultant. Hopefully with her help, we will catch the real rapist."

Frank glanced at the woman he had known as Mandy, seeing no sign that she recognized him, he simply nodded his assent and continued to stare at the table in front of him. For once, Frank thought, maybe forty extra pounds, a full beard, and twenty years might prove to be an advantage. He had slipped his sunglasses off when he came into the room but now placed them back on.

Bryson assumed a seat across from Frank and straightened out some documents in front of him. "This shouldn't take long, Reverend, but I would like to hear your story of what happened at the True Vine Church this morning."

"I'm embarrassed to say that I acted like an idiot. I provoked Mr. Ivory, and he lost his temper. We began brawling like teenagers. The police acted very properly in pulling us apart."

"Since I know the power of your words to provoke people," he said with a wry smile, "I understand how that might have happened. Nevertheless, people are responsible for their behavior. Are you considering filing any charges against Mr. Ivory?"

"Not at all. I intend to apologize to him and hope that he will understand."

Bryson covered some other details. Then he turned to Lieutenant Singletary and asked, "Do you have any questions, Lieutenant?"

Frank kept his head bowed and did not look at anyone.

"Not at the moment. I may have some later, however."

"OK, then that about covers it, Reverend. If you will just wait here a few more minutes, I'll have an officer come and usher you out."

A flood of memories washed over Frank as the officers left the room. In college he knew Officer Singletary as Amanda Billings. He placed his head in his hands and groaned as the movie of that night so long ago played in his mind. It was the second semester of his senior year at college and her sophomore year. Her slightly Asian cast gave her an exotic look, which combined with her tight dark curls and great figure made her an object of notice for the whole campus. She had plenty of dates, but in the lingo of the fraternity brothers on campus, despite their best moves, she was unavailable.

Frank, then called Zeke, took pride in his reputation as one of the campus studs. Ministry, even ethical behavior, was not part of Zeke's thinking. He was out to enjoy life, and collegiate women were just one among several sources of pleasure. What an ass Zeke was, Frank thought. Hopefully his new identity as Frank had made up for part of it. Ironically, his current identity began that night almost twenty years ago.

Earlier in the week, Amanda, then called Mandy, was the topic among his fraternity brothers, as she often was. "I put on my best moves," said one of the brothers, "and if I don't mind saying so, I'm no slouch when it comes to women, but the smoother I moved, the more she became like Antarctica." Other guys related their failed attempts as well.

Frank remembered clearly the shift in conversation. "How about you, Zeke? Has studsville USA struck out as well?"

"Never up to bat and never took a strike," Zeke said. "I know an iceberg when I see one, and I'm not interested in flooding our campus in her tears when she melts."

He thought that had been a rather clever repartee and was ready to move to a new topic, but his fraternity mates were not ready to let the topic go. One reached into his pocket and pulled out a ten-dollar bill. "How about it, guys, let's build a pool for flood insurance. My ten says Zeke can't even get to first base." Within minutes, the pile of money had mounted to $80. "What about it, Zeke, are you all talk or are you willing to put $20 against our $80 that you can get into her pants?"

"Hmm," said Zeke, "I'll admit that $80 could take a significant bite out of my bar bill. That, plus two rounds of drinks at a celebration event afterwards, and you've got yourself a bet."

The memory pained Frank. I was such an arrogant, egotistical SOB raised to the tenth power, he thought.

He thought that he might have lost before he began when he approached Amanda at the library. After some friendly conversation, he invited her to see a movie that weekend, and she promptly turned him down. She was polite but firm. He finally convinced her that he could call her the next night and see if she had changed her mind. She assured him that she wouldn't but agreed that he could call.

With $80 and two free drinks on the line, he began to strategize. He talked to two girls who were eager to please him and promised some special favors if they would talk to Amanda and soften her up in preparation for his phone call. He also did some research on her background and the things that might interest her. He planned his conversation carefully so that she wouldn't have a chance to turn him down before he had a chance to use his best debating techniques to convince her. It still mystified him as he thought back on that phone call. After all that careful preparation, he placed his call. When she answered, he didn't even have a chance to begin before she said, "I've thought about it, Zeke, and I'd love to go to the movie with you next Saturday evening."

Even Zeke was surprised by how responsive Amanda had been to his every move. She did not resist when he put his arm around her in the movie and seemed to enjoy his flirtatious repartee. Then they went for a walk on a deserted golf course under a sky filled with an array of bright stars. He brought a soft blanket along and suggested that they sit on one of the greens and gaze at the sky. She agreed. Soon she lay by his side. Even now he remembered thinking, I am about to win $80 and seal my reputation as the undisputed top stud of my fraternity. He had listened carefully as her initial protestations, "No, we mustn't" to "Oh, no." Then in the midst of gentle caresses and murmurings of endearment, he had deftly released the hook on her bra, and was now unbuttoning her blouse with one hand as his other hand began to caress her almost instantly erect nipples. When her squirming became rhythmic and her "Oh, No" changed into "Oh, Oh, Oh," and her breathing became heavier, he knew he had won.

In a moment, he would begin caressing her stomach in ever expanding circles and would soon be invading her pubic area. He knew her resistance was gone. It was just a matter of time and the natural response of hormones. He removed his own T-shirt and pulled her on top of him so that he might feel her delightful breasts on his chest as he nuzzled her neck.

He was about to move his hands down and massage her buttocks, hoping that as he drew her closer, she would feel his engorged penis straining against his sweatpants, when he felt moisture on his neck. At first he wondered if it was beginning to rain, but the moisture was different from raindrops. As he raised his head, the first thing he saw was Mandy's face. She was crying, and it was her tears that had been the source of the moisture.

It was clear that Mandy was no longer resisting his moves. Her body was even responding with desire. It was also clear that even though Mandy knew what was to come, she felt shame and was hurting. In that moment, Zeke was forced to realize that greed and ego were far more powerful forces guiding his actions than any feelings of passion for Mandy. The impact on Frank was to make him feel very small as a human being.

Almost in the same instant, Zeke looked past Mandy's face to the sky above her head. It was filled with a million twinkling stars on a cloudless night. The vastness of the universe overwhelmed Zeke. Again, he felt very small. It wasn't a voice or any type of clear message, and yet, something deep inside him seemed to say, "Do you really think that this vast universe was created to serve your selfish pleasure? Surely there is more purpose to your life than this."

In one continuous motion, Zeke sat Mandy up, raised himself, and began to gently close her blouse. She looked at him with both relief and uncertainty.

"What are you doing?" she asked, as she looked down at her blouse.

"Mandy," Zeke said. "Look at me."

She looked up, and he looked deeply into her eyes as he continued to button her blouse.

"You are a beautiful woman, and any man would be thrilled to share your love. I was about to rob you of the pleasure of that experience for my own selfish ends."

"I don't understand," she said. For a moment, she seemed almost embarrassed that he didn't want to continue; as if somehow she had done something wrong; that it was her fault.

"Have you told me about your family, or what your major is, or what you hope to do in life?"

"No, you didn't ask," she said.

"That's right. I didn't even care. I only wanted to see if I could get in your pants for bragging rights."

"You would have told someone?" she asked. Her body stiffened as if she was getting in touch with her anger.

"You better believe it. I'm such a selfish, self-centered, son of a bitch that I would have awakened my fraternity brothers just to brag about it."

"That's horrible," she said with increasing brittleness in her voice.

"What is your major, anyway?" he asked.

She was caught off guard by the sudden switch in the conversation and answered without thinking about what had been happening. "I want to be a lawyer. I think lots of people get a raw deal, and I want to do something about it."

"So what if what was about to happen tonight so shattered your spirit and self-confidence that you dropped out of school, and some great court case that would have changed the course of law in this country was never argued?"

"That's a little grandiose, don't you think? I'm just talking about becoming a decent lawyer and helping some unlucky snook from getting jailed for something he didn't do."

"And what if that poor snook, by being saved from jail, went on to open a shelter to care for the homeless?" he said.

"You have a strange way of thinking," she said. "What are you studying to be, some sort of pastor?"

"Ha!" he barked. "Now that would be a miracle. No, I'm just a selfish brat who's been given too much in this life and haven't any idea how I will earn a living. I just assume it will work out in the end."

In a very small voice, Mandy said, "Thank you."

"Don't thank me. I don't deserve it. But, let me give you a piece of advice. You are too valuable a person to be mauled on a green. If anyone ever tries something like that again, scream your bloody head off and do your best to scratch his eyes out." He rose and offered his hand to help her up.

"So what do we do when we see each other on campus in the future?" she asked.

"You," he said with emphasis, "hold your head up high. You have nothing to be ashamed of. By the way, I will make sure of that. I will be very clear with my Neanderthal fraternity brothers that I failed miserably."

She smiled a weak smile.

"And if in time you can find it in your heart to forgive me, I would consider myself very fortunate."

They walked back to Zeke's car.

Now, twenty years later, Amanda Singleterry, that must be her married name Frank thought, was a police officer rather than a lawyer. She was helping investigate the crime of a sexual predator. Frank's secret, which he thought had been buried and forgotten, may well come back to haunt him. I still have a chance of slipping out of here before she recognizes me, he thought.

CHAPTER 15

Explosion and Recreation

As Amanda followed Lieutenant Bryson towards the conference room where the other officers who had questioned Mr. Ivory waited, she knew there was something that she had overlooked, but she couldn't pull it into her awareness.

Four other officers were sipping coffee and making wise cracks about pious preachers duking it out in the church. Their conversation quieted as she and Bryson walked into the room. Her very presence changed the dynamics of the group. While they accepted Amanda as a fellow professional, she was aware that her presence made them slightly uncomfortable. They had worked together over the past month and had learned to trust each other. She was like a new kid at school that no one had figured out yet.

Bryson asked them how the interview with Ivory had gone.

"'bout what you'd expect from someone who considers himself an important public personality," one officer said. "He ranted a little about police brutality and how he was going to sue everyone from the reverend to the chief of police. Like you told us, we just let him erupt like an overripe volcano, and eventually he ran out of steam."

"And that took awhile," another officer joined in. "Then he began demanding a lawyer and saying he wouldn't answer any questions before that lawyer arrived. I think he had watched a few too many crime shows on TV."

"So then what happened?" Bryson asked.

"We explained to him that he had a right to ask for a lawyer but that was going to take extra time, and no one had filed any charges against anyone. Our only interest was to keep a volatile situation under control, and while we were interested in anything he might contribute to our investigation of the serial rapist, we saw no reason to hold him."

"By that time, he had calmed down and began to act more civil. I don't really see that we have anything to gain by holding him," said the first officer.

"Lieutenant Singletary will want to watch the recording of your interview just in case something might have slipped out that will help us," said Bryson, "but it sounds like you handled that quite well. I think the same can be said for the Reverend Franklin Ezekiel Sessions."

Amanda leaped from her chair and shouted, "What did you say?"

Bryson turned with a puzzled look on his face. "I said I didn't see any reason to hold the Reverend."

"His name, what was his name?" Amanda pressed as she felt blood rushing to her head.

"I said," Bryson responded, glancing down at his chart, "the Reverend Franklin Ezekiel Sessions. That is his name. What's the problem here?"

"That son of a bitch," Amanda shouted. She threw her clipboard across the room. "He knew, that son of a bitch knew, and he didn't say a word."

The others stared at Amanda and then almost stumbled over themselves getting out of her way as she pulled her pistol from its holster.

"Lieutenant, what are you doing?" Bryson said, as he also backed away.

Amanda slammed the pistol down on a desk. "You keep that here. If I walked into that room with my pistol, I might plug the son of a bitch."

With that, Amanda whirled about and began to stomp towards the interview room, still muttering curses as she went.

* * * * *

Frank was still considering his options when the door opened with such force that it slammed against the wall. He turned as Amanda advanced upon him.

"Uh oh, I think the lady's memory has returned."

"You're damn right my memory has returned. You are in one shitload of trouble, Franklin Ezekiel Sessions. Did you really think that I wouldn't remember the champion sex king of my campus who almost raped me my sophomore year?"

She stood there, feet balanced as if ready to fight, breathing hard, face flushed, and eyes flashing. Several officers had stuck their heads in the door but were waiting to see how events were going to unfold.

"Mandy, I'm sorry," Frank said. He held his hands up in surrender. "I had already violated most of what I thought were my core ethics this morning. I was forming in my mind my letter of resignation to my congregation for my behavior. Then you walked in the room. I was stunned. It was so surreal that I wasn't sure what reality was anymore."

"Why didn't you just identify yourself?"

"It was stupid of me not to, but I think it would be best if we discussed it in private." He looked over her shoulder at the open door to the room.

Amanda looked behind her at all of the officers who were standing in the doorway. "Gentlemen, I believe the Reverend Sessions is safe from my assault. I would like a couple of minutes alone with him if you don't mind."

She moved towards the door and with some effort encouraged them all to leave. She shut the door and turned to face Frank. "OK, now that we are alone, tell me, I'm listening." She was still flushed in the face, but her breathing was more controlled.

"While I was shocked to see you, I have never forgotten our last meeting and my boorish behavior. I was afraid that if you recognized me, you might decide that I might be a prime suspect for the rapist that you are seeking."

"You still could be." Then she paused and took a deep breath. "No, you're no rapist. I haven't forgotten that night either, but I especially remember how it ended. The Don Juan of the campus discovered he had values that went deeper than a quickie conquest."

Frank stood up and sat on the edge of the table. He looked at Amanda and smiled. "Do you remember what you asked me that night?"

"I wasn't exactly focused on the words that were being spoken," she said.

"You asked me if I was studying to be a pastor," Frank said. "That was the first time that such a thought ever entered my mind. Later when people asked me how I decided to become a pastor, I frequently said it was because of a star and a tear."

"I remember the stars," she said. "The sky was full of them that night."

"Yes, it was," said Frank, "and looking at them, I suddenly realized that I was not the center of the universe but a very small part of something vastly more important."

"And the tear?" she asked.

"One of your tears fell on my cheek while we were lying there, and somehow it penetrated my thick skull that other people were affected by my behavior. I'm sorry about that night, Mandy. I promise you, I've tried to be a better person since then."

"I saw your character that night, both the image you were trying to portray and glimpses of your truer self. You may have your character flaws, Frank, but you are no rapist."

"There is a rapist out there, Mandy, and religion in a very perverted form is part of his madness. If you will let me, I'd like to help you catch him."

She glanced towards the door. "Our first task is to provide a believable story to the squad out there. They didn't exactly see me demonstrate exemplary control as I entered the room."

When they emerged from the room, all of the officers were busy pretending that they were very busy.

Amanda walked over to Bryson's desk where her pistol was still lying. "If this is still available," said Amanda, "I think I will repossess it."

"You scratched my desk when you slammed it down," said Bryson without looking up.

"You are probably wondering what was going on there," said Amanda.

"Not at all, Lieutenant. We have consultants come screaming in here all the time. Some of them almost act like they're crazy. Isn't that right boys and girls?"

"Not all of them draw a gun on us," said another officer, "but I've always heard that Virginia police have a different approach to the law."

The other officers were trying to keep a straight face while they evaluated Amanda's ability to handle the kidding.

"You have a right to an apology, and I apologize. Reverend Sessions and I had a run-in several years back that at first I thought might have a bearing on this case. After we talked, I'm convinced that it didn't."

"I also want to apologize," said Frank. "I'm afraid this rapist has gotten all of us uptight, and I'm sorry that my behavior this morning caused you additional trouble."

"I also think," continued Amanda, "that Reverend Sessions, with his background, might be able to contribute to our investigation."

"So what do you think, Reverend," said Bryson, moving a comb through his blond hair, "is our nut case one of those flaming liberal buddies of yours or is it one of our faithful fundamentalists who has gone off the ranch?" Bryson looked directly at Frank keeping a neutral look on his face.

"Please call me Frank, unless, of course, you are afraid you will be scorched by being so familiar with a flaming liberal."

"In police work," said Bryson, "we have to learn to associate with all types and not let it impair our otherwise impeccable and loving personalities."

"Are you two done sparing with each other?" Amanda picked up the file case. "Is there anyone in this squad room who is interested in solving this case?"

"You got to excuse her, Frank." Bryson nodded his head towards Amanda, "These consultants from Virginia are really hard-nosed. Aside from occasional flares of temper, of course."

"You might want to learn from her interrogation technique, though," said Frank, "I think it makes water boarding by the CIA mere child's play."

Amanda just shook her head. "I'm sorry that I suggested that the two of you might work together."

"Actually, Frank, I am interested in your take on what's going on," said Bryson. "Because of your background in religion and your interest in the sexual angle, you might be able to help us fill in the profile of this nut."

"I do have a couple of thoughts that might be worth pursuing," said Frank.

Bryson held up his hand. "Wait just a minute." He looked around the squad room. "Gather around guys and gals. Let's think this through together."

They all brought their chairs and formed a small circle around Bryson's desk. Sergeant O'Riley brought a carafe of coffee and started passing out some Styrofoam cups. When they were all settled, Bryson waved his hand at Frank. "The way we usually do this," said Bryson, "is that you will throw out your thoughts, but anyone can chime in with either a question or an observation. We keep it pretty loose, if that is all right with you."

"That's the way I'd prefer," said Frank.

"OK, then, share your thoughts with us." He pointed to another sergeant, "Bill, you keep any significant points we come up with on the white board."

"Well, first of all," said Frank, "as you recall, we first learned that this was a serial rapist when what we think of as the fifth victim, Carrie Breakstone, reported her experience to the police, and Brenda Sides broke the story to the media."

"That gave permission for several other victims to come forward," O'Riley said.

"That's right," said Frank. "What some of you may not know is that the reporter, Brenda Sides, had come to me first and wanted me to help her fill in exactly what the rapist had been saying during the rapes."

"Quotes from Bible," said one officer.

"Not just the Bible but from a specific book, the Song of Solomon," said Frank. "What you also may not know is that I'd used some of those very quotes in a lecture that I'd given over at the seminary several years ago."

"So maybe the rapist is one of those seminary dudes," said Bryson.

"That might be true," said Frank, "but in addition there were other pastors from the community there that night."

"Do we have an attendance list?" asked Sargent Riley.

"No, but even if we did, that lecture was copied and is available at the seminary library," said Frank. "It might be of value to see who has checked it out over the last year."

"Why don't you and Amanda do that?" suggested Bryson. "She has the police background, and you might be able to spot someone from the religious community that might be of interest."

"We can do that," agreed Frank, "but there is another event that might prove of interest. Unless the invitation is withdrawn because of my embarrassing behavior this morning, I'm scheduled to give a lecture this Thursday on the religious dynamics behind this case and it's affect on those going into the pastorate."

"Like a moth to the flame," said Amanda.

"What do you mean?" asked another officer.

"Think about it," said Amanda. She got up and moved towards the white board, taking the marker from the sergeant standing there. "Our rapist apparently was affected by Frank's thoughts in that lecture." She put the lecture and its date on the board.

"Several years later, apparently influenced by the thoughts spoken by Frank," she marked Frank's name on the board, "he begins to act out, making use of what Frank had pointed him to in the Bible." She drew a line indicating the time frame.

"A major question," Bryson said, "is what triggered him to act now rather than earlier?"

"Maybe his marriage or his ministry was going along smoothly then," said one officer, "but the ideas kept fermenting in his brain."

"Right, and if the pressure in his ministry or his marriage, or something else in his life went south," said Amanda, "he may have chosen this as a way to release the pressure."

Amanda marked on the board the words "Triggering incident."

"Given our society's emphasis on sex as an act for feeding our personal pleasure, think of this guy as a real narcissist," said Frank. "Sex becomes a reward for all the hard work he does, and maybe a salve for his woundedness when things aren't going very well."

"Sort of like what David did when he got his rocks off with Bathsheba," said Bryson.

Frank smiled and pointed his index finger at Bryson in agreement.

"That's actually a good parallel," said Amanda. "Rape is an act of self-serving power. Bathsheba had no choice when David summoned her just like our drugged victims had no choice when our rapist took them. Power is the aphrodisiac in rape. The sexual pleasure is the dessert."

"Ouch, my preacher never told me about David and Bathsheba in that way," said one of the officers.

"Probably not," said Frank. "Nor did he tell you about David's act with Abigail and others. The point is that for some people sex becomes like an addiction. It's not enough, by itself. Each time you have to enhance the experience with something more."

"Like those politicians who use their position to seduce one of their followers but keep doing it in more dangerous circumstances until they get caught," O'Riley said.

"You guys are good," said Frank.

Amanda wrote the words "Sex addiction."

"Has there been any progression in what your perpetrator has been doing or saying?" Frank asked.

"Actually, there has been a change in tone," said Bryson. "The last victim that reported in to us said that he spoke of something about sex being the first step on a journey to bliss."

"I don't like the sound of that. It could be escalating."

"We've been fortunate, so far," said Amanda, "that he's been so sure of the effect of the drugs disguising his identity that all the victims were allowed to live. He would keep telling them to spread the word that they had been loved by God's spirit, just like Mary had."

"That's disgusting," said O'Riley. "What does he think he is doing, making space for the second coming?"

"That's certainly possible," said Frank, "but this first step towards something else bothers me. Our rapist is getting more delusional. I'm afraid the sexual experience, in which he was seeking transcendence, is no longer enough. Now he wants to take the next step. We may be running out of time."

"There is another thing that is confusing," said Bryson. "What's this about the names. Why does he keep calling his victims by other names?"

"That's a puzzle," said Amanda. "Any thoughts on that, Frank?"

"Not at the moment," said Frank. "Can you give me a list of all the names of the victims and, where possible, what they were being called? Maybe I can come up with some sort of pattern."

Amanda wrote "Name confusion" on the board.

"What did you mean about a moth and a flame?" asked O'Riley.

"What I'm suggesting," said Amanda, "is that if our rapist was influenced by Frank's lecture, but it has been awhile since Frank spoke on the subject, wouldn't he be attracted to hearing Frank's latest thoughts on the subject?"

"So he may well show up at the lecture," said Bryson.

"At least it's a possibility we don't want to overlook," said Amanda.

"I'll make sure the Dean doesn't withdraw the invitation," said Bryson, "and we will have some plainclothes officers there for the event."

"If I'm free to go," said Frank, "I think I'd better start making notes about what I'm going to say at that lecture."

CHAPTER 16

The Apology

A police cruiser provided Frank a ride back to the True Vine Church. The officer, a tall, burley man, was pleasant but not very talkative. He seemed to sense that Frank needed time to sort out his feelings.

Frank's thoughts and the feelings collided like the balls in an old pinball machine. Some pastor I am, he thought. John Knox deserves better. I should resign before this gets any worse. Boy, Amanda looked great. I'd love to catch up with her. I wonder if Eric Ivory will try to take legal action. I need to think about what lawyer I know who could handle that. I should stop in and apologize to Bob Godwin when we arrive. Of course, he may not be there, or, even worse, he may not be willing to speak with me. After this morning's disaster, I can understand if he doesn't want to see me. It's frightening to think that a lecture I gave several years ago could have actually triggered these horrible events. How can something so good, the Scriptures, spawn something so horrible? Religion and love, two of the most creative forces in the world and, at the same time, two of the most destructive. Is there a pattern to these crazy rapes? Can I really be of help to the police in sorting this out?

He was so deep in thought that he jumped when the officer said, "Here we are Reverend Sessions. On which side of the building is your car?"

You can drop me off at the entrance to the church offices. I want to talk to the pastor about what happened and apologize for my behavior." He raised one eyebrow and offered a sheepish smile as he exited the car. "Sorry I haven't been very good company but thanks for the ride."

Frank approached the entry to the offices of the church. In contrast to the bustle of the morning, the hallways were quiet. The large electronic screens were still projecting, alternating between pictures of the pastoral staff and highlighting coming events in the church calendar. A security guard looked up from a desk near the entrance as Frank approached.

"Aren't you…" he began.

"I'm rather embarrassed to say that I am one of the pastors who got into a fracas this morning during the meeting. I was wondering if I might see if the Reverend Godwin is in and apologize for my part in those events."

The guard looked at him for a few seconds and then said, "He may be in. I'm not sure. The main office is up the hallway on your right, and someone there can help you."

"Thank you," Frank said, "I can assure you that I will not be causing anyone more trouble."

The guard smiled. "I'm glad to hear that. As you may have noticed, I'm too old to quell riots."

Frank laughed with him and began to move up the hall towards the large office complex. He noticed the variety of uplifting slogans and Scripture quotes displayed in attractive art forms on the walls as he walked. There was also an honors plaque where various members and staff were highlighted for something they had done this past month. Central to the display was Bob's smiling portrait.

Frank had discouraged his church from displaying his portrait, and his first reaction to seeing Bob's portrait was critical. Then he chastised himself for being so quick to judge. After all, he thought, in a huge church like this, it is important for people to quickly recognize who the pastor is. He walked on down the hall towards the offices.

The office complex was well lit with a big picture window so that those inside could see who was approaching. There were several people bustling in various directions within the complex as they entered and exited various doors that Frank assumed led to more interior offices. As Frank entered, there was soft Gospel music playing, loud enough to hear but not disturb conversation. The décor was tasteful but businesslike. There was a variety of religious symbols and art on the walls. The familiar portrait of Jesus knocking on the door was prominent to the eye of a visitor entering the complex.

A pleasant looking woman in a smart sports suit greeted him with a large smile. "Welcome to True Vine Church. How may I be of help to you?" There was a practiced yet genuine warmth to her greeting. Frank felt nervous, uncertain about how he would be received, but as she greeted him, he began to feel himself relax.

"My name is Frank Sessions of the John Knox Presbyterian Church. I was wondering if the Reverend Godwin might have a few moments. I'd like to speak to him about the events of this morning."

"Oh, that was embarrassing. We were fortunate that the Reverend Godwin thought to have some police on hand. Who would have thought that you would need that at a meeting of the clergy?"

She picked up the phone. "Let me check with his secretary. Did you have an appointment?"

"No, I just decided to take a chance he might have a free moment for me."

He was slightly amused at the exchange on the phone and was fully prepared when she turned hesitantly and said, "You did say that you were the Reverend Frank Sessions, didn't you?"

He put on his best disarming smile and responded. "Yes, I'm afraid I am that Reverend Sessions. In fact I've just returned from the police station."

"Oh," she said, looking uncomfortable, and confirmed the information with Godwin's personal secretary.

"I'll tell him," she said and replaced the phone on the receiver. "If you can wait just a few minutes, the Reverend Godwin will be out to greet you. I guess I should have recognized your name." Then she looked down and shifted some papers on her desk. "I mean, well you look so nice. I just didn't make the connection."

Frank laughed softly. He glanced at the nameplate on the desk. "You mean I don't look like a wild man who would start a fight in a church. I think, Helen, that I should take that as a compliment."

"I'm sorry, I shouldn't have said that," Helen said. "Can I get you some coffee while you wait?"

"No, I'm fine. You go on with your work." He glanced at a plastic holder with some of Godwin's sermon in it. "I'll just glance at one of the Reverend Godwin's sermons while I wait."

Mentally trying to be on his best behavior, he glanced at a sermon dated a month earlier and tried not to fall into the proverbial pastor's trap of critiquing another pastor's sermon. In about ten minutes, a door marked Senior Pastor opened, and Bob Godwin strode into the outer office. He wore a sharply tailored bright blue linen sports coat and a rose-colored, open-collared shirt. He projected energy.

"Frank, good to see you," Bob held out his hand accompanied by a large smile. "Won't you come back to my study?" He turned to Helen and said, "Helen, if you would be so kind, except for an emergency, hold my calls for awhile."

Frank rose, exchanged handshakes, and was ushered through the door marked Senior Pastor. As he passed through the door, he entered a pleasant reception area where Bob's personal secretary was busy at work.

"Rita, may I present to you Frank Sessions, the pastor of the John Knox Presbyterian Church."

Rita turned from her computer with an impish look on her face. "Always glad to meet one of the gladiators from the clergy smackdown event."

Bob's mouth was agape as he turned to see how Frank was responding.

"Whoops, I see my reputation has preceded me." He turned towards Bob. "You've got a winner here, Bob."

Relieved that Frank had received Rita's salvo with good humor, Bob smiled and said, "Rita, could you be so gracious, and I do emphasize the word gracious," he raised his eyebrows slightly, "to prepare some coffee for Frank and me."

"Oops, guess I crossed a line, didn't I? I'm sorry, Reverend Sessions, it just sort of slipped out. I'd be pleased to prepare some coffee for the two of you."

"Rita, I can assure you that if I didn't already have an excellent secretary," Frank said, "I'd try to steal you away from Bob. There is nothing so valuable to a pastor than a good secretary."

Bob proceeded to move Frank into his inneroffice. As the door closed, Bob said, "Rita really is a good secretary, even if her sense of humor gets a little extreme at times."

"I have a slightly cynical but extremely proficient Episcopalian for my secretary," said Frank. "I think one of her gifts is to puncture my balloon once in awhile and keep me grounded. It sounds like Rita may play that type of role for you."

"Rita is a faithful Catholic," said Bob. "I learned, as you no doubt have, that it is good to have a secretary that is a faithful Christian but has no connection with your church."

"You are so right," said Frank. He recognized that what they were doing was discovering connections as colleagues, and it felt good. He looked around the office. It was a spacious, luxuriously decorated office. The walls were full of pictures of Bob greeting some well-known personalities as well as some honorary degrees and a large family picture of Bob, his wife Barbie, and his son David, when he was a younger age.

Knowing that he needed to make some polite conversation while the coffee arrived, Frank turned to the family picture. "That's a nice family portrait. Your wife is lovely."

"Thanks, Frank. That was taken several years ago. Our son David has grown in several ways since then. He went through a strong rebellion stage, as many preacher's kids do. While I'm not wild about the liberal tone of our local seminary, I'm glad to report that David is a student there. He's still trying to find himself, but I think he is headed in the right direction."

"Interesting, my son Jacob is also there. I wonder if they know each other."

As they were talking, the door opened, and Rita came in with a tray bearing two porcelain cups, a pot of coffee, and a few sugar cookies, plus some sugar and cream.

"I hope decaf coffee is alright?" Rita asked as she set the tray down on a table in the sitting area of the office. "The cookies are part of my penance."

"A fine penance it is," Frank said. "The decaf is fine. I think I've had enough stimulation for the day."

Rita smiled, filled the cups, and retreated from the office.

"Bob," Frank began, as he received the cup of coffee and took a sip, "I want to apologize for my behavior this morning. I should not have taunted Ivory like that, and I certainly shouldn't have let it get so far out of hand in the sanctuary."

"Apology accepted, but I'll also admit that you were sorely provoked by Ivory's broadcast. I'm a little worried about this entire campaign of his getting out of hand. I don't mind admitting to you in private that I was a little irritated at the way he roped me into this. I think some of the other brothers were not pleased at being manipulated as well."

"I didn't come to the meeting with the right attitude but what tipped me over the line was a text I received while I was on stage that Reggie Pardella had been killed in prison."

"Yes, that was very sad. You had been trying to help him. I'm not sure that what you were doing would work, but I'm sorry for your loss."

"Reggie was a sick individual, but he didn't deserve to die right while he was trying to turn his life around. Worse yet, it delayed the efforts to catch the real rapist."

"Yes," Bob said, "there is that. Do you think the police are making any progress in identifying him?"

Frank hesitated a second, wondering how much he should say, and then decided that what he knew shouldn't be a subject for gossip. "I think they were embarrassed at jumping too quickly the first time. I know that they are working on it, but we'll just have to wait and see."

"Well, as you have so eloquently pointed out, sex and religion are intricately entwined. I'm not sure what people would say today about the biblical David in our politically correct society, but God used him for good."

That's an interesting take, Frank thought. "You're right," Frank said, "but all the recent sexual scandals in the church are certainly tarnishing the reputation of the church. The rapist's use of Scripture is not making our job any easier."

Frank noticed Bob pull back in his chair. It was almost as if he had been in an intimate conversation and now he was resuming his public persona.

"His utterances are pure blasphemy and need to be denounced by faithful disciples everywhere, as I did in my last sermon. Maybe you'd like to see a copy of it." Before Frank could respond, Bob reached for his phone. "Helen, would you see that a copy of my latest sermon is available for the Reverend Sessions. We'll probably be done here in," he looked at Frank with a question on his face, "oh, about ten more minutes. And get one of those DVDs from the celebration three weeks ago. I'm sure he would enjoy that as well."

"Look, Bob, I know that you are busy, and I have to go back and face my church. Because of the media present, I'm sure this event will be all over the city by evening. I'm thinking about resigning my position to save the church further embarrassment."

"Frank, I know we come from opposite ends of the theological spectrum, but we are colleague in the faith. My advice to you is not to make any abrupt decisions. God may not be through with you at that church yet."

"Thanks, Bob. If I do stay, after this all dies down, I'd like to take the opportunity for the two of us to get better acquainted. I think another scandal of the church is our separation one from the other. Maybe we could learn from each other."

Bob chuckled. "Wouldn't that be interesting? Both of our constituencies think the other is at best a scalawag and at worst the incarnation of Satan. We might want to keep our initial conversations under the radar."

Frank grinned. "There is some wisdom in that, but I at least hope we can have some clandestine conversations and see where it goes."

"I'm interested in that," said Bob, "but let's first get through our immediate problems and take it one step at a time."

They rose together, and Bob ushered Frank out of his office, making sure that Frank had the DVD and a copy of Bob's latest sermon before he left.

CHAPTER 17

Experiencing Church

Frank returned to the John Knox church. Unlike the True Vine Church, John Knox's architecture was traditional. The façade was grey stone that gave an image of solidness. The church had a prominent bell tower with a huge cross that seemed to reach for the sky.

Frank recalled a veteran from Vietnam coming to him once and telling him how the cross provided him stability. When he came back from Vietnam, he was a shattered man. He found a small plot of land just outside the city, built a simple shelter, and prepared to hang out there. One day, as he was walking the grounds, he discovered that at the top of a small hill, with his binoculars, he could spot the cross. When he was at his lowest, he would go to the hill and stare at the cross. "It was my anchor for several years," the man said. It was a humbling reminder for Frank of the power of symbolism.

Frank's sanctuary held about 500 worshippers. That was large for the average Presbyterian Church but was modest compared to megachurches like True Vine. Frank was grateful for this church and the support of its people. They had been patient and held him together during his long, slow, tunnel of grief after Rosie's death. Now he wondered if he had created a scandal that would wound the church he loved.

As he entered the outer office, it was empty. He picked up the mail on the corner of the desk. He could see that the church message box was blinking, but he decided that he wasn't up to answering messages just yet. He was grateful that Marcie, his secretary, had asked for the afternoon off for a doctor's appointment. He didn't want to face anyone, even someone as supportive and balanced as Marcie.

As he moved through the outer office and entered his office, he broke out in laughter. There, sitting on his chair, was a small stuffed tiger with a sign attached: "Even tigers need support, let me know if I can help. Marcie."

He removed the tiger and plopped down into his chair. He was about to sort through his mail when he noticed that his private line was blinking. Most church members left messages on the church line, so he decided to play the message. The familiar voice of his daughter Rachel spoke from the machine. "Dad, heard about what happened at True Vine Church. I know you probably want some alone time first, but when you are ready, I'm available to talk. I love you and am proud that you are my father. If he got a bloody nose, I'll be glad to provide the stain remover."

Typical of Rachel, he thought. It was enough but not too much and laced with a little bit of humor.

OK, time to face the music. He punched in the number of the clerk of session of the church. Wiley McClaren had been his chief lay leader for the last ten years, and Frank had grown fond of him. He had demonstrated a lot of wisdom and patience as Frank slowly worked through his grief. Wiley was caustic and blunt at times, but, when it was important, he was both respectful and compassionate.

When Wiley answered the phone, Frank didn't waste time on pleasantries. "Wiley, I need to see you as soon as possible. I've acted foolishly and placed the church in an embarrassing situation. I need your counsel."

"You didn't get caught with your pants down, did you preacher?"

"No, nothing like that, I . . ."

"Good, the rest we can work out, whatever it is. I've got a free schedule this afternoon. You want to come by my office or should I come to the church?"

"I think I'd prefer your office." He paused and then said, "Don't you want me to explain to you what this is about?"

"No need. I'll hear it when you get here. You're my preacher and my friend. If you want to talk, then we'll talk. See you in about fifteen minutes."

"Thanks, Wiley, you're the best."

As Frank hung up, he felt a gentle breeze blow across his soul. The church expressed its grace in many ways, and this time it was in the form of a crusty old buzzard who knew how to be both honest and insightful. "Thank you, God. No matter what happens, I'm grateful that you have placed people like Wiley in my path," he whispered.

He rose and headed for his Prius. Knowing that there were minimal parking spaces in the lot that served Wiley's building, he looked without success for a place on the street near the office. While, in the past, it irritated him when people claimed that God had provided them a parking spot, or some other trivial item, he did smile with gratitude as he entered the parking lot to see a car pull out leaving an empty spot.

Wiley McClaren was a successful business realtor. From his unpretentious office, he managed two well-operated shopping centers and several office buildings in the city. He was a man of medium frame and often presented the image of a taciturn curmudgeon, but those who dealt with him knew that his word was to be trusted, even when it cost him personally.

As Frank left his car, he breathed in the mixture of air and gas fumes from the street. He enjoyed the smell. It reminded him of the blend of life that made the city exciting. He entered the building and pressed the elevator button for the eleventh floor. As the elevator reached its destination and opened its door, he glanced to his right through a large window overlooking the city. The city spread out before him with a skyline that spoke of business and pleasure. Having taken in the view, he turned left and walked down the hall to office 1123. As he entered, a pleasant, older woman greeted him. She was dressed in a modest grey business suit.

"Reverend Sessions, so nice to see you. Mr. McClaren said that you should go right in when you arrived. Just knock at his door."

Frank knocked and Wiley opened the door. Even as Wiley shook Frank's hand, he pulled him inside his office. "Take a load off, Frank, and tell me what's going on."

Frank described the morning incident and his experience at the police station. Wiley interrupted with a couple of brief questions about details but mostly just let him talk.

When he finished, Wiley burst out in laughter. "Wooee, I'd loved to have been there to see that blowhard Ivory get taken down a peg or two. With all your peacenik sermons, preacher, I didn't know you had it in you."

Frank grimaced, despite himself, and then said, "The problem is, Wiley, there were all sorts of media present. There have already been some news bulletins about the incident. The local stations are using it as a tease to get people to tune in tonight. No doubt, the whole awful story will be featured on the news tonight. The preacher who talks about peace and turning the other cheek is caught in a juvenile brawl in a church sanctuary. How much more hypocritical can you get?"

"Oh, there'll be a dustup or two, but most of the church will secretly be proud of you for being human just like they are," Wiley said.

"You don't think I should resign to save the church embarrassment?" Frank asked.

"Resign, hell no," Wiley said. "Excuse my language, but most people will just be glad you are coming out of your blue funk and showed good human emotions at the unnecessary death of someone you cared about."

"Still, I don't think it was very becoming of a pastor," Frank said.

"Hey, I just made sense out of one of the things you are always preaching about."

"What's that?" Frank asked.

"The priesthood of all believers," Wiley said. Wiley stood up and faced Frank with a stern look on his face. " Frank Sessions, you hopeless sinner, you are no better than the rest of us. Get on your knees, and let me pray that in some unexplainable way God can find it in his heart to forgive you."

Frank starred up at him. He didn't know whether to crack up in laughter or obediently get on his knees.

While he was still thinking about it, Wiley reached down and grabbed his hands and pulled him to his feet. Without explanation, he gave him a powerful bear hug. "Welcome to the God-blessed human race."

Frank felt the tears rolling down his cheek as he enjoyed the feeling of strong arms holding him.

Wiley released him and said, "Look, when it hits the news, of course it will be embarrassing. Have a ready response already written out that you will give to church members who call and a firm no comment to all media inquiries. Be contrite for any embarrassment to the church but unapologetic for defending yourself against Ivory's slander."

They chatted for another half hour and made some initial plans for a session meeting in case someone believed one was necessary.

As he got in his car and headed home, he felt as if the gentle breeze of grace had almost become a full gale. He wasn't sure whether the sun was brighter now, but it did seem as if the trees were more colorful and the sky a little bit bluer. As he drove, he thought about Bob Godwin's mention of having a son in seminary. It's a little surprising that David would attend a moderately liberal seminary, but maybe geography was part of that decision. I think I will call Jacob when I get home and see if he knows him.

He began thinking about what Wiley had said about having a prepared statement to say to congregational members. As he turned the corner on his block, he slowed and pulled over to the curb. Ahead of him, in front of his house, were a couple of TV vans with their antennas stretching above their vans as well as a gaggle of people who he assumed to be reporters. As much as he valued Wiley's wisdom of making no comment, it wasn't in him to be rude. He took a notebook that was in his window pocket and scribbled some notes.

When he drove into his driveway, the reporters eagerly pressed forward until he almost had difficulty exiting his car. He held up his hand in greeting. He tried to make the smile on his face as genuine and relaxed as possible as he edged towards his front door. When he reached the door, he turned to face them.

"I'm just guessing, but I don't think you are eagerly awaiting the announcement of the Scripture text that I'll be preaching from this next Sunday."

There was a smattering of chuckles and someone called out, "Not unless it's about how to avoid a wrestling match in a church sanctuary."

There was some nervous laughter indicating that they weren't sure how he would respond to such a quip.

"I bow to the superior comedian in the group." He did a mock bow. "I don't really have much to say about what happened this morning. I can only say that I was deeply affected when I learned that Reggie Pardella, a troubled young man who was trying to turn his life around, had been brutally killed while in prison for a crime that he did not commit. I acted in a way that was not appropriate, and for that I am sorry. More important than my erratic behavior is the fact that as a city we are still dealing with a rapist on the loose. We need to be vigilant and cautious while the police do their work, and we must be wary of jumping to premature judgments just so we can lessen our feelings of anxiety."

"Are you going to file charges against Eric Ivory?"

"No, I'm not going to file charges against anyone. We both got a little too excited and responded in a way that I expect both of us regret. That's all I have to say at this time. Thank you for your work in keeping the public informed."

Frank turned, unlocked his door, and entered his hallway.

CHAPTER 18

Jacob's Invitation

Just as Frank closed the door on the reporters, he heard the familiar tune of his cell phone. Once his son had taught him that he could place special tunes on his phone as his ring tone, he had thought a lot about what to choose. Finally, after some searching, he chose "Once To Every Man and Nation." It always gave him a small burst of energy when he heard it.

Even during the worst days, in his darkest tunnel, the tune reminded him of James Russell Lowes' stirring poem: "Once to every man and nation, comes the moment to decide, in the strife of truth with falsehood, for the good or evil side." For a moment, he would be lost in the nobleness of life's challenges.

As he lifted the phone from its holder, he glanced at the screen and realized that it was his son Jacob. "Jacob, how are you. I was just about to call you."

"From the rumors going around campus, it sounds like you've had a busy day."

"Sorry you had to hear it via the rumor mill first. That bit about the police offering you a free phone call only happens in the movies."

"So it's true? You really were hauled in by the Gestapo?"

Frank smiled as he thought about how both of his children had learned the art of humorous exaggeration to ease tension. He knew his role was to respond with sanity. "It was the police, not the Gestapo, and while they did invite me to accompany them to the police station, they did not arrest me, and they treated me with utmost respect."

"Kudos to the Fuzz. Now tell me what really happened. And, by the way, Rachel has already called me to check it out, so you will probably be hearing from her as soon as she can figure out how to work her smart phone."

"Actually, I already got a message on my office line from your technologically-challenged sister. I'll call her as soon as we are done."

He paused, drew in a deep breath, and let it out slowly. "Are you sitting down? This may shatter your image of your conservative father."

"I'm all ears, but you should be told that this may be recorded for quality purposes – or blackmail as the situation demands."

"Enough already, I'm about to confess my sins to my son. Do you think that's easy?"

"Actually, Dad, from the little I've heard, I think I'm going to be very proud of you. After that slime ball, Ivory, slandered you on radio this past Friday, if you bloodied his nose, I'm going to personally present you with the *My Hero* award."

"Thank you, but I'm not sure I feel very heroic. I allowed myself to lose control and started brawling like a teenager."

"Let's see, if I remember correctly, I once got a split lip my freshman year in high school. I believe your words to me were 'I'm of two minds, young man. One, you should learn to control your temper. Two, I'm proud that you think enough of yourself to stand up for what you believe.' Other than the young man part, I couldn't have said it better myself, Dad."

"Thanks, Jacob." Frank proceeded to summarize what had happened at the True Vine Church and the police station. He chose to omit the part about Amanda. He wasn't sure that he was prepared to tell his adult children about his past association with Amanda. "Actually it may turn out to have some good aftereffects." Frank said, "The incident was embarrassing, but once I got to the police station, we realized that we can benefit from working together to catch this rapist and restore a measure of sanity to our city."

"I suspect," Jacob said, "that this little contretemps will only add to the attendance at your lecture this Thursday."

"That is unless the Dean withdraws the invitation because I would be an embarrassment to the seminary."

"Not a chance. The students would rise up in protest if he tried that. Besides, he's not exactly a wilting flower when it comes to doing what is right."

Jacob, on the QT, I want you to do me a little favor in preparation for that night."

"Sure, Dad, what do you want?"

"I think we have talked before about the rapist virtually quoting me during some of the rapes. Those quotes came from that lecture I gave several years ago at the seminary. Without calling attention to what you are doing, I'd like you to visit the library and get a list of those people who have checked out that lecture over the last couple of years."

"I can do that. Uh, Dad" Jacob hesitated for a brief moment.

"What is it, Jacob?"

"Can I tell Brandy about what I'm doing?"

"Brandy, who's that?"

Jacob paused, cleared his throat, and then continued.

"Well, I guess you know her as Brenda, you know, Brenda Sides, the reporter."

The image of the reporter with the fiery red hair who had interviewed him with such confidence and yet sensitivity flashed in his mind. "She mentioned that she had met you, Jacob, but what's up with the nickname?"

He heard Jacob breathing into the phone as if getting prepared for what he was going to say. "Well, Brenda first came to me as a reporter, trying to do some background on her story about the rapist. But then we sort of hit it off, and I guess it is a little more than just a reporter doing a story now."

"And the name Brandy?"

"Uh, we recognized that we were entering into some complex territory where the lines weren't always clear, and so we came up with a way to separate when she was being a reporter and when she was just a friend. Brandy is a friend, and Brenda is a reporter."

"The father in me feels the need to raise a caution flag for you, Jacob. I'm not so worried about what you might say to Brenda or Brandy as I am about how you would feel if she wasn't able to make that separation and some of what you told her as a friend appeared in her story as a reporter."

"That's not going to happen, Dad. We didn't intend for this to happen. It sort of surprised both of us. But when we realized how attracted we were to each other, we sat down and had a serious conversation. This is the best solution we can come up with."

"She's a sharp woman, Jacob, and I'm happy that you have found someone that gets your nose out of the books for a while, but I am still nervous about the confused lines between her professional obligations and her personal ones."

"What I'm hearing is that you'd feel better if I didn't mention this library caper to her right now."

"Let's say that when the time is right, she gets the exclusive but don't create a bind for her now by telling her too much."

"Sounds like a plan, Dad. By the way, I had another reason for calling you."

"What's that, Jacob?"

"Well, I can imagine that you and Bob Godwin of the True Vine Church aren't on the best of terms right now . . ."

"Actually, normally I'd agree with you, but after I was finished at the police station, I stopped by his church to apologize for my behavior, and we had a very positive conversation. What's this about?"

"I don't know if you are aware, but his son David is here at the seminary."

"Bob told me that this afternoon. I was going to ask if you knew him."

"I didn't until this morning. He's sort of a combination of a rebel without a cause and a recluse. He dresses all grungy while at the same time sending off the message that he is above all the book learning because he's in touch with the Holy Spirit."

"Sounds interesting. You say you met him today. How'd that happen?"

"I knew of him but never talked to him. We just swim in different streams. But this morning, he stopped by my cubicle at the library and asked if he could talk with me."

Frank recalled Bob's brief reference to David's rebellion and now trying to work things through. "Your description makes him sound like a combination of his father and his anti-father."

"I hadn't thought of that, but you may be right."

"And this meeting happened early this morning, before my disruptive behavior at his father's church?"

"Oh, yeah, this doesn't have anything to do with that. This is before any of that happened."

"OK, I just wanted to make sure. Tell me more."

"There's not a lot to tell. When he heard that you were going to lecture on Thursday evening, he asked me if I thought you might come over early and have a private conversation with him. I told him that I didn't see why not if your schedule allowed and that I would call and check it out."

"Do you know what he wants to talk about?"

"No, he didn't say. He seemed both nervous and intense. I think, whatever it is, he feels that it's very important to him."

Frank trusted Jacob's instincts. "So you think it might be important for me to talk with him?"

"Knowing you as I do, I thought you might like to offer him the opportunity."

"I agree, Jacob. See if you can't set it up for about four o'clock, and then you and I can catch a bite before the lecture that evening."

"I'll tell him. I'll also look for a place where you can have some privacy and get back to you."

"Great, Jacob. I'll check with you later."

After he hung up, he thought Brandy huh. Maybe my son will discover that women aren't always to be avoided.

CHAPTER 19

Casting Suspicion

Frank arrived on the seminary campus about 3:30 on Thursday afternoon. While he was nervous about his speech, those feelings had to be compartmentalized for a while. His first task was to meet with David Godwin. Counseling came naturally to Frank. He had learned through experience that he shouldn't over anticipate what his counselee was going to say. He needed to focus on the other person and seek to hear the real message behind the words. Still, he had not been able to ignore wondering why David wanted to talk with him.

He'd been surprised by his interchange with David's father. He knew that many middle-sized churches, like John Knox, felt threatened because of losing members to the megachurches like True Vine Church. The glitz of the larger church with its high-octane worship and a program to meet everyone's needs offered an alluring alternative to the demands of the midsized church.

While he was amused at Bob's tendency towards self-promotion, he found himself warming to Bob more than he expected. He sensed a genuine human struggle going on within Bob. In the midst of all the liberal-conservative struggles going on among the churches, Frank felt a measure of shared identity with anyone in the ministry. No matter where you were on the theological spectrum, ministry was not an easy path to tread.

When he had commented on the family portrait in Bob's office, he sensed poignancy in Bob's response that he hadn't chosen to respond to at the time. Bob's somewhat rueful reference to his son finding himself evoked a sympathetic chord. While Jacob and Rachel had their moments of mild rebellion, the challenge of coping with their mother's violent death had transcended normal generational differences and kept them much closer than many families experience.

The demands of a megachurch pastor, particularly the pressures of projecting images of success, may have contributed to tensions within the family. He didn't know how David's rebellion had manifested itself. Did Bob see David's choice of seminary as a new, albeit ambiguous, form of rebellion? If David challenged his father with ideas learned from his classes, did that cause family strife? Even if Bob resolved it internally, there was always the public pressure. How would members of Bob's congregation look upon David's choice to attend what to them and to Bob was seen as a liberal seminary?

Two red brick pillars marked the entrance to the seminary campus. As Frank drove down the wide paved lane onto the campus, he noted with amusement that on either side of the lane were large busts of John Calvin and John Knox, as if these two father's of Presbyterianism stood as sentries guarding people and ideas that might influence the formation of the church's clergy. In front of him was a large administration building flanked by six other buildings around a grassy quad. As he parked and began to walk to the left side of the administration building, he noted that this late in August the grass was feeling the stress of the dryness of the season. Several sidewalks provided students with alternative ways to cross the quad, but students often found their own path or enjoyed playing or sitting on the grass and ignoring the sidewalks. An educational institution that offered a major emphasis on ethics was confronted by the bind of wanting things to look nice but wanting to conserve the use of water. There were many brown patches as well as worn areas where the students chose to walk.

He always enjoyed walking on the campus and seeing the students that were preparing for what he knew to be both a challenging and potentially satisfying calling to serve the world. When Jacob chose to go to seminary, he felt torn in his response as a father. On the one hand, he was enormously proud that his son had chosen to follow him into what he continued to believe was a sacred calling. On the other hand, the pain of bearing the sins of the world in your own body, which he knew belonged to the office of any faithful pastor, tempted him to plead with Jacob to find some other profession.

Like a doctor who, in an attempt to shield himself from the pain of his patients, lost his gift for healing, he knew pastors who entered with a call and settled for a profession that soon became a job. Yet he knew Jacob had too much integrity to make that compromise and such faithfulness can be very painful. Jacob was well named. Like the biblical Jacob who acquired the name Israel, Jacob was a unique individual who also wrestled with God and insisted that God make sense out of this crazy world. What made Frank proud of Jacob as a son also scared him as a father.

He stepped to the side of the walkway as two young women and a young man chatted excitedly with each other as they came towards him. He was pleased to see so many women enter the ministry over the last thirty years. The female theologians brought a refreshing challenge that often broke open his thinking in significant areas. He enjoyed working with women in the pastorate, as well. Not only did they bring a different perspective, but also the presence of both sexes affected each other in a positive way.

At the opposite end of the quad was the chapel. As he glanced up at its bell tower, he thought again of the power of architecture. The tower was rectangular with lots of windows. Most of the windows were clear and would allow people at various levels to see out on the campus and community. At intervals, however, there were colored windows placed in a stair step manner that caused your eyes to climb up the tower. Inside the tower, one could see small lounges at various levels, the top ones reached by a spiral stair case. As you looked at it, in its own silent way, the building was saying, "Look up! Look Out! There is more to life than is contained in this given moment."

On the façade of the chapel walls were relief sculptures of religious symbols tastefully displayed on the concrete. The building structure spoke of the mystery of faith.

Jacob had texted him that in agreement with David, he had reserved counseling room # 3 off the hallway to the left of the chapel sanctuary. He opened the chapel door and stepped through the vestibule into the sanctuary. It was not a large space, probably holding a few more than one hundred people if they squeezed in like clowns in the Volkswagen ad of several years ago. The pews had been removed, replaced by individual chairs. The chancel area had been cleared of fixed furniture to enable it to be flexible for emerging patterns in worship. A set of drums sat in a Plexiglas case to modify the sound, a free-standing, small pulpit was off to the left, and a small table to hold the elements for communion was at the base of the steps leading up to the chancel. Amplifying speakers were on both sides. In this small room, he wondered why anything needed amplification. At the front, high up on the wall, was a cross made of rustic lumber. He knew that the Protestant tradition was to have an empty cross to signify the resurrection, yet he sometimes glanced up at the cross almost expecting to see someone there.

On the left side, at the front of the chapel, he saw an exit light and a door that he knew would lead into the rooms and offices in the other part of the building. He paused, said a brief prayer for guidance in what was about to happen, and then walked towards the door leading to the hallway. Once through the door, he quickly spotted the counseling rooms and had no trouble in identifying #3.

He opened the door, found it empty, located the light switch, and flicked it on. There were four upright, cushioned chairs in a haphazard configuration and a modest-sized table against the rear wall. He decided that the intention was to permit people to arrange the room in a variety of ways depending on the intended use. He pulled the table out from the wall and positioned two chairs so that they could sit facing each other and rest their hands on the table for comfort.

He left the door to the room open so that David could see him as he approached and took a seat. He glanced around seeing some interesting contemporary artwork hanging on the walls. While they took different forms and even medium, all the pieces depicted Jesus in the process of healing someone. Appropriate enough, he thought. He hoped that some of that healing power could be present during their conversation.

He heard a light tap on the doorframe and looked up. David's hair was darker than Bob's, and he was slightly taller, probably around six-foot-three, but there was a clear family resemblance. If, as Jacob had mentioned, David walked around campus in some grungy clothes, he had clearly prepared to make a different impression in this conversation. While he retained the five o'clock shadow so prized by many models, his dark slacks were neatly pressed, as was his soft hazel-colored shirt. As he entered the room, Frank's impression was of someone who was hesitant, even shy.

"Reverend Sessions?" He asked.

"Yes, David, come in. Please call me Frank." Since he wasn't sure what this conversation was going to be about and even less sure what David's relationship was with his father, Frank decided not to mention his recent conversation with Bob.

"I appreciate your being willing to make time for me," David said as he offered his hand in greeting. "I don't know your son, Jacob, very well, but he certainly was gracious to set this up."

Frank returned his handshake and indicated the chairs near the table. The handshake began firm, indicating the natural strength of the man, but quickly relaxed to softness as if he had forgotten that he wanted to convey a weaker persona. "Why don't we sit over here by the table?"

Frank observed David glancing at him and then quickly around. After the handshake, he stuffed his hands into his pockets, and then, as if deciding that wasn't polite, he pulled them out and rubbed them together as he looked around.

"Oh, sure, that will do nicely. I don't want to keep you long, with your lecture and all, but I did want to talk to you about a concern I have." He sat down at the table, placed his hands together on top of the table, and stared at them. "I guess I'm not sure how to begin."

"David, in my experience, it is best to just begin, and it will sort itself out."

"This is confidential, isn't it?" David said. "I mean, none of this will get back to my family or anyone else, is that right?"

"This is just between us, David, unless you give me permission to share it, with one exception."

David looked up. His face suggested that he hadn't expected that. "What's the exception?" he asked.

"If you say anything that I determine might lead to physical harm of yourself or others, then if I can't persuade you otherwise, I reserve the right to act to protect whoever might be in danger."

David relaxed. "Oh, yeah, I guess that's OK. I'm stressed, but I'm not going to hurt myself or shoot anyone or anything like that."

Frank smiled, hoping it would help David relax. "I'm glad to hear that. Why don't you begin and try to tell me what is disturbing you."

"Do you know my father and mother?" David asked.

"I've never met your mother. I have had a couple of conversations with your father."

David blushed and stammered a little. "Oh, yeah, the Ivory conference. Of course, you spoke to him there. What a jerk that Ivory is."

"I didn't exactly act like a model of virtue, myself. But, yes, your dad and I spoke briefly."

"I haven't talked to him since all that happened. I hope you won't blame dad too much. I think he got suckered by Ivory. "

"I agree, but that is not why we are here, is it?"

"No, but it does have to do with my dad." David drummed his fingers on the table for several seconds.

Frank waited him out. He knew that if he said anything, he might interrupt David's struggle.

David gripped the table with both hands and looked towards the small abstract sculpture of Jesus healing a blind man. "You just said that you didn't think you were a model of virtue at the ministers' gathering. What did you mean?"

"I preach peace and reconciliation. I went to the conference with malice in my heart for Eric Ivory, and then I deliberately taunted him until he lost it. I wasn't innocent of the scuffle that followed."

"But you recognize it and will try to do better next time," David said. "What if you did things far worse and didn't do anything to change it. Maybe you even kept doing worse things."

"What are we talking about, David?"

"Even before all this rape business became public, you may remember there was a story in the papers this past fall about a clergy having been caught in bed with one of his members."

"Out in Oregon, wasn't it?" Frank asked.

"I don't remember the place but somewhere out there. Anyway it caused a lot of conversation among the students, and someone mentioned that you had given a lecture about sexuality and faith that was in the library." David paused and took a deep breath. "Then, when the story about the religious rapist came out, your lecture came up again among the students and I decided to go take a look."

"Was it known at the time that some of his quotes came from my lecture?" Frank asked.

"That was at least the rumor. But when I went to check it out, I noticed that the librarian had a list of who had checked it out before. She was a friend of mine so, I asked if I could see the list."

Frank could feel himself growing tense as David continued.

"Recently it has been a popular lecture. I looked back even further, and a couple of years ago my father checked it out."

"David, as you have said, lots of people checked that lecture out."

"I know," David said, "but you may not know that my father has a history of not being totally faithful to my mom."

"I'm sorry, David."

"Some people make mistakes and learn from them. I'm not sure that my father did. His biblical hero is David. Naturally, I was named for him. I think, from the way dear old Dad reads the story, David screwed anything that moved and still became God's great servant and friend."

"That must be really rough for your mom."

"My mom was named aptly. She is the Barbie doll personified." David's eyes narrowed, and the lines of his mouth tightened as he shook his head. "Everything is image for her. As long as Dad would tearfully confess and find some rich dude to pay off the other woman, she was content to use his guilt to buy more pretty clothes and some weeks at a health club out in Arizona."

Frank was not sure whether this was what David wanted to tell him, or whether there was more. Was he leading up to something even darker? He wanted to encourage David to continue without leading him in any specific direction. He decided to probe gently.

"You're pretty angry at both of your parents."

"Mom's a fluff. She makes the dumb-blond jokes sound reasonable. My real concern is that Dad's interest in sex might be kinkier."

"Kinkier?" Frank said.

"I was home a few months ago working on a paper, I asked if I could use Dad's lap top. I admit I wasn't being totally honest. I know enough about computers that I know how to get around some basic password protection and trace a laptop's Internet history. It didn't take me long to discover that my Dad's interested in porn. I also found that he kept a collection of all the stories about the rapes."

Frank could feel the sweat build up in his armpits. He knew that for the last several minutes he had been curling his fingers in and scraping the palms of his hands. He tried to keep a neutral look on his face, and his eyes focused on David as he listened. He decided he needed to have David hear someone else say what David had been hinting at.

"David, I'm sure this has been agonizing for you, but I need to make sure of what I'm hearing. Are you suggesting that your Dad's interest in sex may have escalated? Are you suspicious that your dad may actually be the religious rapist?" There, he had said it. He watched closely to see David's reaction.

David's shoulders dropped even as his head thrust forward. "He couldn't be, could he?" David's voice was beseeching. "I mean, my dad may be the chief of hypocrites when it comes to his marriage, but I can't believe that he's a criminal."

"Beyond the pornography on the computer and your suspicions of his unfaithfulness to your mom with other consenting adults, do you have any other evidence that might suggest his connection with the rapist?"

David looked at Frank. Was that a flicker of hope in his eyes? Frank wasn't sure.

"You're right," David said. "I don't have a single fact that would suggest that. I'm just jumping to conclusions. You're right." He looked like a weight had been lifted from his shoulders. "Thank you, Reverend Sessions. I was just way off base. Man, I was going crazy."

"That still leaves you with a very real problem to work through with your father. How you resolve that can have a significant effect on your ministry, David. I urge you to get some serious counseling."

David rose to his feet. "As our savior said, "You shall know the truth, and the truth shall set you free.'"

"I hope so," said Frank, as he also rose.

"I can't thank you enough, Reverend Sessions." David enveloped Frank in his arms and gave him a hug.

As he experienced the hug, Frank realized that David kept himself in good shape and was very strong. "If you decide to talk with your father and want someone present to support you, please feel free to give me a call."

"That would be interesting, to have David play the role of Nathan. 'Thou art the man.' I don't know if or when that will happen, but I appreciate the offer." David smiled. "I look forward to your lecture tonight as I know a great deal of the campus does."

CHAPTER 20

Before the Lecture

Frank left his meeting with David Godwin with a nagging worry that he couldn't quite identify. As was frequently true in ministry, he found his feelings in conflict. Earlier, when he had his conversation with Bob Godwin, he found himself liking Bob and inwardly chastising himself for the negative opinions he had held. He admonished himself for having slipped into envying a colleague who had been successful.

Now, having just finished his conversation with David, Frank was reevaluating his opinion of Bob again. Sexual exposes of clergy infuriated Frank. He knew that each revelation of the failure of a cleric to adhere to ethical behavior soiled the reputation of all clergy. The respect for clergy had fallen dramatically in the last couple of decades.

Living in the fishbowl of a pastor's family, exacerbated by the high profile nature of Bob's ministry, had clearly been hard on David. If what David implied was true, Bob was a disturbed individual. He needed counsel, but Frank didn't feel as if he were in a position to help him.

As Frank stepped out of the chapel, he paused for a moment at the top of the steps and gazed at a number of students that walked along the quad. He had both hope and sympathy for them. He was aware of the tremendous challenge that was in their future. He also knew that if they were effective pastors, they would experience a lot of pain. As he began to walk down the steps and join the crowd on the quad, he felt a strong sense of love for this polyglot student body. He wanted to help them but felt inadequate for the task.

Frank was personally aware of the inherent guilt born by many clergy, conservative and liberal. They frequently judged themselves more harshly than the public. They were charged with proclaiming a gospel of truth. Yet frequently pastors felt hypocritical in their inward thoughts and at times in their own personal behavior. Most times, it was in small failures that others would dismiss as a mere expression of their humanity. Occasionally, however, that inward tension lost its sense of balance and resulted in more extreme behavior.

He noticed a tree off to the side of the walk. Over the years, it had been bent and shaped by the winds, its search for water, and its effort to find the sun. The result of its struggle against the elements was a fierce beauty. In a way, its very presence gave him an element of hope for these students.

He assumed from his brief interchange with Amanda that she had specialized in sexual crimes. He didn't want to speculate what had led to that decision. If he and Amanda were right in their discussion at the police station, it was also likely that tonight he would be speaking to the rapist himself. He wondered if there were particular behaviors or profiles that she would be looking for.

His experience had taught him that it was important to know who your audience is and shape your address to that audience. What made it difficult is that he had more than one audience in the lecture hall tonight. If the rapist were there, what could he possibly say that might make a difference to that demented individual? Moreover, what about the faculty, other clergy, and even the reporters who were sure to be there considering all the publicity around this subject.

Yet he was determined not to allow their presence to distract him from his intended audience: the students who were preparing to be clergy during this confusing time in the church.

He fixed his seat belt and headed towards the restaurant that Jacob had picked for a quick supper before the lecture. He noticed that he was low on gas. Even in a car that sometimes got fifty miles per gallon, you have to fill up sometime, he thought. He had been reading up on the new electric cars. Just plug it in and away you go. It would be just my luck not to be able to find a plug, he thought. I think I will wait awhile before I try one of those. At least I only need less than ten gallons to fill my car. It must really knock you for a loop to have to put twenty or thirty gallons in one of those big ones every time you fill up. He pulled into a gas station, filled his tank, and continued toward the restaurant.

The fear generated by the rapist was only one of the reasons why Frank agreed to speak to the seminary students this evening. He knew that sex and religion were a volatile combination that could explode in the face of the most faithful clergy person. He also knew that when a clergy person stepped over the line, while the public was confirmed in their religious skepticism, faithful church members felt a deep and often wounding betrayal. It is important not only for the clergy but for the faith of church members that pastors face honestly the power and temptation of sex as they engage in ministry. He hoped that he would have some words to say that would be helpful.

He pulled out his cell and gave Jacob a call to let him know that he had spotted the Applebee's on his right just past the stop light and would be there soon. He pulled in and found a parking spot. As he entered the restaurant, he was pleased to see Oscar Ramerez seated with Jacob at the table. "Oscar, I'm glad that Jacob was able to reach you."

"When the Lord said that we should visit those in prison," Oscar said with a smile, "I'm sure that he also meant those who had recently been hauled in by the police as well."

Jacob choked on the Coke he was sipping, spewing some coke on the table. In attempting to reach for some napkins to clean it up, he struck Oscar's glass of iced tea, spilling it over as well.

"Whoa, whose the nervous one around here?" Oscar said.

An alert waitress quickly came over. "Is everything all right?" she asked.

Assured that all was OK, she joined in their laughter as she provided a cloth to clean the table. "Are you ready to order, or shall I get some more clothes just in case?" she said.

They all laughed, and the bond between waitress and customer was formed.

"I think we should order now," said Frank. "We are under a small time bind."

After they had ordered and the waitress had left, Oscar said, "So, have you got your presentation ready?"

"I think so," said Frank. "It's complicated by the fact that the police have decided that our rapist might be present tonight."

"I'd better keep a low profile," Oscar said. "Outside of Arabs, we Latinos are the first suspect in everything these days."

Frank looked over at his rotund friend. "I hate to break it to you, Oscar, but the profile is of a rather tall, strongly muscled individual."

Oscar turned to Jacob. "Do you believe this guy?"

Jacob grinned. "Actually seeing him laugh and tease again is a welcome relief after the last few years. I think this rape thing is horrible, but one welcome, even if unintended, consequence is that my dad is more like his old self."

"He is indeed, Jacob. It is great to be working with him again." Turning to Frank, he said, "Digame, compañero, how do you see this evening playing out?"

"Detective Singletary and a couple of other plain-clothes officers will be there. The only place I see that he might give a clue would be during the question and answer period following my lecture."

The food arrived, and they turned their attention to their sandwiches. While they were eating, Frank turned to Jacob. "Did you have a chance to look up the names of those who had checked out the lecture from the library?"

"Yeah," Jacob said. "I must say quite a few clergy as well as students have looked at your lecture over the last couple of years." Jacob pulled out a paper from his briefcase and handed it to Frank. "I didn't spot anything, but maybe something will jump out at you."

Frank glanced at the names on the paper and handed it to Oscar. "Take a look."

Oscar glanced at the page. "I see your favorite evangelist, Bob Godwin, has read your paper. Also several of my colleagues, but nothing significant stands out for me."

"It's probably only a coincidence, but I'd like you to keep an eye on Bob, just to see if he shows any unusual reactions."

"You know his son is a student here?" said Oscar. "If you get too liberal in your interpretation, he may want to petition for equal time. Can't have a true believer get tainted with your heresies, you know."

"What's your approach going to be, Dad?"

"Since my main focus is on the students and their preparation for ministry, I want to lift up a couple of issues for them. The obvious one is how they cope with religious crazies, such as this person, who will tarnish their reputation as clergy. This is just an extension of the problem created by the sexual scandals that have plagued the church in the last couple of decades. It used to be that both believer and nonbeliever readily entrusted the valued members of their family to a pastor even in the most private of situations. Their children would go off on retreats with clergy. You could visit a widow in the middle of the night in her home, and no one would question that your actions were honorable. Many a clergy would be alone with a person in the church at night, and the only comment was how admirable it was that the pastor would work overtime to help someone. A lot of that culture of trust has eroded."

"That makes it sound like the ministry is a haven for predators," said Jacob.

"Most clergy are honorable and sacrifice a lot to care for their flock," said Oscar, "but there is no question that some sick individuals have also been attracted to the ministry. The question that your father is raising is how do you minister authentically in an age of suspicion?"

"I think I'll stick to my books and hide out in the library," said Jacob.

"You said there were two issues you wanted to focus on," said Oscar.

"Yes, the second one builds on the theme that I laid out in that earlier lecture that seems to have received so much attention."

"Sex and the Bible," said Oscar.

"The Bible reports the religious experience of God's people. There's a reason that there is so much sex in it, albeit hidden by the way it's translated. The core issue is that sexuality is one of the most powerful forces in our society. It has the capacity to both be creative and extremely destructive. If you look around the world, one of the other extremely powerful forces is religious faith. Families have been torn apart, wars fought, nations destroyed because of the forceful impact of religion."

"It makes you wonder if it is worth it. Maybe the world would be better off without religion," said Jacob.

"You aren't the first to raise that question," said Oscar. "The problem is, as I'm sure your father will say tonight, it is pure folly to assume that you can solve the problem created by either sex or religion by denying its reality. They both are present, and the question is how we respond to these powers in the world."

"That's right," said Frank. "Both love and faith are transformative in this world when responded to properly. To deny them and their impact on your life is like trying to deny that breathing is useful. Some of our greatest international follies in recent times have been due to the failure of our foreign policy experts to factor in the power of religion."

"And," said Oscar, "some of the greatest triumphs in our world have been fueled by a faith that would not deny the hope that is within us. Not only individual lives but whole communities have been transformed for the better because of the power of their faith."

"That's a pretty big subject for one lecture," said Jacob.

"True enough, but what I hope," said Frank, "is to focus more narrowly on the volatile combination of sex and religion that a pastor denies to his or her own peril. We are sexual beings and we interact with people when they are spiritually vulnerable. Neither of those powerful forces, and especially their combination, is controlled by logic and reason."

"You're too young, Jacob, but someday you ought to get Upton Sinclair's book *Elmer Gantry* to read; or get the movie. Since your father brought this to my attention, I recalled the powerful scene in that movie where Elmer Gantry approaches a lady evangelist. She had just finished preaching,and she was riding high. Elmer took advantage of her heightened spiritual state and seduced her."

"Both powerful faith experiences," said Frank, "and sexual release are acts grasping for ecstasy and transcendence. It's not exclusive to the pastorate, but certainly our profession makes us vulnerable."

"Is that what the rapist is seeking?" Jacob asked.

"I think that is part of it," said Frank, "but I think we will find out that there is another powerful complicating factor. I just can't put my finger on it."

Jacob signaled the waitress. "Can we get a check and three coffees to go? I think we are going to need them tonight."

"Here's the check," her face broke into a smile. "Shall I put the coffee in spill-proof cups?"

They all laughed with her. When she returned with the cups of coffee, they rewarded her with a generous tip and said goodnight.

CHAPTER 21

Jacob's Affirmation

As they left the restaurant, Frank glanced up at the sky. There was a half-moon and a few stars but also a small dark cloud building in the east. The playful interchange with the waitress and the banter among Oscar, Jacob, and himself had helped him relax. He looked at Jacob, walking at his side. When did that boy grow up to be a man, he thought. You'd be proud of him, Rosie. Whatever else happens, we produced two fine young adults.

Oscar interrupted his reverie. "Since there has been some publicity about this event tonight, I suggest that we park over by Howard Hall, in the back parking lot, and then we can walk across campus and enter Scots Center from the rear door."

"Other than dark glasses and a trench coat," Frank said, "I think you've thought of everything. I certainly don't want to talk with any reporters before the event. I'm sorry that this has turned out to be such a media event."

"As you have been fond of pointing out over the years," said Oscar, "when you combine sex and religion, the media behaves like a thirsty horse smelling water. But, like the Good Book says, 'Happy are those who find wisdom, and those who get understanding.'"

Oscar turned to Jacob, "Why don't you join your father in his lowly Prius and help him avoid an accident on his drive over to the seminary."

Oscar left them and went over to his Chevy van. In bold print on the side, it said, "Iglesia de Jesus Cristo, donde todos son aceptado."

As Jacob got in the car with his father, he said, "If I ever do become a pastor, I hope I can convey the same joy of life and the seriousness of intent that he does."

"He's been a patient and loyal friend. I'm sorry it took me so long to reconnect with him." As they entered the highway, Frank glanced over at Jacob, "I also appreciate the strength you've shown. You're a good son. Thank you."

"When mom was killed, it really scared me. It made me question my faith and shattered my confidence in the goodness of life."

"I know, son . . ."

"No, wait Dad, I've never been able to say this to you but I want to now, especially now, when all this crap is hitting the fan."

Frank slowed for a light and nodded for Jacob to continue.

"When Mom died, especially in the way that it happened, I saw how it was tearing you apart, but I also saw how you found an inner strength to keep going. I knew a lot of that was because you wanted to be there for Rachel and me."

"I think the two of you were what kept me going," said Frank as the green light flashed and he resumed driving.

"I know, but I saw something that I couldn't understand fully. It gave me courage. It wasn't only us, but it was also the people of the church that needed ministry. It was as if in ministering to others, you found a reason for living even when what you most valued had been taken from you."

"I hadn't thought of it that way before."

"I can't believe you weren't furious with God, but like that wooden sculpture in our living room of Jacob wrestling with God and refusing to let go, you continued to cling to God through the people."

"I wouldn't have told you then, Jacob, but there were times in the middle of the night that I wanted to die. Then in the morning either you or Rachel would say or do something, and I thought, OK, I can make it another day."

Jacob shifted in his seat and looked over at his father. "But it wasn't just us, Dad. Something inside of you was sparked when you saw someone being neglected. It was like it made you mad that others were ignoring someone in need and that anger energized you."

"That makes me sound more noble than I am, Jacob."

"No, I'm not saying you always did what was right." Jacob chuckled. "It was the anger thing that at times frightened both Rachel and me, but also I kept noticing how it gave you energy for another day."

"Interesting," said Frank, "anger and sex. That's another combination that drives of life."

"Tonight you focus on sex," said Jacob, "but I just wanted to thank you for allowing the anger to keep you going and for being a great father. When one of my classmates thinks he or she is being sophisticated by questioning the relevance of the faith, I think of what we've been through and know that there is strength in faith that I want to hold on to."

Frank turned into the seminary and maneuvered his way to the back parking lot of Howard Hall. "Thank you Jacob. You were named well. Your mom would be as proud of you, as I am."

Jacob took a deep breath and let it out. "OK, I've been meaning to say that to you for some time. Now I will prepare myself for your lecture on the birds and the bees. I guess it is time for me to learn a little more about that as well."

As Frank pulled the car into a parking space and turned the ignition key, he looked at Jacob and raised his eyebrows, "Is there something more that I should know about?"

Jacob looked out the window towards Oscar's car as it pulled in to the parking lot. "Oh, maybe. I'm not really sure. Anyway, we can talk about it later."

Frank reached over and slapped Jacob on the back. "All right! I look forward to our next father and son chat. In the meantime, I will try to restrain my imagination from picturing who might be the subject of our conversation."

"Yeah, don't get your hopes up too high. It's probably just a passing fancy – won't amount to anything."

"I can dream, can't I?" said Frank. "Come on, let's join Oscar and sneak our way into Scots Center."

As they approached the side entrance to Scots Center, Frank said, "Are you sure the door will be open?"

"As the Good Book says, 'Knock and it shall be opened to you,'" said Oscar. He then stepped forward and rapped a short rhythm on the door. From within they heard a voice, "Un momento."

Frank shrugged his shoulders at Jacob as they waited. Then the door opened and Oscar said, "Quiero presentar Tio Juan, un anciano de mi iglesia. Tio, this is Frank Sessions and his son Jacob."

"Mucho gusto. Entre, por favor."

"Now that is what I would call having the right connections," said Jacob as they entered the door.

They quickly moved down the hallway to a room where they would meet Dean Fairington before the lecture. The room had some comfortable chairs, a small table, and a tray filled with a pitcher of iced water together with six glasses. Off to the left, as they entered, there was a small closet and a coat rack where guests could hang their garments. Ken Fairington came soon after they entered the room.

"Frank, Jacob, Oscar, it is so good to see you. Very clever of you to come through the back door. Though I confess I'm not sure how you arranged that."

"It appears," said Frank, "that Oscar has clandestine connections with the custodial staff."

Oscar grinned. "As God worked through the lowly shepherd to announce the birth of the child, so God often works through those who labor in the night to accomplish good things."

Ken laughed. "Can I quote you? I think that would make an excellent illustration in a sermon I'm working on." He moved to prepare himself a glass of water and passed out glasses to the others.

"It appeared as we drove in that in addition to the students, there were a number of other guests, including a few news vans out front," Frank said. "We figured there would be less hassle if we came in through the rear."

"It is a little bit of a mad house out there," Ken said. "We've already had to scour the building for some extra chairs. Not everyone is going to be able to find a seat, but we have hooked up a remote to another room for the overflow. For some strange reason, there seems to be a lot of interest in what you're going to say."

"I don't suppose having just been hauled in by the police and having the story spread all over the news media has anything to do with it," said Frank.

"They would be even more intrigued," said Farrington, "if they knew that I got a personal call from the chief of police making sure that I didn't cancel this lecture because of your contretemps at the True Vine Church."

"I do hope that my being here is not going to cause you any real trouble," said Frank.

"Let's just say that events on this campus don't normally attract this much attention. Having to set up some more chairs and even feed it into an overflow room is rather unusual."

"Ah," said Oscar raising up his hand with one finger extended, "but you have combined religion and sex, which continues to titillate the public. Go to the grocery store and read the headlines on all the scandal magazines at the counters."

"I guess you're right," said Ken. "Anyhow, whatever their reasons, we are glad to welcome all who come. Well, almost all. Do they really think that the rapist will show up?"

"Probably not," said Oscar, "and even if he is here, he will have every reason in the world to keep his presence unknown."

"Even with these competing agendas," said Frank, "I'm determined to stick to our original purpose and speak to the students."

"I'm with you on that," said Ken. "The students are very interested in what you have to say. In their case, I think there is more than just a prurient interest in this subject." He looked out the door as if thinking of the students who would be present at the lecture. "The recent events with the Scripture-quoting rapist have added another layer to the effect of the sexual scandals on the churches in recent years. For people who want to devote their lives to serving others, it is a heavy burden to suddenly be viewed by the public as suspect and not to be fully trusted."

"That's what really rips at my soul," said Frank. "The vast majority of those who are ordained sincerely want to serve God and humanity. It is not fair that their ministries have been contaminated by the actions of a few sick individuals."

"Hopefully this can be the beginning of several conversations that can prepare them to cope with this atmosphere while being creative in offering authentic ministry to an increasingly hurting world," said Ken. "I really appreciate your being here, Frank, especially in light of the pressures that you are under."

Frank took a final swallow and sat his water glass down on the tray. "OK, It's about time for us to get started. How are we going to play this?"

"You and I will go out together. As we talked about, there will just be the podium for your notes and a small table for a glass of water by its side. I will introduce you and then sit down. After you are done, we will open it up for questions from the floor."

"We can play it by ear," said Frank, "but in light of the media presence and our purpose to serve the students, I think that we should limit the questions to those from the students."

"Agreed. I'll handle that when the time comes. If you are willing, however, because of the media interest, at the end, we may want to make time for their questions as well."

Frank turned to Oscar and Jacob. "Would the two of you join the Dean and me in a brief prayer and then you can go and hopefully find a seat before we begin."

After the prayer, the Dean indicated that he did have a few seats saved up front and indicated how Jacob and Oscar could enter the lecture hall and find them.

Then he looked at Frank. "Let me fix this lapel mike to your shirt. I'm sure this is very familiar to you. You attach this to your belt and turn it on with this button. The sound engineer in the back will adjust the sound." He looked at him and smiled. "May God bless and inspire you, Frank. Let's get this show on the road."

They walked through the door that opened onto the stage. The room was crammed full. Jacob and Oscar had found their reserved seats, and Frank spotted Jacob's slight thumbs up gesture and reassuring smile as he took a seat on one of the chairs to the side. There was an air of excitement and loud chatter echoed off the walls. There was a noticeable shift of attention as Ken moved towards the center of the stage to greet those present and make the introductions.

Frank breathed a small prayer and then consciously ordered his body to relax. He was ready to rise, greet Ken, and move towards the podium. Who knows what will happen now.

CHAPTER 22

The Conundrum of Sex and Ministry

Frank met Ken halfway across the platform, shook his hand, and walked towards the podium. Ample applause greeted him, but he made note of the tension in the room as well. He looked around. The hall was packed, and every face turned towards him with expectation. He was sure that the fire department would not be pleased. He tried to spot Amanda, but he couldn't find her in the crowd. He knew Rachel was in attendance, but he knew only where Jacob was sitting.

He turned on his mike. He thanked the Dean for the invitation to speak. "I'm not sure how the fire department would respond to this gathering, but I want to thank you for coming this evening. Maybe it is right that we begin with prayer and include in that a prayer for our safety." When he had finished his brief prayer, he recalled Oscar's free use of Scripture. Hoping that a little soft humor might ease the tension, he began, "And Adam knew Eve and she conceived." As you seminary students are aware, the Hebrews often used the verb 'to know' as a euphemism for sex. So, pun intended, do you suppose Adam and Eve knew what they were starting or were they just acting out of blissful ignorance?"

There was a soft ripple of laughter in the audience.

"Actually," Frank continued, "I think it is vital to the health of your future ministry that you know, no pun intended, what you are

166

doing and not act out of ignorance, blissful or otherwise." He paused and let his eyes scan the entire audience. "Each of you was created by an act of sex." He noted the smiles on some of their faces. "All of you will be affected by sex throughout your ministry, even if some of you choose the route of celibacy." Now they weren't smiling but beginning to think about their own future in the ministry. He waited a full ten seconds this time.

"Here is the sad truth. Some of you will have your careers, reputations, even your life destroyed by an act of sex." There were a few heads nodding in awareness. "That's not because you set out to destroy yourself nor will you have used reason and logic to arrive at your decision to act." He paused for a full five seconds to let his words sink in. "Don't assume that the corporate leaders, politicians, teachers, pastors, social workers, police, or any of the other professions in which an individual wrecks his or her career and life through inappropriate sexual behavior, set out to destroy themselves. Whatever the cause that leads a person to risk everything that means anything to them for a relatively brief physical experience, it is not because they lacked intelligence. You cannot protect yourself by assuming that you are too smart to do such a thing."

They were listening now. It wasn't just an academic subject. It was their lives that were at risk. They chose to enter this profession full of hope. The reality was that it also held risk and danger for them. What he wanted them to understand is that the danger was real and not to be denied.

He wondered if the rapist was present and what he was thinking as he sat there listening. Was he a seminary student or even a pastor? Had he begun full of hope and idealism? What was it that wounded his psyche so deeply that he could confuse what he was doing with the faith that first generated his sense of call? Was there anything that Frank could say that would make a difference to that poor benighted soul?

There she was. He spotted Amanda standing in a corner down near the front of the audience. She was pretending to listen, but he could see her continue to scan the crowd looking for some clue as to the presence of the rapist. He knew she had at least two other colleagues who were doing the same thing but from different angles.

"You proclaim a faith of love that is incarnated or fleshed out in the lives of people who interact with each other on a physical basis. Many of those people are desperately lonely, not only for the love of another human being but also for the love of God. However crazy it may seem at the moment, you will represent their closest association with God. Whether you want to or not, you will be for them their window onto the divine. Ignore that truth and you will only make yourself blind to the powers that can sneak up on you when you are unaware."

Frank continued his lecture for another half-hour, pointing out how the very practice of excellence in ministry at the same time makes one vulnerable. "The Dean has told me that over the next several months, the seminary is going to include several opportunities where you can learn strategic ways to lessen your susceptibility to problems and resist temptation when it raises its ugly head."

There was some spontaneous applause of appreciation.

"There is a reason why sexual behavior is such a prominent part of the Bible. We not only procreate the human race but also bond ourselves together as a community by this creative power. If you are going to be effective in the ministry, you cannot avoid the power of sex, but you can help people avoid its destructive power and release its creativity."

He was about ready to move into his final section for the evening talking about how as clergy they can overcome some of the suspicion that has fallen on their profession when he sensed rather than saw some commotion near the front left side of his audience.

"Satan, I know who you are."

Frank saw the man rise about four rows back in the audience. His face was fiery red, and his chest was heaving.

"Blasphemer, God will not be mocked."

There was a stunned silence as if events were happening too quickly for people to comprehend them.

Then a woman sitting next to him screamed, "He has a gun."

Frank watched almost as if it were a slow motion movie. Two things happened almost in sequence. First, he saw Oscar launch a hymnbook directly at the man's face. At the same time, he saw Amanda charging down the aisle and using a chair for leverage, launch herself over three people, and land on top of the man knocking the gun from his hand. Four uniformed police quickly entered the hall, handcuffed the man, and escorted him from the building. In real time, all the action took place in less than five minutes.

Ken accompanied the police as Frank called for order. "I know that was a frightening moment for all of you. We certainly need to give a hand of appreciation for the quick action of both the police and my hymnbook-throwing compatriot.

The crowd broke into a resounding applause and cheers. Frank knew that the corporate act of applause would have the effect of expunging some of their fears and reuniting them as one body. His own body was tense, but it was more adrenalin than fear. He wanted to redirect the crowd's attention.

"I must say, Oscar, I didn't know that you had a throwing arm like that. Before you put on all that weight, were you an athlete?"

The audience broke out in laughter.

Both men knew what they were doing.

"Heh, we Latinos don't lose our athletic skills when we gain weight like you gringos do."

Again there was laughter and a few cat calls.

Having accomplished their purpose, Frank indicated that people should be seated.

"Let me say just a few words about the violence that we have just witnessed and the violence that has plagued our city in recent times. If we are going to cope redemptively with the powerful emotions that are disturbing the lives of our people, we need to recognize some simple truths."

Amanda entered by the side door and gave him a thumbs-up sign and a beautiful smile. "Before I go further, I would point out that the police woman who courageously risked her life to protect all of us has just reentered the room and has given me a sign indicating that everyone is safe."

Again there was loud applause, which Frank could sense both pleased and embarrassed Amanda.

"In such a boring meeting, I'm sure it is hard to pay attention to what I'm saying, but I do want to point out a couple of things that I hope you will ponder in the future. First, there is no reason to believe that the man who created the commotion tonight or the serial rapist who is frightening our city are not sincere in their religious beliefs. However distorted we think they are in their understanding, just being religious doesn't protect you from irrational behavior.

"Second, spiritual practices and sexual behavior are not contrasting realities but in a curious sort of way have a symbiotic relationship. Both can be enormously creative and transformative, and both can be tragically destructive. We cannot experience the one and avoid the other and hope to have a wholesome life. What we can do is work to release the benefits and avoid the dangers of both.

"This has been an exhausting evening. I will take a few questions, but with the Dean's permission, I will also return after you have had a chance to ponder what has happened here tonight and enter into a more wide-ranging discussion."

Among the questions asked, one reporter asked if Frank believed that the man who had erupted so violently this evening was, by any chance, the rapist himself.

Frank paused before he responded. "No, I don't think that he was the rapist. First, this man demonstrated a violent tendency while our rapist, while doing horrible things, has so far released his victims. I pray that if there are any other experiences, that will continue."

Frank believed what he was saying, but he also hoped that by saying it, he might dissuade the rapist, should he be here, from escalating into more violent acts.

"Second, this man tonight thought he was defending the faith by denouncing my association of the spiritual and sexual, while our rapist, in what I believe is a distorted way, apparently tends to see a close relationship between his religious beliefs and his sexual acts."

Frank recognized that his own energy was about depleted, and he quickly concluded his remarks. "Because of what has happened here tonight, I want to close this evening with a prayer both for the man that the police have in custody and for their continued work in capturing the man who has committed the rapes in this city."

While he stayed around and greeted some colleagues who were present, as quickly as possible he withdrew from the lecture hall and made his way back to the room where they had gathered prior to the lecture. He quickly filled his glass from the pitcher and took a long drink. The door opened, and he was pleased to see Rachel walk in with a cold can of Coke in her hand.

"I found a vending machine in the hall and thought you might want a jolt of sugar."

He smiled his appreciation as he took the Coke, and then he noticed how pale Rachel looked. He opened his arms, and she flung herself into them.

"Oh Daddy, I was so scared that I was going to lose you too."

"It was scary, Rachel, but it is over now. I know it is especially frightening because of what happened to your mom, but we can give thanks that everyone is OK."

"Daddy, I don't want you to make anymore public speeches."

Frank felt his daughter shivering in his arms.

"Hey there, it's all right now. Can you believe what Oscar and Amanda did? Oscar ought to try out for one of our baseball teams and Amanda, my goodness, she made the karate kid look like an amateur."

It was just enough to break the spell and Rachel giggled. "She was like superwoman flying through the air."

Just then the door opened and Jacob, Oscar, and Amanda walked in, along with Brenda Sides.

"Speaking of superwoman," Frank said, "here she is."

Rachel dislodged herself from Frank and threw her arms around Amanda. "Oh, thank you, thank you, thank you for saving my dad's life."

Then she reached out and snared Oscar in her arms and pulled him in her group hug. "Thank you both."

"Hey, don't I get any thanks?" said Jacob. "I was there yelling to frighten the assailant to throw off his aim."

Brenda was standing off in the corner observing what was happening.

"Uh, Brenda, I don't think this is a time for any comment for the media," said Frank.

"No, I understand. I just followed Jake back here to make sure you were all right. Everything is off the record, as they say in the movies."

"How about we all go to an off-the-record Mayberry's and have a soda or something," Jacob said.

As they were leaving, Frank pulled Jacob back and spoke into his ear. "So, Jake, is it. Is this the subject we were going to talk about?"

Jacob glanced at the departing party with Brenda bringing up the rear. "Well, maybe. We'll talk more later. Right now, some ice cream sounds like it would be some good comfort food."

CHAPTER 23

Looking for a Pattern

Frank was invited to celebrate July 4 with a couple who owned a yacht and had invited a few friends to celebrate the day sailing on Lake Norman. The couple, Ethan and Ivana Rierson, had been a pleasant surprise at the church. Zytegot Industries, a high tech firm, after a long search had accepted Athens' incentive package and established a new plant in the area. The Riersons came with the package.

Ethan was educated as a molecular biologist but had a flair for both organization and entrepreneurship. Zytegot Industries had offered him a handsome salary if he would come to Athens and oversee what was rumored to be some cutting edge biological developments that they believed would offer the world a significant advance in health care while at the same time making Zytegot a significant profit.

Ivana Rierson was a poet and an artist who quickly established her niche in Athens art community. Both of them had been active in a Presbyterian church in Baltimore and were deliberate in seeking out a church that both challenged them intellectually and was committed to service in the community. After visiting John Knox for several Sundays, they called and asked if the two of them could make an appointment to talk with Frank about the church.

Frank was delighted that someone would take church membership seriously enough to want to make an appointment to talk about it. They made the appointment on Wednesday, March 13, and it was one of the more pleasant conversations that Frank had had in awhile.

"Reverend Sessions," Ethan began, "we have visited your church several time over the past few months. While Ivana can speak for herself, I think it is fair to say that we are both impressed by your sermons and we have experienced a warm welcome by your people."

"First, unless it makes you uncomfortable, I'd like you to call me Frank. Most people do in this congregation. Second, I'm delighted that you have been received warmly."

"We certainly have," Ivana said. "Our previous experience in Baltimore was both challenging and stimulating. We want to make sure that our journey continues in a positive manner, so we are being very deliberate in our choice of churches."

"I hope we can provide that same support and stimulation," said Frank, "but from past experience I would caution you that when anyone has had a good experience in another church, it's difficult to replicate that experience as you begin to experience a new church. You will need to give it some time so that you can build relationships and open yourself to new experiences."

"That's wise counsel," Ethan said, "and we recognize that some of the value of a church experience comes as you build relationships. However, we do want to make sure that the general trend of the church offers prospects for the type of experience we had in Baltimore."

"Can you give me a sense of what you are looking for?" Frank asked.

"Two or three things that may seem contradictory at first," Ivana said. "Ethan has been very successful in his professional life and we are very fortunate to have prospered from his talents. I don't know whether we are in the infamous 1% category but we are quite comfortable. We don't want to apologize for our wealth but we also don't want to be looked at as a rich catch for the church we join."

Frank nodded his head and raised his eyebrows slightly. "That is pleasantly forthright. We have families with a large variety of incomes in the congregation and I think you will find that most of them feel as if they are all treated as descent people without reference to their income."

"As you have just experienced," Ethan said, "my wife is not shy about expressing herself and I guess that leads to the next subject. While we are, as Ivana expresses it, comfortably prosperous, we are somewhat more liberal than some of our colleagues and we want a church that is not afraid to push us on the issues that are facing our society. We don't have to agree but we do want challenged to grow, and we want room to express our own opinions as well."

The conversation continued in the same open vein and the result was that the Riersons had joined John Knox church in late April. They also occasionally invited Frank out to dinner and continued their dialogue on the issues. In June, after the incident at the second forum at True Vine Church, the Riersons were among some of the first people to reach out to Frank in support.

One of the Rierson's indulgences was to belong to a yacht club that was established on Lake Norman, a large lake constructed by Duke Power. The lake was large enough that one could really feel as if one had stepped outside the busy world and could just relax. As part of being supportive, they invited him to spend the fourth of July on their yacht.

The Riersons had called on Saturday June 22 to issue the invitation. He remembered because it was the weekend following his lecture at the seminary. He was feeling drained by all the events of the past several weeks but given Rachel's strong response to the attack at the lecture, he thought he needed to spend some reassuring time with both Rachel and Jacob. When the Riersons suggested that Jacob and Rachel also were invited, that sealed the deal.

Everyone on the yacht recognized that this was a time to step outside the pressures of the world. Even though it would be hard not to be aware of the issues that were frightening the city, the conversation was generally about lighter things. Some knew of Frank's involvement but that too was avoided for the trip. That evening, they sat on the deck of the Riersons yacht, watched fireworks over the water, sipped margaritas, laughed, and affirmed the joy of life. For a few hours, Frank could compartmentalize both church responsibilities and the mysterious rapist, and just savor family, food, friends, and a panorama of nature's beauty that filled his spirit.

They returned to Athens about midnight. Jacob returned to the seminary but Rachel asked if she could use the guest room at Frank's house. "If you will make me some of your delicious pancakes for breakfast before you leave in the morning. As strong as Rachel appeared to be, Frank knew the event at the seminary had deeply shaken her.

The next day, Friday, after a fun filled and delicious breakfast, Frank returned to the church to finish his preparations for Sunday. He also wanted to make three hospital calls in the afternoon and begin an application form for a sabbatical grant that was due in about three weeks.

Saturday and Sunday went well. People had relaxed about the incident at True Vine Church and now enjoyed kidding him about the flare-up. He also received some heartfelt hugs after worship. Many had heard about the incident during the seminary lecture and were concerned for his safety. Humor seemed to be the best way they could reach out to him and offer support. While over the years he had received a fair share of complaints about this or that issue, it was clear that they were united around any threat to their pastor.

He was feeling fairly good on Monday morning when the phone rang. When the call identification screen identified the call was from the police department, he felt a mild twinge of concern.

"Frank, it's Amanda. There has been another rape. It happened on Saturday this time. The victim was processed Saturday and was checked out at the hospital on Sunday. We asked if she was willing to have a more extensive conversation with our task force, and she agreed to come in this afternoon. We all thought that you might like to be in on the conversation. It's scheduled for three this afternoon."

"Thanks, Amanda, I'll be there."

There's got to be a pattern to all of this, he thought; some clue that can break this open. But what is it?

When Frank arrived at the police station, the desk sergeant immediately sent him to the conference room where the rest of the task force was already assembled.

As he entered the room, Lieutenant Bryson greeted him with a big smile. "OK, now that we have theological truth on our side, I think we are ready to proceed."

As Frank entered the room, he glanced at the conference table around which the officers were sitting. A stab of pain went through his body. He bent double. He had trouble getting his breath.

Amanda cried out, "Frank, what is it?"

She was too far away to reach him but another couple of officers leaped up and grabbed him before he fell.

Though doubled over, he reached up and waved his hand. "The cookies, please get them out of the room. I can't stand to be near chocolate chip cookies."

The officers were stunned but O'Riley, reacted first and grabbed the cookies and took them out of the room.

Bryson pulled a chair up so that Frank could sit on it. "Should I call an ambulance? "

Amanda had come around the table and had her hand on his artery to check for his pulse. "Frank, talk to us. Is this some type of allergy?"

Frank raised his head but his eyes were still tightly closed. He raised his hand again to stall their questions. "Just give me a moment and I'll explain. No need to call an ambulance. It just caught me off guard, that's all."

He opened his eyes and looked around at the startled room of officers. "I'm sorry. It was just the sight of those cookies. My wife died trying to buy some chocolate chip cookies. I can't stand the sight of them."

"What, no donuts? I thought that was a required part of any gathering of Athen's finest," Frank commented.

The conference room was slightly better furnished than many of the interview rooms. The table was a rich mahogany. The chairs matched each other and were cushioned. The room was well lighted and some appropriate pictures of police operations or honor events were hung on the walls. Frank assumed that this was the room where events involving significant public figures took place. He was impressed that they would choose this setting to talk with a victim of crime.

The others greeted him with smiles and high-signs. Even if Bryson was still chafing from their initial encounter, Frank knew that they all valued his presence. He glanced in Amanda's direction and received a slight raise of her eyebrow along with a small smile.

"We tried to get a Starbucks franchise but the politicos didn't think the public would accept that as a valuable use of their tax dollars," said one of the officers. "We do have some reheated black sludge available, if you would like."

"Sounds delicious," said Frank. "What type of background can you provide me before our guest arrives?"

Amanda spoke up. "Not a lot, I'm afraid. The rape, as near as we can figure, took place in a cornfield. There just doesn't seem to be any recognizable pattern to these incidents."

At that moment, there was a light tap on the door and an officer stuck his head in to announce the arrival of Janice Long, the latest victim of the serial rapist.

Amanda rose and exited the room to receive Janice while the others shifted in a way that provided her space to enter the room and take a seat near the door through which she would come. Again, Frank was impressed with their professionalism. While Amanda was gone, Frank noticed that another officer brought in some fresh coffee and a few donuts on a plate, together with some napkins. They knew that this would be a difficult moment for her and wanted to make her as comfortable as possible and convey the impression that this case was of high priority for them.

Amanda ushered Janice into the conference room. Janice was dressed in a dark suit. She was about five-foot four, with ash brown hair that hung about two inches above her shoulders. She kept her eyes focused on the table before her, held her hands at her side with her fingers curled in, and greeted the officers present with a mumbled "good morning."

They did their best to return her greeting with words of welcome, and Lieutenant Bryson stepped forward with a smile. "Please sit here, Ms. Long. We appreciate your being willing to come in and talk with us."

As she approached the table, Frank noticed that she was bent forward and winced slightly as she took her seat. One of her hands came forward as if protecting the area just under her breasts.

O'Riley also stepped forward. He was physically the most imposing figure in the room but his kind eyes and jovial tone often put people at ease. "Ma'am, the division has perked some fresh coffee in honor of your presence, and since we officers rarely get to taste good coffee, we'd like to thank you and offer you the first cup."

It was the right tone, as the other officers smiled and a few said, "Here, here."

Janice's face relaxed, and her hunched shoulders seem to lower a little as she responded. "Coffee with cream and one half of one of those donuts would be nice. And please call me Janice."

Once the coffee and donuts passed around the table, Amanda took the lead in the conversation. "Ms. Long," she hesitated a breath, "uh, Janice, we are the task force set up by the police chief to investigate and apprehend this criminal. As I mentioned to you, I'm actually a consultant from Richmond. These other officers are part of the Athens' Police Department with the exception of Reverend Sessions."

Janice nodded at Frank. "You were the one who helped the reporter write that first story about these rapes, weren't you?"

Frank nodded. "Yes, I was. I'm very sorry for what you have experienced. It takes a lot of strength to come in here and go over your experience with us. Thank you."

Amanda continued around the table identifying each of the officers.

Janice acknowledged each of them as they were introduced. Her words were soft and hesitant.

"Janice, it is important that we have as complete a picture of the event as you can provide," Amanda said. "Even those details that you think are unimportant might provide us with a clue, so please tell us anything that you can about what happened to you. After you finish, we will follow up with some additional questions."

"Well," Janice began. It was almost as if she were swallowing her words as she spoke. "I guess it was pretty dumb of me, but I went out to my uncle's cornfield to get some kernels that I often use to feed some birds at my home." All of the task force leaned in to hear her.

Amanda reached out and placed a hand on Janice's arm. "Janice, let me interrupt just a second. First, let me encourage you to speak a little louder so that everyone can hear you. Second, there is no way that this was your fault. What you did was very natural. The blame is entirely on the criminal that did this to you. Please continue."

Janice proceeded to tell her story. Many of the details were familiar from the story of the other victims: being drugged by ether, taken to an isolated place, awakening but not fully in control of her decision making, hearing the rapist spout religious words as she was being molested, and then being released with some arrogant reminders that she had been filled with the love of God.

There were some ominous differences, however. The cornfield was large, over 50 acres, and included in its bounds some groves of trees on slightly raised hills in the midst of the field. They were preserved to prevent soil erosion. Apparently, Janice had been taken to one of those groves where the rapist had prepared a rapidly inflated air mattress among the trees.

"Did he carry you to the trees? I ask because that would indicate that it was fairly close by," O'Riley said.

"I guess he carried me deeper into the cornfield, but after I awoke, we still had to walk quite a ways." Janice said. "It was weird. It was almost like we were out for a hike together. I remember that he had his arm around me and occasionally his hand would slip down on my..." she blushed and looked down.

"It's alright," Amanda said, "We know this is difficult."

She raised her head, and her face tightened. "He would lower his hand and squeeze my buttocks." She looked defiantly at the officers. "No one does that to me, but I just let him. It's so disgusting."

"Janice," said Bryson, as he reached out both hands towards her keeping his hands some distance and face up. "This man is insane, and he took liberties that he had no right to take. You were drugged. It's not your fault."

Janice continued to describe her experience. Near the end, her story took an unexpected turn that caused all of them to listen even more intently.

"He had taken off my blouse and shorts. I was lying on my back on his airbed. I knew he was going to take off my bra and panties next, but then he reached back and picked up a knife."

"Can you describe the knife?" one of the officers asked.

"I was reared on a farm and watched meat being prepared. The knife was like one of those large butcher knives used to cut slabs of beef. I remember wondering if he was going to kill me like a human sacrifice."

"Please go on," Amanda said.

"Well, he didn't kill me. He started mumbling something about death not being able to hold him. He slipped the knife under my bra and cut it off exposing my ...," she hesitated and put one of her hands in front of her breasts as if to shield her, but then she continued, "my breasts.

Frank felt a chill run through him. He recognized some of the signs of escalation that he had feared might occur.

"Then, while still mumbling something about the fountain of life that will not be repressed, he stuck the knife under my panties and slit them open. I knew that he was going to rape me, and," again she looked down at the table. "I know you say I was drugged, so it wasn't my fault, but I saw what was going to happen, and I just laid there."

"He had a knife," Bryson said. "You didn't have any choice."

"While staring at my exposed body, he undressed himself. He was clearly aroused. Then he raised the knife up in the air." Again, she blushed slightly but seemed determined to continue. "I wasn't sure at that moment what was going to be plunged into me."

A couple of officers coughed trying to prevent a chuckle while others smiled acknowledging her use of humor in a difficult moment.

"Then it gets even weirder." she seemed to gain confidence as she told her story. "He lowered the point of the knife to my belly and began chanting, 'Marie, my beloved Marie.'" She paused and looked up with a question on her face. "Do you suppose he lost someone he loved named Marie, and all of this is part of him still grieving over her?"

Some of the officers looked intrigued by the possibility and made some notes. Amanda, not wanting to interrupt the flow of her story, encouraged her to continue.

"He carved some marks into my chest. It's a little like a cross with some wings attached. It's really strange." She looked towards Amanda. "Do I have to show the marks to everyone?"

"No," Amanda said. "When we are through here, I will have a lady officer take a photo of where he cut you. For now your description is enough."

Frank decided it was time for him to ask a question. "Did he say any words while he was carving the symbol onto your chest?"

"Something about a dove and violating a cove or something."

The task force looked mystified, but Frank continued, "Was it something like, 'Oh, that I had wings like a dove! I would fly away and be at rest.'?"

"Yeah, that sounds like it. What does it mean?"

"It's from the Psalms," Frank said, "but I'm not sure what it means to the rapist except it's part of his religious delusion."

"I can't believe anyone who believes in God would act like that," said Janice.

"Nor can I," said Frank. "He is a very sick individual. And you have been very brave to come in here and tell us your story."

When the conversation drew to a close, each of the task force members came forward to shake Janice's hand and assure her that they were going to do everything possible to catch him and put a stop to all of this.

Amanda gave Janice her card and emphasized that she should call if she thought of something else, no matter how small. She then led her out and instructed a woman officer about having the scars on her chest photographed.

When Amanda returned, the officers were still sitting there. The room was strangely silent as each officer tried to process what he or she had just heard. These are veteran officers, Amanda thought, but they still seem stunned by what they heard.

"Well," she said.

"That is one tough lady," one officer said.

"You got that right," O'Riley said. "I'd like to get my hands on that bastard. I'd ring his dick off and toss it to the moon."

There was a chorus of laughter around the room, and the tension seemed to be broken.

"Amanda," said Bryson, "we may have given you a bit of a hard time, being an outsider and all, but you have more training in this sort of thing than we do. I think I speak for all of us, just tell us what to do, and we'll do it – on or off the clock."

They all nodded in agreement. "The gloves come off," said another officer. "Let's get this bastard."

"I agree," said Amanda. "Let's begin by reviewing what we have and see if we can find some type of pattern that will give us a clue to where he might strike next."

"Uh, Reverend," Bryson began, "I know that we fu…er screwed up on that Pardella fellow, and I'm sorry about that, but I still think we need to check on other registered sex offenders. This guy is clearly off his rocker."

"I don't disagree with that," said Frank, "but just be careful that we don't jump to conclusions too quickly. This guy is clearly different from your normal sex offender."

"What do you mean, Frank? Amanda asked.

"First of all," Frank said, "you know the cases better than I do, but aren't most sex offenders that we have on record, people who go after children? If it's adult rape, and we catch them, then they are in prison, not registered and living in the community."

"You've got a point," said Amanda. "In most cases that I know of, the pervert doesn't switch back and forth between children and adults. Still, we've got to cover all bases, so we should assign someone to check on the registered sex offenders in Athens, but with caution."

"What about the dates when the rapes occurred?" an officer asked. "Is there any pattern there, so we can at least know when the next rape is coming?"

"They seemed to start with the new year," Bryson said, "at least as far as we know. The first one was on January 27."

A screen of calendar months was flashed up with the dates circled in red. "These are the dates that we know about. Does anyone see a pattern?" asked Amanda.

"The most obvious one," said Frank, "is that they seem to occur once a month."

"If that's right," said O'Riley, "that means we have at least four weeks to catch the guy before he strikes again."

"And if we're lucky, maybe more," said another officer. "They don't always occur the first of the month."

"That's right," said Amanda. "The January rape was the last week of the month, February was the second week. Then March went to the last week, but April was the third week."

"Here's a possibility," said Bryson. "The first one was in the twenties, the second in the teens, then the twenties, then the teens. Does that help?"

"It would if we didn't have the last one on July 6, which breaks the pattern," said Amanda.

"What about the idea that Janice had about this being a grief thing?"

"That interested me at first," said Amanda. "He does often call the victim by another name, like he was pining for someone, but if you look back, they aren't the same names."

"Guess that sucker has had a lot of broken relationships in his life," said one officer. "Though somehow I don't feel very sorry for him."

"What about the religious angle, Frank?" Amanda asked.

They all turned to look at him.

"I've been thinking a lot about that and also my role in all of this?"

"Explain," said Bryson.

"While I reject the radio host Ivory's accusation that either my liberal theology or my program to help ex-offenders played any part in these horrible incidents," he looked at Bryson, "there is a way in which I, and my liberal beliefs, may have played a significant part in this man's actions."

"In case some of you don't know," said Bryson, "when I first was assigned to this case, O'Riley and I had, shall we say, a rather contentious interview with the Reverend. However, I've come to understand that while we may have our differences, he is someone to listen to."

"Thanks, Bryson. I've come to respect you more as well. You handled yourself with real sensitivity in our conversation with Janice. Maybe there is hope for both of us yet."

"You were about to tell us how you may be a part of all of this," Amanda said.

"Yes, well we all know that the rapist quotes passages from Scripture while he is raping his victims. As we talked about earlier, some of those quotes may have been taken from a lecture I gave several years ago at the local seminary."

"The Bible talks about rape?" one of the officers asked.

"Actually it does," said Frank, "but the quotes that I am referring to speak of the relationship of our yearning for God, or spirituality, and our yearning for physical closeness in our sexuality."

"So our rapist probably heard your lecture, is that what you are saying?" asked O'Riley.

"He may have heard it, or he may just have read it," said Frank. "The seminary library keeps copies of lectures available to check out. The point, however, is that maybe our rapist is connected with the seminary in some way."

"Does the library have records of who attended your lecture and even who checked out your lecture to read?" asked Bryson. "That would at least give us some people we could zero in on."

"It was a public lecture, so there is no help there, but they do have a check-out list at the library." said Frank. "I asked my son, who is a student there, to look at the list and see if anything popped out. I didn't see anything right away. I'm sure the library would give us a copy. We can also get a list of the students who were enrolled at that time and see if that helps."

"We didn't want to advertise that we were looking in that way before his recent lecture in case we could spot someone attending that looked suspicious," Amanda explained.

"What about that nut that tried to shoot you at the lecture?" asked O'Riley. "The one who discovered that Detective Singleton is faster than a speeding bullet."

"Up, up, and away," said another officer.

Amanda felt herself blush but was also pleased by the comment.

"Amanda's quick acrobatic skills probably saved my life," said Frank, "but since that man was in jail during this last rape, he has eliminated himself as the serial rapist."

Amanda, trying to move the conversation away from herself and back on the crime, said, "So what have we got? So far, it seems that the rapist only acts once a month but not on the same day or even week."

"We also know that he is strong, quick, and clever," another officer said.

"And that his religious fixation may be associated with the Reverend's lecture in some way," said Bryson.

"Do you have the list of the names of the victims and the names the rapist called them," said Frank. "I think there has to be a clue there. I'd like to ponder that some more."

"O'Riley can get that list for you," Amanda said. "We will have some officers check on the background of those who checked your lecture out and interview some of those we know attended to see if they can identify other people who attended. This is a full court press, people."

There came a knock on the door, and an officer stepped in and handed Amanda some copies of the photo taken of Janice's scars. Amanda passed them around to the task force. The rapist had cut the skin enough to bleed but not enough to risk her life. As each of them examined the photo, the room grew silent.

The scars depicted a crude cross with what looked like wings fixed to the arms of the cross as if preparing it to fly upward.

"That is disgusting," said one of the officers. "What does it mean?"

Amanda turned to Frank. "Frank, when Janice was telling us her story, you said that the quote was probably from the Psalms, but you didn't know what it meant for the rapist. Have you had any further thoughts?"

"I'm afraid I had other thoughts even then, but I didn't want to frighten her."

Everybody looked up and waited for Frank to continue.

"Janice recalled that the rapist said something about a dove and violating a cove or something. I think he was quoting from Psalm 55 where the psalmist is complaining about the treachery of a friend. At one point the psalmist cries out, "O that I had wings like a dove! I would fly away and be at rest;…""

"The wings on the cross," said O'Riley.

Everyone looked at their photo with the crude wings attached to the cross on Janice's chest.

"I think so," said Frank, "but as you read the psalm, it may give us a hint to the rapist's thinking. If I'm right, we may be in for even more trouble."

"I'm not sure I like where this is going, but go on," said Amanda.

"Part of my interest in this whole subject of sexuality and spirituality was why people who had achieved a lot in their lives would risk it all for a sexual encounter, consensual or not."

"Like the politicians and corporate big-wigs we talked about earlier," said Bryson. "It's like they suddenly turned stupid."

"Something like that," said Frank, "only, as I said, I look at it more like an addiction.

"Say more about that," said O'Riley.

"You can be addicted to things other than drugs," Frank said, "but drugs give us the pattern to look at. Some people will experiment with drugs but then decide there are other things in life and just move on." Frank smiled. "Probably if we had a lie detector machine in here, we would discover that some of you have tried some marijuana or something even stronger. But then you realized that it could risk your career, so you stopped using."

There was some shifting of chairs, a few sheepish grins, and some elbows shoved into a fellow officer's ribs.

"Even without a lie detector test, I will confess that back in college I tried the weed more than once," Frank said. "But when I got married and had kids, I knew that I had to put that chapter behind me."

"I knew those liberal preachers were messed up," Bryson said.

"But for some people, use doesn't decline," Frank continued. "Not only do they not give it up, but it escalates. The original pleasure is not enough, and they keep wanting a stronger and stronger experience."

"So, if a politician has begun to dull out on the game of politics, he may add an affair or two to enhance the experience of pleasure?" asked Bryson.

"What could be riskier for a person whose career is dependent on public approval than to engage in an affair that could blow you out of the water?" Frank asked.

"So why don't they just buy the sex from a safe hooker and keep it quiet?" asked an officer.

"Some do, but that's like sticking to weed. Pretty soon even that pleasure is not enough, and you want to take it to the next level. So you add a little more danger."

"OK, but what does this have to do with our rapist?"

"If my theory is right, and the psalm is my pattern, the rapist was trying religion for his search for ecstasy, but then he suffered a severe disappointment -- some form of betrayal if the psalm is reflecting his experience."

"Is that really in the psalm? Does someone have a Bible in this police station?" Bryson asked.

With a sheepish look on his face, O'Riley pulled a small Bible from his breast pocket. "What psalm are we talking about?"

"Psalm 55," Frank said. "If I remember correctly, about half way down, it begins to talk about being betrayed by someone who you have trusted."

"Well, I'll be da... oops, I guess I'm just very surprised," said an officer reading over O'Riley's shoulder.

Everyone burst out in laughter.

"My concern," Frank said, "is that the psalmist begins to talk about how his enemies surround him and the covenant has been violated, but that God will protect him from death."

"And that is the escalation you are talking about," said Bryson.

"What if the sexual pleasures are not enough and now he wants to take his victims through a higher level of pleasure, the passage from death to life?"

"And cutting Janice was a first step?" said Bryson. "That bastard is off the chart loony."

"Janice didn't say," Frank continued, "but my guess is that after he cut her, he probably entered into some weird rhythm of sucking on her breasts and sucking on her blood. We are just lucky he wasn't ready to take it to the next step."

"We might not be so lucky next time," Amanda said. "We are on this full-time, people, and we will meet here to coordinate at the beginning and end of the week and always be on call if something new is discovered."

Frank remained seated as the rest of the officers filed out.

Amanda turned to him. "You know, we've both come a long way since that amorous tryst on the golf course."

"I'm still embarrassed by my behavior on that night. Knowing what I know today, you should have had me arrested and thrown away the key."

She placed a hand on his arm. "If I had, we might not be here today stopping this maniac from harming others."

"You are very gracious, Amanda. I guess it proves God is a redemptive God as I've been telling others over the years."

"Frank, there is something else about that night that I need to tell you about."

"There's lots we need to talk about. Why don't we find a time when you can come by the house. I know you've met my kids but I'd like you to know them better."

"Is that the adult equivalent of taking me home to meet your parents?" She noticed some color filling his face. "Why, Frank, I think you are blushing. I'd love to get to know your kids better – and you."

There came a knock on the door, and an officer who stuck her head in said, "Officer Singletary, you have a call on line four."

"Got's to go. See you at our meeting on Friday if not before, and I look forward to having supper with you.

CHAPTER 24

Clues Come Together

"Dad, stop treating me like a child. I know I'm your daughter, but I'm also 23 years old, graduated from college, and have a full time job. The rest of the world treats me like an adult with a brain, and I'd like you to do the same."

"You're right, Rachel. It's just that when your mom died, I made a promise to myself that I would do everything I knew how to make sure you and Jacob had a bright future. I wish you didn't have to deal with the seamier side of life, that's all."

"Dad, if one of your parishioners came to you and said, "I want to protect my adult child from exposure to the shadow sides of life, what would you say?"

Frank looked at Rachel for a long moment. Even though she was taller than Rosie was and had a different color of hair, he could still see reflections of his wife in her. It was the intensity with which she faced him, the compressed lips, the refusal to blink, and the set of her shoulders prepared for any argument that most reminded him of his wife. As he had often done with his wife when she bested him in an argument, so now he grimaced, stuck out his tongue at his daughter, and made a sputtering sound. "I don't like it anymore now when my daughter has the better argument than when your mom did."

Rachel laughed. "I always loved it when I saw you do that with mom because I knew that the tension of your argument was over, and you were strong enough to show her the respect that she deserved."

It was Wednesday afternoon, August 21, and Rachel came by his house for a visit and an offer to fix supper for her father later that evening. Their conversation naturally turned to the investigation. Frank was not sure how much he should share with Rachel, but she kept probing with her questions.

The effort to identify the rapist had floundered. Frank and the task force had spent endless hours examining every lead. Then on Sunday, August 11, the rapist struck again. This time the victim was a woman named Alice. The rapist called her Claire. When he heard that, something planted itself in Frank's mind. Like a small pebble in a shoe, it bothered him, but he wasn't sure why. Now, under Rachel's probing questions, he began to review what had happened.

The task force had gathered to review what had happened. In this latest incident, the rapist decided that the perfect setting for the consummation of their relationship would be a Catholic grotto on the grounds of a nunnery where many people came for their weddings. When he had stripped Alice of her clothes, he began to chant. Alice remembered that he said something about an imperishable body and death with a sting.

It didn't take long for Frank to identify the quote for them. It's from Paul's letter to the church of Corinth," he said. "The rapist has clearly moved from focusing on climax to ecstasy."

"Read us the quote," Bryson said.

Frank opened his Bible and read, "When this perishable body must put on imperishability, and this mortal body must put on immortality, then the saying that is written will be fulfilled: 'Death has been swallowed up in victory.' 'Where, O death, is your victory? Where, O death, is your sting.'"

"This guy is really sick," one of the officers said. "Now I see what you mean about this escalating. We've got to find this guy."

"What I don't understand," said Frank, "is how she escaped unharmed. He seems really primed to take this to the next level."

"Lucky for Alice, he got a little careless this time," said Amanda. "What he had not planned for was the arrival of another couple who were looking for a romantic place for their own liaison. He must have heard them coming through the woods."

"The way Alice tells it," said Bryson, "she heard this giggly laughter coming from down the trail. He suddenly stopped what he was doing. He grabbed his clothes, bent, kissed her pubic area, and said, 'I thought you were the one to accompany me on this blissful journey, but I guess I will have to wait for another.' Then he took off through the woods."

"The romantic couple got quite a shock," said Amanda, "when they saw the naked Alice lying on the inflated mattress in the grotto. Fortunately, the woman of the couple had read about the rapes and rather than run off, they immediately called 911."

Now as he described the task force conversation with Rachel, Frank knew that the next victim wouldn't be so lucky. He felt frustrated with their lack of progress. "OK, I will tell you what I am thinking about the serial rapist, but you are not to get involved. This is police work."

"Sure, Dad, I'll leave it to the police just like you do."

"That's different ... Oh, never mind. Maybe telling you about it will help me clarify some of what I am thinking."

"Do you remember when we used to play Clue as a family? Sometimes you'd let me play as your partner when I was younger and we'd think it through together." Rachel said.

"Yeah and you got pretty good at it. I finally became your assistant rather than the reverse."

Rachel pulled two Budweisers from the refrigerator and set them on the table. "So what are the clues we are working with?"

"The first thing you look at is what doesn't seem to fit into the normal pattern. What are the oddities? What do they mean?"

Rachel took a sip of her beer and said, "The first odd thing I heard about was that the rapist kept using wrong names to address his victims. Detective Singletary suggested maybe he just wasn't good with names, but you said there was something more."

"I didn't know what it meant at first, but I told Amanda that it was important."

"Amanda, is it? Am I picking up a clue to a different mystery here?"

Frank felt his face flush, and he quickly reached for his own beer. "Don't go jumping to conclusions. We've been consulting with each other a lot in the last few days, and it just seemed natural for us to be on a first-name basis."

"You are blushing, Dad. She is a very attractive woman. It may not lead to anything, but since you were busted at that preacher's forum, you've shown more energy than Jacob and I have seen since mom died."

Frank remembered when his children had encouraged him to try meeting someone with an Internet dating program. "You remember what a disaster it was when I tried that a few years ago?" Frank said. "I think Officer Singletary is a useful ally in solving this case. That's all there is. Let's move on."

Rachel smiled at him. "Just so we are clear, whether it's Officer Singletary or someone else, Jacob and I would be thrilled to see you in a relationship again."

"I know, honey. It's just … let's move on, shall we?"

"You came up with a theory about the names?"

"At first, names like Catherine, Margaret, and Mary didn't mean much, but I kept remembering that at the April incident, he called the victim Bernadette. That's not a very common name."

"At least he didn't call someone Mother Theresa. That would have been too much."

"You are closer then you think," Frank said. "Who was Mother Theresa?"

"She's a saintly woman who went about helping the poor and helpless in this world."

"OK, keep playing with that thought while I get us some crackers and cheese to go with the beer."

"How about another beer while you're up?" Rachel asked.

"That's another new experience, knocking back a few brewskies with my daughter."

"What do you think it's like drinking with your preacher?"

Frank got the cheese slicer and prepared a plate with cheese, crackers, and bits of smoked salmon. He brought it to the table together with two more beers.

As he was sitting down, Rachel's eyes lit up. "Saint Theresa. Are all of these women saints?"

"Not the women themselves but the names he called them. The latest victim, Alice, he called Claire. At first that didn't mean anything, but on my drive home, I suddenly remembered that Claire was one of the Catholic saints. St. Claire had been a beautiful Italian woman who rejected her wealthy family for the path of poverty. She declared that she wanted to be the bride of Christ.

"So when I got home, I pulled up a saints calendar on the Internet. The dates and names all fit."

"We know that Alice or Saint Claire was very lucky to escape with her life," Rachel said. "We're clearly running out of time. Whose names seem likely for September, and what are the dates?"

"Remember, there are lots of saints each month, so it is easier to see the pattern when looking back," Frank said. He shifted in his chair, and his fingers drummed on the table.

"Dad, what's wrong? I know when you are trying to hide something. You think you know who the next saint will be don't you?"

"Sometimes you see connections that aren't there, Rachel. I could be very wrong about this."

"Tell me, Dad, and let's think this through together."

"There are four women saints on the Catholic calendar for September." Frank hesitated, drew in a breath, and looked again at Rachel. "I could really be wrong about this, Rachel."

"Wrong about what? Dad, what did you find?"

"On Wednesday, September 4, the saint celebrated is Saint Rosalie."

Rachel caught her breath and looked down at the table for a moment. Then she looked up at Frank. "In everything we have been through, and many of my own experiences that you don't know about, there was a constant truth that you taught me, Dad."

"What's that?"

"In every situation, good or bad, God can speak to you if you are willing to listen."

"But is our connection with Rosie so strong that we are jumping to conclusions?"

"Of course we can be wrong, and God doesn't run the universe just for us, but we have to take seriously that God might be giving us a personal clue."

"God, I miss your mother."

Rachel came around the table and hugged her father. "I do too, Dad, but I also know Mom would want us to do whatever we can to get this frigging idiot before he does more harm. Don't stop now, tell me what else you've been thinking?"

"Do you know where he gets most of the quotes he keeps spouting?"

"From the Bible, I guess."

"Oh, it's based on the Bible, but the way he chooses and what he says in addition ... Rachel, those ideas come almost directly from a lecture I gave at the seminary a few years back."

"No way."

"Yes, and that's why the police thought of me as a suspect. Think about it. A preacher who has demonstrated an unusual interest in the relationship between sex and the Bible, who hasn't handled the death of his wife very well, perhaps even demonstrating some mental health problems and some asocial tendencies as a result."

"That's ridiculous. Sure you've had some difficulty with Mom's death, but you're not a psycho."

"I know that and I'm glad you know that, but it's reasonable for the police to think otherwise."

"And Amanda, what does she think?"

"I think she was confused at first. I haven't told anyone this, but we actually knew each other in the distant past and, quite frankly, we didn't part on the best of terms."

Amanda popped a cracker with cheese into her mouth and looked at her father. "Come to think about it, I don't know much about your early history. Were you lovers or something?"

"Let's just say for now that the 'or something' category might fit. Someday I may tell you more, but, for now, it's important that we figure this out before September 4."

"That doesn't give us much time. Only a little over a week. Where do we begin?"

"I want to go back and look at the saints and their history to see if we can get a clue as to where the next rape might take place."

"Why don't we include Jacob and let him help us? He's really into that theology thing. I think he's thinking about going for his doctorate after he gets through at the seminary."

* * * * *

The next evening the three of them gathered at Frank's house. Jacob had an early evening class at the seminary, so it was nine o'clock before they got together in the living room.

"If you don't mind, I'd like to wait a few more minutes before we tell you what we have in mind, Jacob. I've invited someone else to sit in on our meeting."

Before anyone could react, the doorbell rang. "That must be her now."

"Who's our mysterious guest?" Jacob asked.

"I'll bet I know," Rachel said with a grin on her face. "If I'm right, it's someone from Dad's mysterious past."

"It's Amanda Singletary, the lead detective on the case," Frank said., "And, Rachel, let's ditch the mysterious past bit for now. I'm not sure how Amanda would respond to our talking about it."

"OK, for now, but I am dying to hear more of the story later," said Rachel.

"What are the two of you talking about?" Jacob asked.

"I'll tell you later, maybe," said Frank as he got up to open the door and greet Amanda.

"Detective, it's good to see you. Jacob and Rachel are already in the living room."

Frank and Rachel explained their theory to both Jacob and Amanda.

"That's very promising, Frank," Amanda said. "And I like the idea of seeing if we can find a clue as to where this might take place. I don't know much about the saints, but I'm sure the information is available."

"There is something else you all should know," Jacob said, holding up his hand.

They all turned and looked at him.

"Dad, you remember when I arranged that meeting a couple of months ago between you and David Godwin?"

"Yeah, he was worried that his father might have something to do with all of this, but I have serious reservations about what he said," Frank said. "I'm not a fan of Bob Godwin, but it sounded to me more like a wounded son witnessing some marital problems between his dad and mother."

"Wait a minute, I hadn't heard about this," said Amanda. "Frank, I thought we'd agreed that there would be no more secrets between us on this investigation."

"I just didn't want to get someone in trouble because his son feels underappreciated."

"By someone, you mean another pastor. You do realize that this whole crime centers on a demented person who is very religious – that just might include pastors, don't you think?"

"OK, Amanda, it probably wasn't a good call on my part."

"Zeke, I've cooperated with you because I thought you could help. I'm beginning to think that pastors are as bad at covering for each other as police are."

"Zeke," Rachel said. "Who's Zeke?"

Frank watched as Amanda's face turned scarlet red. "I mean Frank. Zeke is someone else I once knew. Tell me about the Reverend Bob Godwin and his son David."

"Before we have that conversation," Jacob said, "I think you ought to hear what I was going to say before you two started tearing into each other."

"Sorry, but we are going to come back to this," Amanda said. "What were you about to tell us, Jacob?"

"Well, David, that is the Reverend Godwin's son, who is a second-year student at the seminary, came up to me after he heard that Dad was going to give a lecture at the seminary this past June. He asked if I could arrange for him to have a private meeting with dad before the lecture."

"We had that meeting, and he shared his concerns and fears about his father," Frank said.

"What he told you may be very important," Jacob said, "but that's not what brought this to mind. Rather, it was when you all started talking about the saints."

"What about the saints?" Amanda asked. She had taken out her notebook and was making notes as they talked.

"Well, it got me to thinking about David," Jacob said. "I've not witnessed this personally, but I hear David is part of a peculiar little group at the seminary." Jacob hesitated as if not sure how to go on.

"Jacob," Amanda said with a police officer tone to her voice. "Despite what you hear, as a police officer, I am capable of listening to information without jumping to wild conclusions. I know this is a classmate of yours, but as I need to remind your father, just because they are clergy, or studying to be clergy, doesn't mean there isn't a bad apple among them."

"I know. It's just that it sounds rather weird, but maybe it's important. You see David is part of a seminary group that is exploring a new form of prayer life."

"I'm not sure that I'm following you," Amanda said.

"Even though they are Protestants, they have decided that as a spiritual discipline, they will take up the Catholic practice of praying to the saints."

"Zowie," said Rachel. "Maybe we have a whole clan of religious nuts at the seminary."

"I think it's pretty clear we are dealing with a single culprit, but this could offer us a clear group to look at," said Frank. "Maybe, if I call the Dean tomorrow, I can get more information on the individuals in the group."

"I want to be in on that conversation," Amanda said. "If you are right about the date of September 4, we don't have a lot of time. In the end it will be the police that will have to handle whatever we find out."

"I'll call the Dean tomorrow," said Frank, "and set up an appointment for us. Are you available in the morning?"

"Anytime after roll call," said Amanda. "Let's say from ten on."

"OK, maybe that is enough for tonight. Jacob, you and I will do some research on the saints and look for any clues in their backgrounds that might give us a hint as to the places for these rapes. If you get some ideas, run them by Rachel. She's pretty good at seeing patterns in random thoughts."

As they all moved towards Frank's door, Rachel held back enough to give Frank a hug. As she did so, she whispered into his ear one word, "Zeke." She looked at him with a look that told Frank he was going to have that conversation sooner rather than later.

CHAPTER 25

Saints Preserve Us

Two days later Rachel, Jacob, and Amanda met at Frank's house. After supper they gathered around a table in the living room. Jacob came with a briefcase stuffed with papers. He set his laptop on the table and looked for an available outlet.

"I'm ahead of you this time," Frank said, as he reached under the table to pull up a power-strip and placed it on the table. "I figured each of you techno geniuses would be wired and low on battery power."

"I'm good," said Amanda. "My iPad is charged and ready to go. What have we got?"

"First," said Rachel, "we have a theory that we want to check out. Amanda, can you pull up a list of the previous rape victims and whatever is known about the places where the rapist took them?"

"We haven't been able to locate all the places, but we have a pretty good idea of many of them. What've you got in mind?"

"Like we said last time," said Frank, "we think that our religious friend has a fascination with the saints, and we want to see if he picks his spot with a particular saint in mind."

"Fortunately for us," said Rachel, "the male chauvinistic tradition of the church works in our favor this time. There are far less women saints than men, so that narrows our search."

"My sister's right," Jacob paused for a couple of seconds and then added, "for once."

Rachel poked him.

Jacob continued. "If you look at the September calendar, which is our focus for now, there are only four women Catholic saints recognized on the general calendar."

"Wait a minute," said Amanda. "I was raised Anglican, and they recognize saints as well. Who's to say that this nut is only interested in Catholic saints?"

"Like you said, Dad, she's sharp." Jacob grinned at his dad and then turned to face Amanda. "You're right. Not only that but different countries have different Catholic saint days. That stumped me at first, but Dad had a good thought about that."

"If our suspicion is correct," Frank said, "this is somehow connected with our local Protestant seminary. We are guessing that it is either a student or faculty member, or perhaps a local clergy who frequents the school. That narrows the field somewhat. I suggested that if it is a Protestant who has become fascinated with saints, the first thought that likely will pop into his mind is to look for Catholic saints."

"Just to be sure, I pulled up an Anglican and an Orthodox calendar of saints, but when I pulled up the Catholic calendar, the names seemed to fit best," Jacob said.

"This could get interesting. Maybe I should deputize the two of you as deputy detectives," Amanda said.

Rachel cleared her throat and pointed at her father. "What about him?"

Amanda raised an eyebrow and said, "The jury is still out on him."

"Gee, thanks. Where exactly would you be if I hadn't gathered this august body together in the first place?" Frank asked.

"Maybe you could make him a probationary deputy detective until he demonstrates more skills," Rachel said.

"I think I'll put on some coffee while the three of you continue this discussion," Frank said as he headed towards the kitchen.

"Operating on the assumption that this fascination with saints may be a new enthusiasm," said Jacob, "I figured that the simplest way for a novice to begin was to go to an Internet calendar of the Catholic saints. So I did the same to see what we could learn about the ones whose names he used. For example, wasn't the first rape victim that we know about a woman that he called Catherine?"

Amanda worked her iPad while Jacob and Rachel fidgeted and waited. "Yeah, she was raped on February 13 at …"

"Wait," Rachel held up her hand. "Let us first tell you about what Jacob found out about Catherine and see if it relates to the place before you tell us where it was."

Jacob pulled up a document on his computer. "Two things stand out in the article I read. The most unusual thing was that she experienced an ecstasy of passion each week from noon on Thursday until Friday at 4."

Both Jacob and Rachel watched Amanda to see if she saw any connection with the place of the rape.

"I'm not sure I understand what that means, but I also don't see a connection with the place," Amanda said while looking at her iPad.

"What about the fact that she was a lover of prayer?" Jacob asked.

"Spot on," said Amanda. She didn't try to hide her excitement. "We are pretty sure that the first rape took place on February 13 at an outdoor chapel in the woods at a Catholic retreat center about fifty miles outside the city."

"All right," Rachel shouted and gave a high five to her brother. "Maybe we are on to something."

Frank entered the room just as Rachel shouted. "This humble, probationary, deputy detective thinks there are indications that you may have had some success. Can I be so bold as to ask if I am correct?"

"If you sired these two," Amanda said, "then I think we will have to advance you through your training and make you a full-pledged deputy," she paused, looked at Jacob and Rachel, and smiled, "albeit with low seniority on this particular team."

"If you can find some Splenda for my coffee, I'll agree with that suggestion," Jacob said.

"So low on the totem pole with this group means I'm the gofer for food and drink. Is that the way it is?"

"I think you've got the picture," said Rachel. "How does it feel to be the powerless one, for once?"

Frank glanced at each of them and then grinned. "As long as you all remember the importance of demonstrating mercy and kindness to your lesser minions."

"Dad, it looks like Rachel was right. At least the location for the rape of Saint Catherine fits with her biography."

"Let's check out March," Rachel said with growing excitement.

"OK," Amanda said again checking her iPad. "Sally, aka Saint Margaret, was raped on March 26. Tell me what you know about her."

"She was born in England," Jacob began. "Interesting enough, her parents were Protestants, but she converted. She was arrested for harboring some Catholic priests. When she wouldn't repent of her dastardly deeds, they tortured her."

"Nothing fits at the moment," said Amanda.

"Oh, shoot," said Rachel. "I knew it was too good to be true."

"Don't give up yet," Frank said. "What form of torture did they use on her?"

"A rather gruesome one, I'm afraid," said Jacob. "They put her in some type of contraption that slowly pressed her to death."

"That's it," cried Amanda. "From what Sally described, she was raped at a vineyard in a nearby county, and she remembers that it was near a wine press."

"We're on a roll," said Jacob. "I'll wager that St. Bernadette's rape was either in a garden near a hospital or near some natural spring, perhaps associated with healing."

"The healing spring near the Sisters of Mercy monastery," said Amanda. "I think you've hit upon the pattern. This can really be helpful."

"What about Cary, aka Mary?" asked Frank.

"That stumped us for awhile," Jacob said. "Then Rachel came up with an idea. Tell them Rachel."

"Mary was known for her sassy talks with Jesus where they would tease and joke with each other. He wanted to give her a crown of thorns but she kept insisting on a crown of roses."

"It ironic," said Amanda, "since Carrie was the one who first made us aware of the serial nature of this crime that we haven't been able to pin down the spot. The way she describes it, it was certainly out in the woods and with lots of flowers around. The next victim, Barbara, aka Emily, was raped in a child's tree house. How weird is that?"

"It fits," said Rachel. "She had been neglected by her own parents and devoted herself to children."

"And Marie? Amanda asked as she looked at her iPad. She was raped in her uncle's cornfield outside of the city."

"She was a farmer's daughter," said Jacob.

"OK, in retrospect we can tie the victim with the spot, but can we predict the future spot based on the saint's biography?" Frank asked.

"That's more difficult," said Jacob. "And we have to be careful. We've been focused on September 4, but it could be Sept 2, 5, or 8 as well."

"That's right, there are four female saints in September," said Amanda. "Why did you think the likely one was on September 4?"

Rachel and Jacob both shifted in their chairs and looked down as if waiting for Frank to speak.

"It's OK," said Frank looking at his children. He rose from the table. "Objectively we don't know which one of the saint days will be chosen. They are all possibilities. The reason my children and I picked September 4 is more emotional than rational. The saint on September 4 is Saint Rosalie. As you will recall from our previous conversation, my wife, their mom, was Rosalie."

"We'll have to watch all four dates," said Amanda, "but I wouldn't ignore your intuition either. Let's explore possibilities for Rosalie first, and then we can look at the other three as well."

Throughout the rest of the evening, they brainstormed possible scenarios for the four potential saint victims.

Amanda stretched and shut down her iPad. "This has all been very helpful. I'm going to return to the station and review what we have. So far, the victims have all been taken from locations in and around this city. That makes sense. The rapist doesn't want to stray far from areas where he is familiar. I will arrange for high alert vigilance on September 2, 4, 5, and 8. In the meantime, I'd appreciate it if you all would continue to brainstorm possible locations that might be used for the actual rape. If we are lucky, we just might stop him this time."

"You think that Theresa on the 5th or Mary on the 8th might be more likely victims, don't you?" asked Rachel.

"I think the temptation to choose either Theresa for her fame or Mary because of her being the mother of Jesus is likely," answered Amanda. "However, who can figure how the brain of a nut works."

"She's right," said Frank, "and we may be too close to this to see with clarity. He might even pick Ingrid on September 2nd."

"This may be a stretch," said Jacob, "but if this is someone associated with the seminary and with Dad's work, we shouldn't overlook the fact that he might know of our mom and that might be a deciding factor."

"We'll keep that in mind," said Amanda. "I'll run a background check on members of the saints prayer group and see if that turns up anything."

CHAPTER 26

Preparation for the Park

Frank, Amanda, Rachel, and Jacob gathered at Frank's house to review the case.

"Boy, I was nervous all day yesterday," said Rachel. "I was just sure that we had made a mistake, and Ingrid was going to be the victim."

"That was the least likely on our list. We still have three more possible dates to go," said Amanda.

"Amanda," Rachel said, "don't the police have small little GPS systems that a person could wear on the inside of their clothes?"

"Rachel, what are you thinking about?" Frank said with a worried look on his face.

"I was just thinking that if the next victim was wearing one of those GPS thingies, then the police could track her and find out where the rapist was taking her."

Frank stared at her, but she didn't continue with anymore explanation. "The next thing we are supposed to ask is how can we know who the victim will be so that we can plant a GPS on her, and then you are going to answer?"

"I was just thinking out loud. I've also heard that there is a counter agent that a person could take that wouldn't allow the drug the rapist is using to have such a strong effect. The combination of a GPS and a built-up resistance to the effects of the drug would allow the victim to better protect herself and improve our odds of catching the guy."

"Rachel, we are not going to risk you as bait to catch this monster," Frank said.

"If the message our last victim reported is any indication, he is growing increasingly dangerous," said Amanda.

"What do you mean?" Jacob asked.

"You recall" said Amanda, "that Janice Long, the victim from July, had a symbol of a cross cut into her chest."

"Didn't you say, Dad, that maybe that meant he was escalating? asked Rachel.

"I am worried that may be happening," said Frank.

"Now we have our August victim," said Amanda. "Apparently only being extremely lucky saved her life. Her name is Alice, and she was called Saint Claire. Another couple was wandering in the woods near the grotto where he had her, and it scared the rapist off. I'm afraid we may be running out of time. Alice was very rattled when we interviewed her, but she did report that our rapist, in addition to quoting Scripture about love and passion, started talking about death and something about a sting."

"Probably 'Where, O death, is your victory? Where, O death, is your sting?'" said Jacob.

"That's what your father thinks," said Amanda. She shivered visibly. "This guy is really weird. He asked her if she would like to accompany him on a heavenly journey and experience the ecstasy of God. He cut her a little more deeply than Janice and also cut himself and mixed their blood."

"Amanda, we've got to stop this maniac," said Frank, "before we are dealing with murder as well as rape."

"We are doing our best, Frank. What I'm trying to do is have officers on alert but not in a way that will scare the rapist and push him to move on to a new location. We are very close. I'm just not sure what else we can do."

"That's where I was going before," said Rachel. "Now I want you all to stay calm and not over react until I'm done explaining my idea."

"I don't think I'm going to like this," Frank said.

"No, you won't, but if you will hear me out, I've thought a lot about this. The victims have always been young solo women, and the spot of their abduction has usually been in some sort of nature setting with easy access to a road so that he can carry them off in a car."

"I'm with you so far," said Amanda.

The problem has been that he carries them off so fast that no one can find his special spot, which is usually secluded. Since his victim is semidrugged, she can't cry out even if someone was close enough to hear her."

"From Rosalie's biography," Jacob said, "Rachel and I were thinking he might choose a cave somewhere this time."

"But we don't know where the cave is," said Rachel, "so here's my idea. We'll get one of those little GPS thingamajigs that Amanda has and sew it into my underwear."

"Wait a minute. Rachel, you are not going to become the bait for this monster," said Frank. His voice rose almost to a shout. "I won't allow it. Mandy, tell them this is too dangerous."

"Mandy?" Jacob said.

"Your father's right, Rachel," Amanda said. She couldn't hide a small smile at Frank's use of the name he had called her so many years before.

"Look, Dad, I am not your helpless little girl. I'm 23. I've got my second degree black belt, and I have a little wrist container of mace just in case I need it. Besides, this is the modern age; I can wear a little radio so that the police can follow whatever is happening."

"This isn't the movies, Rachel. This guy is nuts, and now he is talking violence as well."

"You're right, Dad, and if we are right, he is going to dishonor my mother's name in the process," Rachel said. She was standing tall and staring at her father. "Tomorrow morning I'm going running in the park. I need the support of both you and Amanda, but I'm doing it anyway."

"Dad, it's the best chance we have," said Jacob. "I'd do it myself, but he shows no inclination to go after men, and I'd have a hard time impersonating a woman."

"You don't even allow yourself time to get close to women to know what they look like," said Rachel. "When this is over, we need to focus on getting your nose out of the books and teach you how to smell the perfume."

Frank was trying to stay focused, but one look at his son's face turning red and he collapsed onto the couch in laughter. Even in the most serious of times, his children and their bantering reminded him of the precious gift of life and the wonder that he had two of the finest.

"Rachel, we are talking about you and your safety and not about my love life. I can take care of myself, thank you," said Jacob.

"Amanda, help me out here," Frank said.

"I won't cooperate unless you give your permission, Frank, but with the precautions she is suggesting, it might be our best chance. Even if he succeeded in subduing her, we will still be able to follow wherever he takes her."

Frank got up, walked to the window, and stared out at the backyard for several moments. He thought about his fearless Rosie and how she always faced challenges head on. He hugged himself and shook a little before he turned around and looked at them. They were very still, waiting for him to speak.

"This is crazy. If I say yes, I'm going with you to the park, and I get one of those radio whatchamacallits so that I can listen in to everything that is happening."

"You can come to the park. That will look natural. But once we get started, you've got to let me run on ahead so that I will be alone on the trail."

Jacob guffawed. "A few years ago that might have had to be an agreement, but I don't think that will be a problem currently."

A pillow hurled by his father came flying towards Jacob's head.

"Which park are you thinking of?" Amanda asked.

"The large greenway on the west side of the city with the long, winding pathway. Normally it might be full of people, but this idiot has got people so scared that a lot of people are avoiding it these days," said Rachel.

"OK, I'll get the radios and the GPS signal for you," said Amanda. "It may take me a little while to trace down the pharmacist I have in mind and get the antidote, but I promise to be back with all our equipment by no later than eight this evening," said Amanda.

"I don't want you to start running before 6 a.m. We can't risk putting too many visible officers around, but I will have plainclothes officers on side streets all along the way. You'll wear the radio on your sleeve and say the word squirrel every ten minutes. If I don't hear that, I'm sending people in regardless. If you see anything the least bit suspicious, say robin, and I will put people on hyper-alert. We will always be within ten minutes of you at all times."

"Sounds good to me," said Rachel.

"It doesn't sound good to me," said Frank, "but if we get the son-of-a-bitch, I'll know that fervent prayer is answered."

"Even a lapsed Anglican might become a believer if this works. I'll be back with the equipment this evening. In the meantime, I'd encourage you to get as much rest as you can. Maybe go to a movie or something."

CHAPTER 27

September 4

After Jacob and Rachel had moved out, Frank had purchased a smaller house that only had one guest bedroom. Jacob was quick to suggest that Rachel needed the guest room, and he would sleep on the couch.

"So all we have to do is figure out how to fill in the time between now and then," said Jacob. He was trying to be lighthearted, but it was clear that he was as nervous as the rest of them.

Rachel looked around the living room. There was a stack of books near her father's favorite chair along with some back issues of the *New York Times*. A sweater hung on another chair. She brushed some crumbs off a coffee table. "I think we could spend a little time cleaning up around here. How can you live like this, Dad?"

"I always knew when your mom was nervous or upset," Frank said. "She'd go into a cleaning frenzy. If we stick to making the house presentable and not slip into the spring cleaning mode, I'll help."

"I have a plan," said Jacob. "We will devote an hour to house cleaning to satisfy my fastidious sister, and then we will order a pizza and download a couple of the best old time comedy movies we can find on U-Verse. Humor is the best antidote for whatever ails you."

"Let's go really back and get some Marks Brothers, Lucille Ball, and maybe some Jack Benny routines, and I can introduce the two of you to comedy when it was really funny," Frank said.

"I think I read about some of them in one of my ancient history texts," said Rachel. "Are those silent films or just in black and white?"

"I'll tell you what," said Frank. "Let's have a little wager riding on this. I'm about to introduce the two of you to a time when comedy was real and not just crude references to body parts. If you can watch them without laughing, I'll buy the pizza, but if you crack a smile, the meal is on you."

Jacob tossed Rachel a dust cloth. "Let's get to cleaning; I can just taste that free pizza now."

They were so absorbed in their cleaning tasks that there wasn't much conversation for about an hour. Finally, Rachel looked around and said, "Well, it still looks like a pigsty but at least it's a clean pigsty."

"Great," said Jacob. "I'll order the pizza, and Dad can look through the on demand channel of U-Verse and see if he can find something funny."

An hour later, they were all three sitting on the couch, munching pizza, and watching the films that Frank had chosen.

Frank couldn't decide which he enjoyed the most: watching the Groucho Marx film or watching his two adult children trying to keep solemn faces as they watched it with him. It was a half-hour into the Lucille Ball movie when Rachel finally cracked up and that released Jacob to do likewise.

There was clearly a puzzled look on Amanda's face when she walked in at 8:30 to the sound of hilarious laughter bouncing off the walls. "What have you guys been drinking?" she asked. "Remember, I'm with the police. If you've been smoking weed, I don't want to know."

"I know that it would shock my peers," said Rachel, "but I think I've gotten higher on these old-time movies than I ever got on weed. Opps," Rachel put her hand on her mouth and looked guilty first at Frank and then at Amanda. "I mean, higher than what some of my decadent peers say they get when they smoke that nasty, disgusting, and clearly illegal marijuana, which I personally would never touch."

"You are clearly the worst liar that God ever created," Jacob said.

"At least I don't hide away in a musty library," said Rachel. "You're a good-looking guy, Jacob. When was the last time you even allowed a woman to notice?"

"Not all my research is devoted to books," Jacob said.

"OOO, breaking news, the scholar awakens from his slumber. X-rated moments in the library stacks, news at 11."

"OK, guys, you can have that argument later," said Frank. "I'd even be interested in where it goes. But right now let's help Amanda with her packages."

They moved to the dining room table.

"Wow, what happened to this table? I can see my face in it," said Amanda.

"OK, Amanda," said Rachel. "Your detective eye has clearly picked up the area of improvement that our probationary deputy detective has to work on before he can be a full member of our crack investigative team."

"Enough, all ready," Frank said with a mock frown on his face. "I'll go get four beers while Amanda unpacks her wares." He headed off to the kitchen.

As he returned, Amanda is explaining the way the GPS works and how the double-sided tape is used to stick it in her underwear. "It should send out a strong signal for at least a couple of days, which is far longer than we will need it. My only concern is the caves and how they affect the signal."

"Wait a minute," Frank said. "I thought this was just so we can tell where he accosts her and then we move right in and capture him."

"That's the way it is supposed to work," Amanda said, "but I want to be prepared for any eventuality. This guy may be nuts, but he is also very clever."

"It's OK, Dad. Amanda's just being extra cautious," said Rachel.

"We will be reading the signal as you move along the running path, so we will always know exactly where you are," Amanda continued. "At the same time, we will also be listening to your verbal report over this small radio that will attach to your running blouse. It's not set up for two way communication. We can hear you but if he should subdue you, we don't want him hearing us. Hopefully he will just think the wire is some sort of IPod or something."

"OK, and as long as things are normal," said Rachel, "I keep reporting on squirrels I see along the way, but if something is unusual, I'll suddenly see a robin, right?"

"That's it. Now, in the very unlikely case he gets away with you, we don't want you to be in the lethargic state of the other victims," said Amanda. "My pharmacist friend has provided me with these small pills which will act to prevent the drug he is using from having its full effect."

"How long will they last?" asked Frank.

"That's a problem," Amanda said. "Obviously it's best if the pill is taken very near the time when the drug is introduced. Since that is not possible, this is what I suggest. Take one of the pills right as you start running but I also want to fix another of the pills inside your mouth under your tongue. I'll also give you a couple of extras in a bag to have in your pocket."

"That's a good plan, Amanda," said Rachel.

"I know it sounds a little James Bondish, but I think it can help cover our bases regardless of what happens," said Amanda. "Most of the victims reported that they could still function but just didn't have the will to resist. I'm hoping you will still have the ability to take one of the pills if it gets that far."

"And what happens if she can't take the pill?" Frank asked.

"First of all, Dad, it is not going to get that far," said Rachel, "but even if it does, you and Amanda are going to be following us on the GPS, so you will know exactly where we are."

"I tell you what, sis," Jacob said, "if you pull this off, I'll let you introduce me to some of your ditzy girl friends, and I'll introduce you to some decent men who aren't zoned out on drugs. We can even have a double date."

"The guys I date aren't zoned out on drugs, but you've got yourself a deal. I'm holding you to it."

"Now, as master detectives who are alert to the subtlest of clues, Jacob and I have agreed that there is another mystery we would like to solve. Don't you think it is time, Detective Jacob Sessions?"

"I do, Detective Rachel Sessions, and I do believe we have the prime suspects right here in this room," said Jacob.

Frank raised a quizzical eyebrow, took a swig of his beer, and said, "You know, we have a big day tomorrow, and it is important that we get a good night's sleep."

"Do you notice that little twitch over his left eye, Detective Sessions?" said Rachel.

"I did," said Jacob, "and did you notice how said suspect has tried to distract us while being evasive in his response?"

"I'm not sure what's going on here," said Amanda.

"Perhaps this might clear that up," said Rachel. "Detective Sessions, I think it might be a good idea to have suspect Zeke and suspect Mandy take seats in the witness chair. Could you provide them those chairs?"

"Uh oh," said Amanda, her face took on some color. "They're your children, Frank."

"Frank? We are not addressing a Frank here. We are talking to someone called Zeke," said Rachel. "Although if you have another alias, we can add that to our case record."

"OK, guys, it is probably good to clear this up. What do you want to know?" Frank asked.

"It's pretty clear," said Jacob, "that the two of you have known each other in the past, apparently under the aliases of Zeke and Mandy."

"That's true. We were classmates for a couple of years at UNC in Wilmington. And yes, I was known by a shortened form of my middle name, Ezekiel. So, now that that's cleared up, maybe we can get some sleep."

"Aw, the classic half-confession, where the accused tells a partial truth and hopes we will be distracted," said Jacob. "Did you catch that, Detective Sessions?"

"I did," said Rachel. "Perhaps we need to ask the other witness and see if their stories are consistent with each other. Ms. Amanda Singleterry, how do you describe the relationship with Zeke Sessions?"

Amanda looked down at her feet for a second, then up at Frank. "I would describe our prior relationship as competitive." She smiled. "Wouldn't you agree, Zeke?"

"Uh, yeah something like that." Frank shifted in his chair and took another drink from his beer.

"Would you care to elaborate on your answer, Ms Singleterry?" Jacob asked, clearly enjoying their discomfort.

"Let's just say that your dad as a senior had a reputation as the top stud on campus."

"Dad! You, a minister, were considered a stud on campus?" Rachel exclaimed, giving up the charade of the investigating detectives.

"I wasn't planning to be a minister at the time. We had a date. It didn't work out. That's about enough information. I don't want to embarrass Amanda."

"What'd she do? Make you lose your status as top stud?" said Jacob.

"Yeah, something like that." Frank smiled at Amanda. "Though we only had one date, she actually was part of changing the whole direction of my life."

"Wow," said Rachel, "you must have been one powerful date. You put him in his place and he found his place."

Frank laughed. "I think that about sums it up. Look, now that you have stripped us of our most embarrassing secrets, don't you think it's time we let Amanda go and get some sleep ourselves?"

"It is getting late," said Amanda, "and I've still got some details to set up for tomorrow. Why don't I come by and check things out about five-forty-five tomorrow morning."

CHAPTER 28

Running the Trail

Rachel was up early after a restless night. She was grateful that Jacob had given her the guest room. At four o'clock, she decided she wasn't going to sleep anymore and might as well get up. While she was determined to follow the plan, she knew that it was going to be dangerous and, as Amanda had warned her, she needed to expect the unexpected.

She carefully pulled out two sheets of paper and wrote a letter to both her dad and Jacob. She hid them in her backpack, knowing that it would only be unpacked if something bad happened to her. In such a case, she wanted each of them to know how much she loved them and that they shouldn't feel guilty about what was fully her decision. She knew they would feel guilty anyway, but she wanted to say it to them as clearly as she could.

She hesitated and then pulled out a third sheet of paper. This one she addressed to Amanda. While she didn't know her well, she sensed that something significant could develop between Amanda and her dad and wanted Amanda to know that she fully approved. She also wanted her to know what a comfort it had been to have Amanda share in the family frolic the night before.

With those three notes written and safely hidden away, she got up and stretched while she looked out the window into her father's backyard. She noticed a bright star shining through the trees and thought of her father's old saying, "A star and a tear." She had asked him about what he meant several times over the years. His only response was that a star reminded him that there was something bigger to life than our hopes and fears and a tear reminded him that the something greater could only be glimpsed if you acted in compassion towards others. As she stared at the star, she realized where the source of that something bigger had always been for her father.

I wonder, she thought, if it's not too late for me to be in touch with that same source. She turned, knelt beside her bed, and prayed. She stayed there for at least twenty minutes, not trying to form anything into words but simply releasing herself into the hands of the God that had sustained her father through all the challenges of his life. When she rose, she felt calmness come over her, and she knew that she was ready, whatever the day held.

She chose a pink, tight-fitting pair of running shorts and a flowered T-shirt. She hoped the flower pattern might hide the little microphone pinned to her shirt. She taped the GPS into her underwear as Amanda had shown her, pulled on her shorts and T-shirt, and chose her favorite purple running shoes. Finally, she carefully placed the small microphone on the T-shirt and pinned the battery pack under her T-shirt where she could easily reach it. "Oh, there is a squirrel." "Wow, aren't squirrels great climbers." "I think that is a robin." She practiced several ways of trying to make the comments without seeming unnatural. Tying her hair into a ponytail, she walked out of her room.

Her father was sitting at the table with a cup of coffee. The lines on his forehead broadcast his concern, but he smiled. "Ready for our little run today?"

"Let me have a banana and some OJ, and I'll be ready to go. What time is Amanda coming?"

"I think she said about five-forty-five," said Frank. "We still have about fifteen minutes. Can I get you anything else?"

"You wouldn't have a bagel and some jelly in there, would you?"

"I must have known you were coming. I stopped by the Bagel Den day before yesterday and picked up bagels and even some cream cheese."

Jacob rose from the living room couch. "Bagels. I could use some good carbohydrates for energy. Dad, do you suppose for next Christmas, instead of buying each other gifts, we could all pool our money and buy you a decent couch?"

"Next family reunion, you get the guest room," Rachel said.

Jacob came over, pulled his sister to her feet, and gave her a long hug. They had always been close, but this unexpected affection almost cracked through her outwardly calm veneer.

She was grateful that the doorbell rang and she had an excuse to turn away and answer the door. Amanda was dressed in her official detective outfit. She smiled but tried to act as a professional and not a friend.

Once their hurried breakfast was done and Amanda had checked out the equipment, Rachel said, "I remember that during the most difficult times of mom's tragedy, one of the comforting things we did was have family prayer together. Amanda, would you join us for a little prayer before we begin."

"I don't know how to pray very well, but I'd be glad to be a part of your family prayer. I'm assuming that Frank will lead us."

"No," said Rachel, "I want Zeke to lead us."

Both Frank and Amanda smiled, and Rachel was pleased that she had been able to distract them from what was about to take place. "Just so you know," Rachel said, "I know there is more to that story than we have heard and Detective Jacob Sessions and I are relentless investigators, so neither of you are off the hook yet."

Amanda took Rachel's hand and moved towards where Frank and Jacob were standing. "I'm game if Zeke is," she said and winked at him.

"Just remember a star and a tear, and we will all get through this," Frank said.

"And you are going to have to explain where that phrase came from as well," said Jacob. "I've heard you say that several times during our life, but you never explained the source."

"For now," Frank said, "just remember that you are part of something far more important than you realize and that it is easiest to understand when you are being compassionate to others. If I didn't believe that, I would never agree to what we are about to do."

Amanda gave Frank a receiver and showed him how to use it. "Remember, you will be able to hear Rachel, but you won't be able to communicate with her. Don't panic when she doesn't respond to what you say."

"OK, folks, it's time to move out," said Amanda. "Give me another 30 minutes to get my people in position before you separate. Rachel, don't take any more chances than necessary. If you can, use your karate and run like hell. We'll know the general area, and we'll get him."

"It's OK. I have a good feeling about this," said Rachel. "And thank you all. Each of you has given me the support I need. St. Rosie will be with us."

She gave Jacob and Amanda a quick hug and climbed into the car.

She watched as Frank said a few quick words to them and climbed into the driver's seat. "OK, dear, as scared as I am, I am enormously proud of you and your mother would be as well. Let's get this bastard."

As they drove towards the greenway, Rachel turned to her father. "Why does someone do this dad? Is he really religious or just crazy?"

"A little of both, I'm afraid," said Frank. "However you interpret the story of Adam and Eve in the garden, it speaks of the two great voids in a human's life. In the first case, we are separated from God. We feel the limitations of our finiteness and yearn to be part of the whole. In the other case, we are separated from each other. We are not complete without the other, but we also fear that which is different from us."

"So sexual intimacy is a way of seeking that wholeness?" Rachel asked.

"My guess is that our rapist, in his own distorted way, is seeking to be reunited with that which makes him complete. By focusing on saints, he thinks he is uniting with that which is both human and holy."

"It almost makes you want to turn your back on both religion and sex," Rachel said.

"Sex and religion," Frank said, "are our central source of hope and meaning. Think of it, people sacrifice power, wealth, reputation, security, and their very life in response to either one."

"They both have been powerful in your life," said Rachel, "haven't they?"

"Yes. The loss of your mom and my feeling of impotence to do anything to save her almost destroyed both my faith and my capacity to love. At the same time, it was my love for you and Jacob and the patient faithfulness of the people of John Knox that held me together."

"Whatever happens in the next several hours," said Rachel, "never forget that because of our love as a family and the faith that you taught us, it has all been worthwhile. And, we will make it through this. I know it."

"I pray that you are right, Rachel. Here we are. Let's go for a run."

They pulled into a parking lot that was deserted of cars. "The other thing this crazy man has cost this city is our freedom to enjoy the beauty of nature," said Rachel. "OK, turn your little machines on and check the blip that will be your daughter as she runs away from you."

"And what is my speedy daughter going to be saying at least every ten minutes?"

"Oh, look mommy, there is a little squirrel. Can I take him home with me?"

Frank shook his head. "I think we are as ready as we can be. Let's go."

They got out of the car, did some stretches, commented on the beauty of the morning blue sky with a scattering of white, fluffy cumulus clouds, and slowly began running down the path together.

After about one-half mile, Rachel could tell that her Dad was beginning to wear down. Spotting a bench up ahead, she said, "I think that should be our resting spot."

Frank didn't disagree. Huffing and puffing, he came up to the bench and flopped down. "This is where I have to let you go, huh?"

"Strange, isn't it? said Rachel. "If we are unlucky, you'll see me in about an hour back at the car. If it goes as we planned, it will be a little longer."

Frank rose and took his daughter into his arms. "I love you and am very proud of you but I'm also terrified."

Rachel kissed him on his cheek. "I know, Dad, but we have to do this. Just keep listening for those squirrel reports and perhaps a robin or so."

Rachel turned and ran down the trail. As she went, she said "Oh, look Mommy, a little squirrel. Can I take it home with me?" Then she waved and went around a corner.

She could see through the trees that Frank was staring after her but knew that he would soon turn and start back towards the car to wait. The early morning chill was refreshing and running helped her with her own nervous energy.

The path narrowed somewhat as she turned a corner and came upon a small bridge built by the city to get people over a stream. The water was clear and made a gurgling sound as it passed over the rocks beneath the bridge.

When she was just a little girl and went with her family through similar woods, she used to fantasize that they were the first humans to arrive on this planet. She would search through the trees and around every large rock trying to spot the native life of the planet, which she was sure would be friendly. Now, as she ran on, she searched through the trees, but this time the creature she was looking for felt sinister and evil.

The calm that she felt envelop her during her early morning prayers stayed with her. She was nervous but not terrified. She trusted that whatever happened, she was here for the right reason. When her mother had been killed because she happened to arrive at a store during a robbery, Amanda had felt so helpless. She had watched her father be strong for her and Jacob even as the loss of their mom had torn him apart. She had learned from that terrible loss that life was not always fair but sometimes you needed to be strong for the sake of those you love.

Her thoughts were interrupted by a movement near a big tree ahead. At first, it startled her and then she realized with a laugh that it was indeed a small squirrel racing up a tree. "Wow, look at that squirrel go up that tree," she said knowing that it would relieve both her Dad and the police to hear her report in.

Even though she knew that she was taking a risk, it felt good to be doing something against an evil in the world. She saw a small tree lying across the path ahead and sped up so that she could leap over the tree. She recalled her mother coming to one of her cross-country meets her first year in high school. Those were good years, she thought. Watch me leap over this tree, Mom, and on St. Rosie's day, too.

On any other day, this winding path through large trees that provided rich shade and delicious shadows would have been wonderful.

"Look at those two squirrels chase each other up a tree. They look like they are having so much fun," she said as if talking to the trees. "I don't believe in reincarnation, but if I did, I think I might choose to be a squirrel for one of my trips through the circle of life." The sun grew brighter and pierced the leafy canopy of the path providing welcome warmth at various points along the path.

She rounded a bend and saw that the path straightened out for a couple of hundred yards. She was just about to speed up when she spotted something pink on the path ahead. "I doubt if it is anything, but there is a robin ahead on the path," she said aloud to alert her listeners that there was something different occurring. "Aw, it looks like a child's change purse that must have fallen out of her pocket while she was running. What a shame."

She slowed and bent over the small purse to examine it. She sensed a movement behind her and just had a chance to say robin again before she felt a blow behind her knees knocking her to a kneeling position on the path. Her eyes were still on the small pink purse. She let out a small yelp as a cloth bag was pulled over her head. She realized that there was also a strong smelling rag being held over her nose and mouth.

She had tried to picture how this would happen and how she would respond. In her imagination, she would refuse to breathe in what she assumed was a form of ether and draw upon her karate skills to quickly dislodge her attacker. Once she was free of his grip, she assumed, her skills could protect her until help arrived.

Being knocked to her knees so quickly and the disorientation from the darkness of the bag over her head, threw her careful plans into disarray. Before she recognized what was happening, she even took in a breath and felt herself beginning to lose consciousness. In her dazed state, she was still aware of several things taking place. First, he immobilized her by wrapping his strong arms around her and lifting off the ground. Second, she tried to dislodge the small pill from its spot under her tongue. Then darkness descended. She felt a rolling motion as if she was floating in a large ocean buffeted by waves.

* * * * *

Jacob had accompanied Amanda and agreed to coordinate the radio communication among the various parties as events developed. He was feeling guilty that he couldn't be out there defending his sister but understood that she had to be alone if this was to work.

When the sound of Rachel's struggle began, Jacob and Amanda adjusted their receivers in order to hear what was taking place. Amanda bent forward to catch every sound that was coming over her receiver. At first, she heard a small yelp and the sounds of a struggle taking place.

Then a calm, yet agitated voice spoke. "What's this? A microphone. Damn, Rosie, saints are supposed to be holy, not deceptive. You may have to be punished for this."

Then there was silence. The receiver went dead. She knew that it had been pulled from the unit and that there would be nothing else to hear.

Glancing at her GPS receiver, she went into high gear. "Units 5 and 6, block access roads L and M. Make sure no one gets in or out. Then send a detachment down the path in a pincher movement. The rapist has his victim. Proceed with caution. I'm on my way."

"Detective, this is unit 3 over on 8th Street. We have an empty Chevy Malibu that doesn't appear to belong to this neighborhood. Plate is Ralph, Edward, Victor number seven, seven, seven. Running it through DMV now."

"That's Reverend Godwin's plates," said Jacob. "I'm almost sure of it. Do you think he is the rapist?"

"We'll soon find out," said Amanda. She spoke again to her officers. "The guess here is that it will register to the Reverend Bob Godwin, but whoever it is, see if you can make contact."

Amanda's ATV was already moving down the trail as Jacob studied the forester's map to give her the shortest route to where Rachel had been accosted. She called Frank, who she knew would now be near panic. "Zeke," she hoped the old nickname would calm him, "this is Mandy. I know you heard the same thing I heard."

Jacob looked at her with a smile on his face but didn't comment.

"Mandy, what the hell happened," shouted Frank. "She said robin and then my receiver went dead."

"I think our subject spotted the microphone and pulled it out of its battery pack but thanks to the other GPS, we still have a tracer on him."

"Where are you?"

Trying to project a *everything's under control* tone that she didn't feel, Amanda responded, "Jacob and I are headed towards the spot now. If you will take your car to the Lombard Street entrance to the greenway, you will be close. The police will stop you before you enter. Just tell them to call me for permission to enter. Keep calm, Frank, the police are nearing the spot right now."

"If he's hurt Rachel," Frank said, "I'll beat him to a pulp."

"I've got to be in touch with my officers, Frank. I'll see you at the site."

As Amanda maneuvered her ATV on the trails, Jacob glanced at the GPS receiver and noticed that the two signals had separated. "What does that mean?"

"My guess," Amanda said, "is that he has tossed the mike with the one GPS as far as he can throw it and doesn't know that the other one is still sending out a signal."

She radioed to both units who were converging on the site. "Unit 5 and 6, report in."

"Unit 5 here. Nothing got out or in. On path nearing site. Can't see any humans about."

"Unit 6 here. The same."

"Unit 5 and 6, the signals would indicate that he has left the site and headed into the woods. If he is carrying a body, he can't move fast. Look for point of ingress. My ETA is about 3 minutes."

"We hear you coming, Detective."

It didn't register at first. Then it struck her. I'm in an electric ATV. What are they hearing?

She didn't have time to process that before she saw her units up ahead examining the various entrance points into the woods. She braked her unit and leapt out. "What were you hearing?" she shouted as she ran towards them.

"Just the sound of your . . .oh, your ATV is silent. I thought I heard something just as we came up on the site."

"Trail bike," Amanda said. "There are deer trails everywhere. I just hope the tall trees don't mess up the GPS signal. Mine's a 4-wheeler, and I'll bet his is just a dirt bike so he can move on trails that we can't."

"We're on the edge of the city, and it's a large national forest to the north of us," said Sergent O'Riley. "I used to hike in there as a kid. We'll move slower than he will, but with the signal guiding us, I think we can follow him."

"Lieutenant Bryson, radio in and find some trail bikes. We'll keep contact so that you can deliver them to us up ahead. OK O'Riley, let's go."

Just then Frank came up and leaped out of the car to join them. "Frank, come with O'Riley, Jacob, and me. He's taken off through the woods. He has Rachel with him. We think he may have a dirt bike."

Frank began running towards the woods.

Amanda called after him. "Frank, slow down. If he has a dirt bike, we can't outrun him. We need to steadily follow him until he stops. We don't want to wear ourselves out in the process. Remember, we have him on our radar. He won't get away."

Frank slowed as O'Riley, Jacob, and Amanda caught up, and they entered the woods at a brisk pace. O'Riley was reading the GPS receiver in his hand. "He is clearly headed north, and if I remember correctly, there used to be some caves up there that we used to explore as kids."

"That fits with what I thought he would do," said Jacob. "I remember those caves. We went spelunking there when I was in college."

"With luck," said O'Riley, "he won't know the trails as well as I do, and he might take a few wrong turns that will slow him down. We can head directly to the cave area." He handed his receiver to Jacob. "Jacob, you keep your eye on the GPS as we walk just in case he decides to go another way."

For the next hour, the four of them force marched along the trails that O'Riley picked and moved steadily towards the limestone caves that were indicated on the map. Occasionally they thought they heard the sound of a dirt bike, but there was nothing but nature sounds when they arrived at the base of the hill.

"There are multiple caves in this area," said Jacob, "but the larger ones are in this direction." He started to lead them off towards the right side of the hill.

"Let me radio in our location and get some units out here to monitor the exit paths in case we choose wrong and he tries to escape," said Amanda.

"We can't wait for the units to arrive," said Frank. "We have no idea what he might be doing to Rachel."

Amanda thought back on the words she had heard over the speaker earlier , "You may have to be punished," rang in her ears. "You're right," said Amanda. "We'll have to split up and search the caves in pairs. Frank, you go with Jacob. He knows these caves. Promise me that if you discover anything, you will radio us and wait for one of us to arrive."

"Sure," said Frank, but Amanda knew that it was unlikely that he could wait if he saw Rachel in danger. She could only hope and, yes, pray that she and O'Riley would find them first.

"Jacob, any suggestions on which caves to try first?"

"The two caves we most liked to explore are just up ahead. The entrance ways are very close together. They may even connect back in the mountain somewhere."

O'Riley gave a meaningful glance at Amanda who gave a small nod.

"Rev., here's the first entrance. You will find a lot of rock formations and some deep drop-offs so proceed with caution," O'Riley said.

Jacob held up his hands. "Wait just a minute." He reached over and grabbed several handfuls of grass and flowers. "I know this sounds like Hansel and Grettle, but stuff this in your pockets. Whenever you have to make a turn, put a little grass down to guide you back home. Believe me these caves can be rather disorienting."

Each of them gathered some grass and flowers to stuff into their pockets.

"I knew there was a reason why I read you those fairy tales when you were a kid," said Frank.

"We don't know how dangerous this guy will be, so be cautious about giving your position away with your flashlights and conversation," said Amanda.

As they approached the second cave entrance, O'Riley said, "They're both pretty smart, aren't they?"

"They read the tea leaves pretty well," said Amanda. "I was glad you didn't say anything about that bike track back there. If we are lucky, we'll find them before Frank and Jacob do."

O'Riley nodded as they approached the entrance to the cave.

"O'Riley, I know you are fully prepared to go into this next cave with me, but given the erratic signals, I think it would be helpful if you stayed outside and guided the backup units in. Also, you may be able to hear what's happening to Frank and Jacob out here."

"I don't feel right about you not having backup, Detective."

"It will be safer for all of us if you are both getting our signals and guiding the units into the caves when they arrive."

"OK, Detective, but if I don't hear from you every 15 minutes, I'm coming in."

As Amanda approached the entrance to the cave, she thought she noticed how some of the dirt had been brushed over as if to cover tracks.

CHAPTER 29

An Altar to the Gods

Amanda shivered slightly as she worked her way back into the cave. Truth be known, she never liked close spaces, and the dampness didn't help any. She remembered as a girl going with her parents to the Mammoth Cave in Kentucky and how eerie it was when the guide turned off all of the lights. It was so dark that she couldn't see her father next to her. Holding his hand was the only thing that kept her from freaking out.

Now she was on her own. As they followed the trail here, Jacob had told all of them what to expect when they entered the caves. Now, that was very helpful. She kept the light pointed down so that it didn't shine too far ahead but still warned her about any outcropping of stalagmites or stalactites that might pose a hazard. She couldn't remember which was which, but she knew that one grew up from the floor and the other hung down and both could be hazardous to your health. Every hundred yards or so, she would turn off the light and keep very still trying to sense any indication of where Rachel and her captor might be. As she was forced to make turns, she was grateful for Jacob's idea of spreading some leaves or seeds on the ground. They would be useful when the backup unit came in behind her. It was about a half-hour into the cave when she thought she caught a glow around a bend in front of her.

She almost banged her head on a stalactite but saw it just in time as she crept forward. As she approached the bend in the passageway, she began to hear a voice that seemed to be chanting. It was not English.

She wondered if it were Latin and was part of the rapist's fascination with Catholic tradition. Or was it just a chant that he made up. She had heard about people speaking in tongues. It had something to do with being filled with the Holy Spirit. This religion thing, she thought, can sure get confusing.

Not knowing what she would find, she tried to look around the bend and still not be seen by someone in front of her. This time, she was grateful for a couple of large stalagmites that allowed her to creep forward unnoticed. As she made her way forward, she saw ahead of her a larger space, almost like a room. Huge stalactites hung down like large pillars in a cathedral. The glow she had noticed was caused by two lanterns that had been placed in small outcroppings on the walls. The echo of the chant she heard bounced off the walls and created an eerie cacophony of sound. It almost felt sacred.

She looked further into the room. She could see Rachel lying on a slab of rock with a man standing behind her. The slab looked like an altar. The man was chanting and moaning as if he was in a spiritual trance. Oh my God, she thought, I'm too late. Then relief flowed through her as she heard Rachel moan and move.

"Now Rosie, just lie there peacefully. You are so lovely. Those pink little shorts and beautiful blouse with the flowers are just what I would expect Rosie to wear. When they come off, I know that your body will reveal God's beauty." He began to stroke her legs. "How graceful are your feet in sandals, O queenly maiden!" He moved his hands up to her thighs. "Your rounded thighs are like jewels, the work of a master." He lifted her T-shirt, revealing her taught stomach. "Your navel is a rounded bowl that never lacks mixed wine." He bent to kiss her navel. As his hands moved in wider circles, he continued, "Your belly is a heap of wheat, encircled with lilies." He moved a hand up higher towards her breasts, still seeming lost in his trance. "Your two breasts are like two fawns, twins of a gazelle." He seemed to interpret Rachel's moaning and movement beneath him as her own responsiveness to his touch. He continued his slow, rhythmic seduction scene, part physical and part spiritual. "Oh my dove, in the clefts of the rock, in the covert of the cliff, let me see your face, let me hear your voice ..."

When Rachel did not respond, he hesitated and stepped back as if uncertain. "Before I consummate this sacred act, I need to know why you were wearing a microphone? For us to journey together to the great beyond, I must be sure that you are my beloved Rosie."

His face moved from a beatific glow to a frown. "Maybe you really aren't Rosie but an evil Satanic imposter sent to disrupt this sacred union with the holy." He reached down and fondled one of her breasts. "You have such lovely bosoms. I look forward to tasting them, but for us to journey to the fuller life, I must know that you are my lovely Shulamite, a gift of God and not some evil imposter."

As Amanda watched, she searched for a way that she could move closer. He seemed to be in such a dreamlike state that she tried to move behind a rock formation just inside the entrance, but her movement seemed to awaken him.

He picked up what appeared to be a butcher's knife and held it close to Rachel's neck. "I think we have visitors, Rosie dear. Whoever you are, you had better show yourself right now, or we are going to have a sacrifice before its time."

Amanda knew she had to make a quick decision. The man standing behind Rachel couldn't be more than 25 so that ruled out Bob Godwin. The license plate on the Chevy Malibu that had been reported suggested that the stranger before her was from the Godwin family. She wasn't close enough to rush him before he hurt Rachel, so she decided to play another game.

She punched in her warning signal to guide her backup unit and set her radio behind a rock. She shifted her pistol into her waistband behind her back, stood up, and moved into the light.

"Who are you?" David demanded.

"It's OK, David. You've come to celebrate St Rosalie's day. It's not your fault that you got the wrong woman."

David looked confused. "What are you talking about? You come any closer, and I will slit her throat." He moved the knife closer to Rachel's neck.

"To sacrifice the wrong person in worship is wrong," Amanda said, trying to make her voice sound holy, as she imagined a saint would sound.

David stared, as if trying to see her more clearly.

She moved forward slowly, more into the light where he could see her. "David, you are not into violence. You know that it is in the sharing of holy sex that you draw closer to the Divine. I am the true Rosalie, sent by the Holy One to share your journey."

David's mouth came open as if to speak, but before he could say anything, Amanda continued. "Don't you find me attractive, David? Wouldn't sex be far better with one who gave herself to you than one who was drugged and passive?"

"What are you talking about, and how do you know my name?"

"I know your name, David, because you are faithful to the saints, and we appreciate it."

The knife was still dangerously close to Rachel's neck. Amanda knew that she had to do something dramatic to change the dynamics. "David, you appreciate the sacred beauty of a woman's body. How about we play a version of strip poker?" She slowly unbuttoned the top buttons on her blouse even as she arched her back.

David's eyes widened just a bit, and his focus was clearly on Amanda rather than Rachel.

"Instead of cards, our form of strip poker will be an even exchange, David. I don't want this young innocent girl hurt – it offends the saints for the innocent to suffer."

"I'm not stupid, you know."

"Of course not, David, but you would like to see some more, wouldn't you?" Amanda casually stroked between her breasts. "For your first move, why don't you raise your knife just ten inches away from her neck. You're still in control, David, but you get to see more."

David hesitated and then slowly moved the knife up several inches, but it still hovered over Rachel's body.

"That's good, David. You deserve an award. How about I remove three more buttons." Slowly she unbuttoned the next three buttons and pulled her blouse open a little to reveal more of her cleavage. "It's your turn now, David. How about putting the knife down by your side. You're still in control and can raise it anytime you want to."

"OK, but next time you are going to have to remove your blouse." Slowly David lowered the knife to his side.

It would be just like my backup units to wait and see how this is going to play out, she thought. She kept her eyes fixed on David's face, holding his attention. Just then she saw Rachel open one eye and look at her. I think my gal is playing a little possum, she thought. Good girl. Let's take another distracting step. Slowly Amanda unbuttoned the last button and let the blouse hang open.

"Open it the rest of the way," David said. His eyes were fixed on her breasts in anticipation.

"If I do, will you take a step back from your altar, David. I need to see that you really want me and not her."

"Take it off and we'll see," David said.

No one taught me how to be a strip artist in police academy, Amanda thought. Too bad I don't have some exotic music to move to. Keeping her movements slow and what she hoped was seductive, Amanda peeled back her blouse and let it slip to the floor. "What do you think, David? Can this be a holy moment?"

David took a step back, and his eyes were now fully fixed on Amanda. "More, I want to see more. Take your bra off, too."

"Can I step forward so that you can see me more clearly as it comes off, David?" Even as she said it, she took a couple of steps closer and shifted to the balls of her feet so that she could leap forward at a moment's notice.

As she moved forward, she saw out of the corner of her eye, an opening on her left. There was a slight movement, but she couldn't be sure whether it was a person or just a trick of the lights reflecting off the walls.

Jacob had mentioned that the caves might connect back in the mountain, so she assumed that Frank and Jacob had found a connecting tunnel. David was still too close to Rachel for any surprises. She hoped that Frank and Jacob would not make any sudden moves but give her a chance to play this out a little longer.

David shifted the knife in his hands. "That's close enough. I can see you right where you are."

"OK, David, but we really are going to have to think about what you are going to exchange for this." Amanda reached behind her and released the bra. Slowly she reached up one hand for the shoulder straps and began to pull them down."

Just as her breasts were fully exposed, Rachel rolled forward off the table. As David started to react, a stone flew out of the darkened opening of the tunnel Amanda had spotted. The stone struck David on the face. He screamed and turned towards his right to look into the other tunnel.

A loud voice boomed from the tunnel. "David, stop." The loud, deep voice echoed off the cave walls and sounded like a Hollywood version of God speaking. Before David could decide who was speaking to him, Jacob leaped out of the tunnel and flung himself on top of his sister. A small stalactite came flying out of the tunnel, forcing David to back away from the altar.

Amanda saw her opportunity. Even as she was retrieving the gun from her waistband, she ran forward, leaped on the rock slab, and pointed it at David. "Don't even think about moving, David, or I'll blow you apart starting with your balls."

Seconds later, O'Riley and three other officers dashed into the room from the tunnel that Amanda had used.

"It took you long enough," Amanda said out of the side of her mouth while she kept her eyes focused on David, who was now curling against the wall.

Bryson stepped towards David, quickly kicking away the knife that had fallen on the cave floor. "Hey, detective, we'd never seen a Virginia officer perform. You've certainly got all the right moves."

"Be careful, Detective, my finger could slip and shoot your balls off instead."

"O'Riley, I believe it might be appropriate to haul this slime bag out of here," Bryson said.

Jacob and Frank were checking Rachel for any injuries. Amanda, still standing above them on the rock altar looked down. "She's all right, isn't she?"

Frank looked up. "Uh, Amanda, for an undercover cop, you are rather exposed at the moment."

Amanda looked down at her naked breasts and then back up at Frank. "It's not as if you've never seen them before."

"What is it with you guys?" Rachel said. "You've got more secrets between you than Apple has aps."

"No one has that many secrets," Frank said as he handed Amanda her blouse. The other officers were trying to pretend they weren't looking while stealing a glance as they secured David.

CHAPTER 30

The Sins of the Father

David was led down the hillside and placed into a squad car as the rest of them emerged from the cave.

"We need to call his father," said Frank, "and tell him what has happened."

"If you have the energy," said Amanda, "I think it would be best if you called him, being a colleague and all."

Frank grimaced and said, "I think you're right, but I don't look forward to it." His arm was protectively around Rachel. "If anything had happened to her," Frank said, "it would not have been a nice conversation."

"But nothing did happen, Dad," Rachel said. "Now it's almost like they are losing a child instead of you, and you know what that can feel like."

As the rest of them headed down the hill to get into the waiting cars, Frank punched in the number for the True Vine Church. Helen's cheerful voice greeted him.

"This is the True Vine Church. How can we be of service to you in the name of our loving savior."

"Helen," Frank said, "this is Frank Sessions, please put me through to Bob. It's an emergency."

"I'll connect you with Rita, his secretary."

Rita answered and Frank explained that he needed to talk with Bob right away. Rita hesitated a moment and then explained that Bob was in conference but should be free later in the afternoon.

"Rita, this is Frank Sessions. It doesn't matter what Bob is involved in, you need to interrupt him right now and let me talk with him."

She started to protest and then thought better of it. "I'm sure that you wouldn't insist if it was not an emergency. Hold for a second, and I will try to reach him."

Frank paced at the entrance to the cave as he waited. The sky was blue with cumulus clouds dotting the sky on this warm fall day. How can such beauty be present at a time of such tragedy, he thought. He picked up a small rock and hurled it into the cave, listening for its echo as it fell.

"Frank, this is Bob Godwin, what's the emergency?"

"Bob, trust me on this. I want you to make sure that you are in absolute privacy as we continue our conversation."

"Well, OK, just let me shut the door to my office."

Frank could hear him explaining to Rita that he didn't want to be disturbed and then the door closing.

"OK, I'm completely alone, Frank, now what's going on?"

"It's your son, Bob. He's just been arrested in connection with the rape cases. As we speak, he's being taken to the police station on Arlington Boulevard. We can sort out the details later, but I urge you speak to the best lawyer you know and then meet us at the police station. We will be there in about one-half hour."

"I don't understand, Frank. Not David. That's impossible."

"Bob, no matter what else is true or isn't true, right now David needs you, and he needs a good lawyer. The rest can be sorted out as we go along. Trust me on this. I've got to go. I will meet you at the police station.

There was nothing else that either of them could say, so the conversation ended. Frank headed down the hill towards the police cars that were waiting.

When they arrived at the police station, Bob and his lawyer were waiting for them.

Amanda stepped forward. "Reverend Godwin, my name is Amanda Singletary, the lead detective in this case. As I think Frank has already explained to you briefly, your son has been arrested, and he will soon be interviewed in interrogation room number 6."

"This has got to be a mistake," Bob began.

"I'm afraid there is no mistake. He was caught in the process of molesting Rachel Sessions, the young lady over in that corner."

"Rachel, Frank's daughter? That's crazy. Frank, tell them it's not true."

"Bob, listen to the rest of what she is saying. It's important."

Amanda continued. "In a few moments your son will be brought up to this room. You are certainly free to greet him and talk to him for a few moments, but then we will have to proceed with the interrogation."

She turned to the man standing next to Bob. "You are Reverend Godwin's lawyer?

When he nodded in assent, she told him, "You are certainly invited to be present during this interrogation. Once father and son have had a chance to speak with each other, I think it would be best if Reverend Godwin just watched from the viewing room and you accompanied David during the interrogation."

While Bob and his lawyer were discussing these arrangements, everyone saw an officer bring David into the room.

Bob immediately went towards him. "Son, I don't know what this is all about but I have the best lawyer in town. We will get this resolved as fast as we can."

"Resolved?" David looked at him. "You mean covered up so that it won't tarnish your precious reputation, don't you, Dad?"

There was a crazed look in David's eye, and he cackled as he pointed the finger at Bob. "Thou art the man – the womanizer who has broken the covenant with his wife but bought out his accusers so that his precious image could be preserved. Absalom may have raped his sister, but your son David has raped the city. "

Bob looked at his son, and his face lost all of its color.

"You won't be able to hide this from the pious hypocrites that make up your congregation, Dad. Your own son is the Secular Evangelist that has terrorized the city and disgraced your ministry. Tell mom there will be no more Barbie doll clothes for her. It's rags and ashes from now on for both of you."

"David," Frank spoke in a forceful voice as he stepped forward. "Your parents have made many mistakes, but they are still your parents. You almost harmed my daughter, yet I forgive you. By all that is holy, do not cut yourself off from your parents."

David looked around, first at Frank, then at Rachel huddled over in a corner, and then back at Frank. "Your daughter? Rosalie is your daughter? I didn't know. Oh, my God, I didn't know."

Her name is not Rosalie but Rachel. She is not a saint, David, anymore than any of the other women you harmed. Your namesake, King David, was a mighty king and a terribly flawed sinner. Yet when he acknowledged his sins before God, God didn't give up on him but worked through him for the sake of the people."

"You said that you would be here when I confronted my father. I guess you were true to your word," David said.

"Like your namesake, you will pay for your sins, David, but be a man and like him take responsibility and allow God to work through you."

David stared at him for a long time and then turned towards his father. "Tell Mom I love her even if she is a fluff." Then he turned to the policeman at his side. "Let's get this over with."

Frank watched David and his lawyer being led into the interrogation room. Bob was frozen in place.

"Stay with him now, Bob. He needs you. Later we will meet and sort some of this out."

Frank turned and walked towards his family. "Let's get out of here. Amanda's got work to do, but I've asked her to come by for supper tomorrow night."

CHAPTER 31

Epilogue

Frank had invited Amanda to his house for supper the next night. He deliberately invited Amanda to come at 6:30 and asked Jacob and Rachel to stop by the Stallion Steak House and pick up his order for supper at 7:15. The doorbell rank exactly at 6:30, and Frank opened the door.

"You're right on ti…" He stopped in midsentence and stared.

Amanda laughed. "You didn't think I was going to come in my police uniform did you?" Her dress was floor length with a paisley pattern of bright orange, yellow, and brown swirls. It had a scoop neck and was sleeveless which accented her warm brown olive complexion. Her dark hair had that freshly washed sheen accented by multiple tight curls.

"I only wish that I had three months notice so that I could have lost forty pounds and gotten into better shape. You look absolutely lovely," Frank said.

"I see that you have shaved off your beard," said Amanda. "Is that the first step towards the new you?"

As Frank took her hand, he also reached up with his other hand and rubbed his cleanly shaven jaw. "It is definitely the first step, Amanda. I think this whole incident has helped me break through the fog that I've been living in." He smiled as he gazed at her. "I think this may be the second time that you have played a role in changing my life."

She kept hold of his hand and pulled towards him as she entered the house. She came up on her toes and kissed him lightly on the cheek. "I don't know what the wild bush country felt like, but that's nice."

"I feel about ten pounds lighter," he said. "As you enter the house, I want you to notice that even though it's been a couple of days since Jacob and Rachel have returned to their homes, it is still neatly picked up and dusted. I've even purchased some new wine glasses polished to perfection."

"I like the direction this new you is taking. What type of wine are you offering?"

"Rachel helped me pick it out. She is definitely the wine connoisseur of this family. We. have a very special chardonnay that shows just a hint of violets and a shade of walnut husk. It's considered one of the premium wines made by the Brothers of Ezekiel Monastery in Colorado."

"You've got to be kidding," she said as she grabbed the bottle and began to read.

"Truthfully, I don't know how it tastes, but when we saw that on the bottle, we couldn't resist."

"Do we wait for Jacob and Rachel, or do we try it now?" she asked.

"I think now would be appropriate to toast old memories. They know most of the story, but I don't have the nerve to tell them the whole story."

He carefully opened the bottle and brought their glasses to the couch where they could sit next to each other. He had also placed a tray of crackers, cheese, and green peppers with dip on the table before them. He filled their glasses and then raised his to hers. "Here's to fond memories and the proof that even the most boorish of behavior can have a redemptive future."

They both drank slowly. Then she turned to him. "Zeke, there is something about that night that you don't know. It's embarrassing, but it might at least help you to realize that you weren't the only one who was acting inappropriately that night."

His neck drew back and a couple of creases formed on his forehead as his eyes narrowed. "I'm not sure anything could have been worse than the way I behaved. I'm only grateful that I came to my senses before I completely abused you."

She set her glass down on the table and turned herself with one leg folded underneath her dress so that she was facing him on the couch. She hesitated, reached out, grabbed the wine glass, and took another drink before setting it down again.

"Amanda, what is it?"

"Do you remember how I responded when you first spoke to me in the library?"

"Do I? It was like the Rock of Gibraltar that wouldn't be moved. I thought I'd lost the …" He hesitated, "…lost the bet before I'd even started."

"And then what happened?" she asked.

I offered my best winning smile to convince you that I could call again that night to see if you'd changed your mind. I even did some research to know what you were interested in so that I could demonstrate what an interesting guy I was."

"And then…"

"That was strange. I didn't even get a chance to try out my winning arguments. I never did understand that. When I called, you said yes almost before I could get the question out."

"Did you ever wonder why I changed my mind?"

"It flashed through my mind, but when I picked you up, you were so responsive that I think my hormones just took over."

She reached out and took another drink of wine. She placed the glass on the table, turned back and reached out for his hands. She grimaced and then said, "That's what I'm about to explain to you now."

"I don't understand. What could be so difficult to tell me? After all, I'm the one who had the bet."

"Not the only one," she said.

"What are you talking about?"

"When I got back from the library, I happened to let it slip to some of the girls that you had asked me out. They started ragging me about how everyone knew that no girl was safe around you."

"I guess I did have a pretty bad reputation."

"I sort of had a reputation, too," Amanda said. "Only mine was that no guy could get near me."

"Well, yeah," Frank said. "That was sort of what the bet was about."

"The girls in the dorm thought that your reputation trumped mine, and I got stubborn. One thing led to another, and they soon had $75 betting that I couldn't let you get to my breasts and then turn you off and walk away."

Frank sat in complete silence and stared at her.

"So now you know the whole story," she said and looked down. "You're not the only one who needs forgiveness for that night."

Frank fell back on the couch behind him and began to howl with laughter. "You had a bet? There were two bets that night?"

"It's really not that funny. I've carried that guilt for years."

He pointed at her, grabbed his stomach, and rolled back and forth, finding it difficult to stay on the couch. He continued to laugh.

Frank pulled back slightly. "I do have one question, though?"

She looked at him, tilting her head slightly.

"Who won, then?" he asked. "I mean, I did make it to the breasts, and fine breasts they were, but it sounds like you intended for it to get that far. So if I hadn't stopped, would you have simply gotten up and walked away?"

Her eyes began to twinkle. "I guess we will never know for sure, will we?"

They both burst out in laughter and Amanda picked up a pillow and began pounding him with it.

Just then the door opened and Jake and Rachel walked in. Seeing them on the couch, holding on to each other, and cracking up with laughter, Jacob and Rachel hesitated.

"Uh, are we interrupting something," Jacob asked. "We could come back later."

"No, you are just in time. We had just remembered something very funny about our past relationship."

"How'd you like the wine?" Rachel asked. "Wasn't that cool?"

"That's what brought back the memories," Frank said.

Amanda stood up to greet them.

"Amanda," Rachel said, "you look gorgeous." She came over and gave her a big hug.

Jacob set the packages for the supper on the table and came forward to greet Amanda. "If you two can behave yourself, we could set this supper out before it gets cold."

Once the meal was on the table, they all gathered around. This time it was Jacob who poured the wine. In the middle of the meal, Rachel began looking at Amanda.

Suddenly Rachel leaped to her feet. "The song, Jacob. Get your guitar."

"What do you ..." and then he glanced at Amanda again. "Oh yeah, I think you're right." And they both started laughing.

Amanda looked perplexed, and Frank colored even more. "Uh, Amanda, would you like a refill of your wine? It actually is very good wine." He rose quickly to reach for the bottle.

"I think I'm missing out on something here," said Amanda.

Both Jacob and Rachel started humming as Jacob started picking at the guitar.

"After our mother died, Dad did an excellent job of being a father and a mother to us," Rachel said, "except he wasn't near the fun he used to be."

"Yeah," said Jacob. "Dad used to love to sing, but after mom's death, the music seemed to disappear."

Frank nodded but didn't say anything.

"But then," said Rachel with a smile, "about two months ago Jacob and I came by the house to take Dad out to supper. When we walked into the house, we heard that familiar voice singing again."

They looked mischievously at their father. "He was singing an old-time song. Want to guess what it was?"

"I haven't a clue," said Amanda.

As Frank's face turned a bright red, Jacob began strumming his guitar, looking for the right chord. "OK, you lead Rachel."

With a giggle, Rachel began, and Jacob joined in.

"She had a dark and a-rovin' eye-eye-eye) And her hair hung down in ring-a-lets She was a nice girl, a proper girl but one of the rovin' kind"

Now Amanda blushed as well, and almost involuntarily she reached up and touched her dark curly hair. "Nice of you to remember, Frank."

They laughed and teased each other for another hour.

"Amanda," Rachel said, "you will never fully appreciate all that you mean to me. Not only did you save my life, but you also were part of restoring my father's health and happiness."

"I'm going to have to get on my way," said Jacob, "but I second my sister's sentiments. I hope we will continue to see a lot of you. Despite the picture my sister painted of me, I do have a life as well. In fact I've got a date tonight, so I'd best say goodby."

"You've got a date?" said Rachel. "Do I see images of bright red hair flashing in the moonlight?"

Jacob blushed. "I did tell Brenda I'd help her with some of the final details of her story."

"All right," said Rachel. "I've become a convert. I believe in miracles."

* * * * *

After Rachel and Jacob had gone, Frank turned to Amanda. "It's a beautiful night. Would you like to take a walk?"

"I think a walk would be great. Any place special you had in mind?"

"I was thinking of a golf course near here," Frank said with a deadpan expression on his face.

"That sounds good to me," Amanda said, "as long as it's understood that all bets are off."

9 798891 940505